LOVE
IN
FOUR
DOTS

JUAN M. GARCÉS

LOVE
IN
FOUR
DOTS

———

A NOVEL

———

Translated from the
original in Spanish

by
Juan M. Garcés and
Linda D. Garcés

Love in Four Dots is a work of historical fiction. All the events and the narration as well as the characters are a creation of the author, excluding a few notable historical figures whose roles are also fictitious.

Published in the United States by Kindle Direct Publishing, an imprint of Amazon Kindle, a division of Amazon.com Inc. Seattle, Washington. Amazon and Kindle are trademarks of Amazon.com Inc.

Grateful acknowledgement is made for permission to use previously published material to: Fundación José Ortega y Gasset-Gregorio Marañón (FOM), to quote from the Meditaciones del Quijote, by José Ortega y Gasset; HMH Books & Media, to quote from "The Unexpected Universe" by Loren Eiseley.

Garcés, Juan M., 1945–.
Love in Four Dots / Juan M. Garcés.
Translation from the original in Spanish / Juan M. Garcés and Linda D. Garcés
    p. cm.
References included.
ISBN 978-1-7347478-2-9 (paperback)

Photography by Donald Boys

Book design by Martha Garcés and Mayfly Design

First Edition Juan M. Garcés
www.juanmgarces.com

Printed in the United States of America
10 9 8 7 6 5 4 3 2 1

For Linda

CONTENTS

Introduction

The novel *Love in Four Dots* was inspired by six letters written in code with faint pencil dots between the lines of volume III of an 1844 Spanish edition of *Don Quixote*, that I discovered in my years as a student in the 60's in Cali, Colombia. They were written by Federico, a political prisoner and Sofia, his lover and confidante in Popayán, Colombia, during the One Thousand Days War (1899–1902), perhaps the bloodiest of all the civil wars in the political history of the Western Hemisphere.

Until the early years of the twentieth century, Popayán was the capital of the Old Cauca State, an immense territory that occupied about half of Colombia, with an area comparable to that of Spain or Texas. It was surrounded by the Pacific Ocean to the west; the Caribbean Sea and Panama (then part of Colombia) to the north; Ecuador, Peru and the Amazon River to the south; and the rest of Colombia plus Venezuela and Brazil to the east. The city played a key role in the political history and cultural evolution of Colombia from the beginning of the sixteenth to the end of the nineteenth century. Early in the twentieth century, general Rafael Reyes, then president of Colombia and adopted son of Popayán, changed the territorial division of Colombia and the city of Popayán became the capital of the Department of Cauca, whose territory became less than ten percent of that of the Old Cauca State.

The Plaza Mayor has been the historical center of Popayán since its founding in 1537. The Government House to the north is a symbol of the state power; to the south, the Cathedral, the Archbishop's House and the Clock Tower, represent the Church and time; in the east, the City Hall and the banks that house the civil and economic powers; and to the west there are homes of important citizens and some businesses. Popayán is also known as the "White City", because of the color of most of its buildings. Some have named it the "Literary City of Colombia" as the city was also the birthplace of many presidents of Colombia and of famous poets and distinguished intellectuals.

The Clock Tower is a massive brick structure that has ruled over time there since 1682. It houses a clock that operates by a single hand that counts the hours and has six bells that chime them. There is even a legend that claims that the remains of Don Quixote are hidden there, an ideal metaphor for the city's soul.

Love in Four Dots is a work of historical fiction that follows the content of the coded letters written by Sofía and Federico and makes use of historical records modified to fit the chain of events. The raw materials for the story came from various sources, including: the coded letters, my childhood memories, tales heard from relatives and even from the maids in my parents' home and from a variety of historical sources and documents in the public domain.

The coded letters secreted in *Don Quixote* were transcribed and translated to English respecting the original text created by the lovers. Punctuation was added to facilitate the reading of the letters. The quotations from *Don Quixote* were translated into English from the original text in the 1844 Spanish edition of *Don Quixote* or from the electronic public domain version in Spanish of *Don Quixote* from the Centro Virtual Cervantes (CVC). The narrator, Ramón, is the alter ego of the author, living in an imaginary time fitted to the contents of the letters and the historical events associated with the novel. The characters and their roles are fictitious and were given names and family names that mimic those of historical persons.

Perhaps the most unique feature of the novel is to include a second secret code, not based on the pencil dots between the lines of the text but on the actual dialogues of Sancho and Don Quixote, which are part of the pages where the pencil dots were written. The interpretation of this second code is, by definition, subjective and hence the readers are free to create their own. It's a fascinating exercise.

PART ONE:

DISCOVERY

A pencil point was an intrusion into this universe for which no precedent existed.

—Loren Eiseley, *The Unexpected Universe*

I: A Marvelous Find

In my hands is a book: *Don Quixote,* an ideal jungle.

—José Ortega y Gasset, *Meditations on Quixote*

That day I couldn't resist the temptation and entered into the narrow hallway, where I waited for a few moments allowing my eyes to adapt to the penumbra, whose upright steps would lead me to *The Oasis,* a used books and antiques business located upstairs. Hernando Tancredo—a retired anthropologist with the looks of a French musketeer—was the owner and soul of the business. He had a magical touch for dealing with customers interested in books, antiques, or interior decoration; an uncanny ability to guess what his clients needed or to find something to sell them. He greeted his clients with such charm that they felt obliged to make a purchase of something before leaving. When he saw me, he held out his hand.

"Ramón, how are you?" he said. "How can I help you?"

The question was unnecessary. He knew what I was after. I had visited *The Oasis* many times, always looking for interesting old books at the right price. We exchanged a few pleasantries and without further ado I got lost in the forest of bookshelves, pre-Hispanic relics, and odd furniture pieces. It was a familiar forest.

On one of the shelves I spotted a little book that piqued my attention. It was the third volume of an 1844 edition of *Don Quixote,* (in the original Spanish), from the printing house of don Alejandro Gómez Fuentenebro. I had in my hands a *sui generis: Don Quixote,* the ideal book of the Castilian language—a worn-out volume with spectacular etchings (Fig. 1). I imagined enlarged photos of the etchings on the walls of my home, and on the spot I decided I had to buy it.

It had a light brown cover made of faux-leather and it was missing the spine so that its ribs were exposed.

Fig. 1—Photocopy of an engraving from the 1844 edition of *Don Quixote.*

A typical old book that, like a stray dog, needed a friend. I bought it for a few pesos. During my bus ride home I thought about how to take photographs of the engravings and frame them for display.

*   *   *

A YEAR LATER I WAS STUDYING FOR A FINAL EXAM when I was overcome by Cali's midday heat and took a break. While taking a sip of

I knew I was the witness to a new creation. In an eternal moment I had traveled through a sequence of scenarios, going from my studies to a lizard, a fly, a cup of cold coffee, and to two lovers hiding between the lines of the text of *Don Quixote* waiting to escape from their prison like the genie from Aladdin's lamp.

By following Don Quixote and Sancho on the road to El Toboso and centering my attention on what was *yet to come* I had stumbled onto the key to exhume the story buried for many years in the leaves of the little book.

Fascinated by this find, I proceeded to peruse the entire book, and found more and more pencil dots, and even a few scattered letters, written with pencil in the margins of the pages or within the text. The feeling that somebody was spying on me was unbearable.

In a truly frenetic manner I transferred the individual letters above the dots onto scratch paper. After putting them in the right order, they became words and phrases, and eventually gave birth to six intriguing letters hidden for a long time until that magical afternoon. *How did they exchange the letters? How could I find the other books they mentioned in the letters? When were they written?*

The letters, apparently consecutive, were written only in certain sections of the book. Nothing could be found in the first one hundred pages or so, and nothing in the center or at the end of the book. Probably the lovers were trying to avoid detection by someone who might be inspecting the book, searching for hidden messages. I realized how lucky I was when I happened to open the book in the right place. There, I found the first four dots that led me to the word LOVE. Also, the paragraph in chapter VIII that contains the four dots used to write *love* is where Sancho says to Don Quixote:

> Where I saw her for the first time, when I took her the letter about the antics and mad deeds I left you doing in the heart of the Sierra Morena.

This strongly implied that the selection of the starting point for the letter was not accidental. Moreover, it suggested a connection between the conversations of the lovers and the dialogues between Sancho and Don Quixote within the text where the dots were written. I could never have imagined that the letters included two secret codes, entangled like the fibers of a rope.

Interestingly, close to the end of this letter the writer revealed her name: *Sofía*. She encoded four of the letters using four pencil dots and the letter *f* handwritten in the margin in cursive. After reading and re-reading the letters I felt like a blushing child peering wide-eyed through the keyhole of a door, seeing something I was never supposed to see. But being like a child, I couldn't take my eyes off the page. The spectacle was irresistible and I continued searching for more surprises. It was addictive. I felt compelled to continue reading.

I became the operator of a radio receptor pulling in distant voices from the past as my hand moved the dial and stumbled onto a magical frequency. The words of people long dead arrived like the night's light arrives from distant stars and inscribes a message on the astronomer's photographic plate to tell him a story. Was the message from the woman that was spying on my reading? She couldn't talk to me but had left her words and thoughts hidden in the book to share them with me and used the star's light to send me her story.

That day, the starlight touched the pages of the little book of *Don Quixote,* and was reflected into my eyes and converted into letters, words, and ideas as fresh as when written by the secret lovers. To read is to love, to enter into an amorous relationship with another creature.

In the letters I found several names and family names, but only a few complete names. The name Pedro Lindo[1] was one of them. I found out that he actually had lived in Popayán, worked at a bookstore also as a government accountant and as a doctor, and had died there in 1907 from a contagious disease contracted from a charity patient. This placed the letters in Popayán around the time of the One Thousand Days War. Other family names found in the letters also suggested they were written in Popayán.

Reading about Pedro Lindo and his fate, I wondered what else did I know about the One Thousand Days War. I remembered that when I was a child, around 1938-1940, and visited my grandfather, Antonio Ramos, in his room where he told me about being captured as a prisoner and taken to jail, barefoot and chained, along the streets of Popayán during the One Thousand Days War. While he drank coffee in bed, he would invite me to enter into the large armoire of his room by walking through its mirror into the enchanted world of his stories. While doing so, I could hear again the echo of the bullets passing close to my grandfather when he was hiding behind a wall or in a trench, scared to death, to avoid being shot to death. In fact, in my child's imagination, I became a pretend veteran of the One Thousand Days War. In my childhood mind, to imagine my grandfather in chains was like looking at Christ carrying the cross on his way to Calvary. I would have given any money to have him next to me at that moment but he had died in 1945. I wondered if it was his soul who had helped me to open the little book in the right page when I was sitting in his director's chair.

As a boy I couldn't distinguish between stories and memories. Everything my grandfather said came from a kind of wonderland. I was still at an age when—like *The Little Prince*—I had just arrived on this planet and everything I saw, heard, and felt was new. It was like experiencing everything for the first time, the world of children, artists, and inventors, the kingdom of imagination.

*   *   *

THE LETTERS, A MIXTURE OF LOVE NOTES and political intrigue, were signed simply *S* and *F*. Luckily for me, *S* used her first name once in her first letter and that of her lover in the second, leaving two very clear footprints in the sands of time: Sofia and Federico. Ever careful apart from these two indiscretions, she never revealed their family names.

Federico was a liberal political prisoner. Sofia was his lover, in charge of delivering his confidential messages to the outside world, at the same time that they interchanged tender and amorous words. They were like soldiers, taking risks that could result in the loss of their freedom and their lives.

After I decoded, copied, and made copies of each letter in the little volume of *Don Quixote,* I returned to *The Oasis* hoping to find another book—or more than one, with any luck—with dots. Sofia and Federico mentioned other books they used in their correspondence, and I wondered if some of them could still be at the bookstore or in the hands of the person that had sold the little book to Hernando.

Returning to the bookstore was another step in my adventure in search of the identities of the authors of the letters. After climbing the long staircase, I took a deep breath and entered into the space of *The Oasis.* I greeted Hernando and, without mentioning my reasons for being there, got busy searching for more books with dots but couldn't find any. Then, I approached Hernando and asked:

"Who sold you that little book of *Don Quixote* that I purchased from you for a fortune about a year ago?"

Hernando looked at me as if he wondered what I had in mind and invited me to approach his desk where he started looking into a large ledger of purchase transactions. He ran his hand over the pages, searching for the name of the seller, and when he found it he said, "Here it is. His name is don Emiliano Rimas. He is an old man who comes here to buy and sell books and he sold me the 1844 edition of *Don Quixote* that you own now."

As soon as Hernando described the man, I left the store and went to find a pay phone in the Plaza de Caicedo—Cali's main plaza—where phone books listed names, addresses and phone numbers. After I found his address and was trying to decide what to do, a taxi driver guessed my need. Pulling his fancy blue 1942 Chrysler to the curb, he called from the open window, "Where can I take you, sir?"

I jumped into his taxi and gave the man directions to don Emiliano's home. It turned out to be a new two-story corner house with a small garden separated from the sidewalk by an ornamental iron fence.

A small brass plate indicated that don Emiliano lived upstairs. I rang the bell and waited. I rang again and there was no response. I looked at my watch and cleaned my glasses. It was siesta time. I waited a little longer and rang the bell once more and soon I heard footsteps; I could hear somebody slowly coming down the stairs.

A tall and robust older woman, with a noble face crowded with dark moles and a tight bun of white hair on her head, opened the door. I asked if don Emiliano lived there and she answered by nodding without saying a word while observing me from behind her cloudy eyes. She asked for my name, told me to wait, and started closing the door while still looking as though she was trying to remember my face forever and she went slowly back up the stairs as she dragged her feet.

It was a hot day, about four in the afternoon. The gentle breeze from the Farallones de Cali† was not yet coming down from the mountains. I shifted back and forth on my feet. Finally, when I thought I would not see the woman again, her slippers slapped each step, announcing her return and she descended. She opened the door and told me that don Emiliano said to go upstairs.

We went up slowly. I followed the woman, trying to be patient while observing the yellowish callouses under her heels every time she placed a foot on the next stair. She was not in any hurry. She had to be around eighty years old.

---

† Part of the western branch of the Andes mountains in Colombia.

Upstairs, don Emiliano stood waiting for us in the hallway. He greeted me with a friendly face and a firm handshake, saying, "Who sent you here?"

"Hernando, the owner of *The Oasis*. He said you buy and sell books at his shop. Hernando and I are friends; I am interested in hard to find books. Older volumes, rare editions."

The old man confirmed that he did business with Hernando and asked who my parents were. When I told him, he said, "I know who you are,"—and he kept nodding and smiling as he stared not quite at me, as if looking into a memory over my shoulder. I felt at home, welcomed. The old man had let me into his circle of trust.

Don Emiliano was a typical Old-Cali character, somebody like a Nelson Mandela born in Cali. He asked me to follow him into his library, which occupied better than half of the second floor. The immense room was filled with bookshelves and bookstands in all sizes, colors, and styles, crowded with books about every imaginable topic. The important things were the books, not the shelves.

Don Emiliano slept right there in the library. There was an iron cot with a white cotton bedspread nestled in a corner. Next to his bed there was a tombstone made of white marble with information about the dead person. A photo nearby showed a woman in her funeral casket, her head peacefully resting on an embroidered white pillow. I did not dare to look at the details.

Of course, I did not ask don Emiliano about the woman in the photo and did my best to hide my surprise by moving along the bookshelves, pretending I wasn't troubled at all. I had never seen anything like that in a bedroom or in a library.

In the center of the room there was a comfortable cowhide armchair. Above it hung a single uncovered light bulb illuminating the whole room. Don Emiliano sat himself there with a book in his hands, looking at me while I was searching through the bookshelves trying to spot other old books with pencil dots within the text. What was he thinking about?

Little by little we began to talk about books and people. Don Emiliano had read extensively and knew several generations of people in Cali. He treated me as an equal, ignoring our age difference. I learned don Emiliano was the owner of several rental properties in central Cali. He looked to be between 70 and 80, and exuded independence. We had common interests: we enjoyed owning old books.

"They are the best company," he said.

He told me that his routine started at about 4 a.m. and continued until 10 p.m. He took a siesta after lunch and rests after meals. Some afternoons during the week, he was occupied by caring for his rental properties. Soon, I learned that he knew where every book was in his library and that each book had handwritten annotations using numbers and letters to rate the book and this helped him to locate any topics of special interest. Surprisingly, the little book of *Don Quixote* that had been in his possession for some time had only two annotations. Perhaps, he did not discover the letters because he couldn't see well or missed the pencil dots; at his age he probably had cataracts.

As we became closer friends in subsequent visits, don Emiliano gave me several books that I treasure to this day. The last time I saw him, the old man asked an impromptu question.

"Ramón, tell me, what are you looking for?"

I became quite surprised and nervous, thinking that the old man suspected I was hiding something from him—which was true. But I plunged ahead.

"Don Emiliano, do you remember a little book of *Don Quixote* that you sold to Hernando?"

"I certainly do. I only had the third volume of that set of four."

"The exact one. I purchased it from Hernando. I fell in love with the engravings in the book and wanted to have the complete set of that edition." I said, but did not reveal my secret.

The old man looked at me intrigued, wondering about my reply, and squinting his eyes said, "I bought it years ago from *El Cojito*. He had his bookstore in one of those old two-story houses near the Plaza de Santa Rosa. It's been a while since I saw him. I really bought that book from him out of pity. It was three in the afternoon and he hadn't had breakfast. He asked me to buy it for a few pesos and I did. I could not stand looking at an old man suffering like that."

He didn't say more, but I felt by the way he looked at me that I had lost don Emiliano's trust and didn't dare to ask him more questions. I didn't have the guts to go back to see him, but I had the little book and he had given me a new clue, a nickname: *El Cojito*. I had to find him.

*   *   *

EARLY IN THE MORNING THE NEXT DAY, I took a bus downtown and began to look for any information about *El Cojito's* bookstore by talking to the book dealers around the Plaza de Santa Rosa. It was market day. The sidewalks and the streets were crowded with people, some killing time on the cement benches under the shade of the trees, and others shopping or looking for entertainment in the cafes and bars around the plaza. The drivers of the horsedrawn carriages, along with their frail and tired horses waited for clients, in competition with the buses that drove by, perfuming the air with the vapors of their diesel engines. I'd been there many times before with my father looking for bargain books. I asked the dealers if they knew where I could find *El Cojito* or his bookstore, but nobody could help me.

Finally, when I was about to take the bus home I asked an old lady who was sitting on the sidewalk selling religious books. She squinted up at me and said, "Nooo, young man, he was killed by a bus right there at the corner. Nothing was left of his shop. He was a noble man and a true gentleman. Poor dear, he was walking around distracted or preoccupied with who knows what when the bus killed him. It was something horrible. God bless him."

Right there, looking at her surrounded by cheap old books, I felt I was at a dead end. Neither Hernando, nor don Emiliano had more books with pencil dots and *El Cojito* wasn't alive to tell me more about the little book. I thanked the old woman for the information, took a bus and went home. I had done my job and had accomplished my goal but I wasn't happy with the outcome.

At home, I made a clean handwritten copy of each of the six letters in a notebook and put it away, along with the photos of the engravings, with the intention of looking for other ways to find the identities of the authors of the letters.

In the following months I visited several libraries and talked with a number of scholars familiar with the culture of Old Cauca. I also discussed the letters with relatives and friends but could not make much progress. The story of the letters turned from being an obsession to becoming a theme of conversations with my college friends while having a beer during the weekends. Eventually, I left the book aside but not forgotten. My studies took me abroad—along with the book—, and then my career and later on my family obligations dominated my life for many years. It wasn't the time to be looking for footprints in the sands of time. But I couldn't stop asking new questions about the story of the coded letters when I thought about the little book of *Don Quixote*. In a way, more than once, I felt guilty for not taking more time to continue my adventure in search of *what was yet to come*. Eventually, when I least suspected it, *what was yet to come* came to me as a surprise in my own home.

II: *Another Great Surprise*

... and you don't have to pay attention to these enchantments...
which, given they are invisible and fantastic, ...

−Don Quixote, Part I, Chapter XVII

O n a very cold winter day, while sitting by the fireplace, I again stumbled upon the 1844 volume of *Don Quixote* on the bookshelf and it attracted my attention. But this time I had new reasons to look into it. Soon, I was going to retire and would finally have time to write something about the story of the coded letters. Perhaps, with help from the Internet, I would eventually find the identity of Sofia and Federico. Outside, swirls of snowflakes like diamonds happily danced in the wind flying around the rigid ash trees and the playful evergreens above the snow-covered ground. The fire crackled and popped in the fireplace.

Wondering if in my early youth I had been mature enough to pay serious attention to such a precious gift, I sat in my favorite chair next to the fire and decided to take a new look at the old book. Once again I returned to Chapter VIII in the Second Part of *Don Quixote* and read:

"From this point on begin the feats and pranks of Don Quixote and his squire: he convinces them to forget the ingenious hidal-

go's previous knightly deeds and set their eyes on those yet to
come, that from now on are starting on the road to El Toboso."

Moved by these words, I returned to the theme of the letters, setting
my mind on what was *"yet to come."* Following my old habit of browsing
books and magazines from the last to the first page, I started looking at
each page over the light of my reading lamp in search of anything I had
missed. Finally, on the back of the title page, I detected a faint signature:

Miguel Wenceslao de Angulo.

I looked at it again, and again, until there was no question that the
signature was as real as the text in the book. It was only visible by shin-
ing the light through the page: somebody had signed his name with invisible ink (Fig. 2) under the words POR MIGUEL DE CERVANTES
SAAVEDRA.

The name was familiar. I had seen the Angulo family tree and knew
where to find it: slipped inside the cover of a precious book I had received as a gift from my father, don Joaquín Bastos Romero. It was the
1866 edition of the *Geografía General de los Estados Unidos de Colombia*
by General Tomás Cipriano de Mosquera, printed in London in 1866.
I retrieved from the book the paper I was looking for and unfolded the
handwritten document with the Angulo family tree. As I expected, the
name was there. Moreover, I was able to find more information about
Miguel Wenceslao de Angulo in the genealogy book by Gustavo Arboleda quoted before, where I had found information about Pedro Lindo.

I learned that Miguel Wenceslao de Angulo Días del Castillo[2] had
died prematurely in Popayán in 1864 due to the abuses he had experienced as a prisoner of war in Cali during the violent civil war of 1860.
He was contemporary with the 1844 edition of *Don Quixote* and probably the first owner of the book where he left his signature. Of special

interest was to find he had married doña Antonia Lemos Largacha, a distinguished woman from Popayán, and that their daughter, Sofia Angulo Lemos, had married don Rafael Reyes Prieto, president of Colombia (1904-1909).

Her first name and the connection to her family name to the invisible signature made me hope that she could have been Sofia. But I read on and found that Sofia Angulo Lemos had married Rafael Reyes in 1877 and had died in Bogotá in 1890, years before the One Thousand Days War. Hence, she couldn't have been Sofia, the author of the letters.

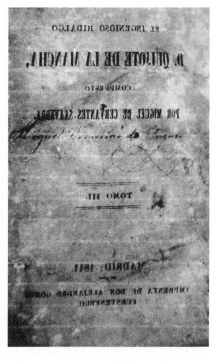

Fig. 2—Photocopy of the invisible signature of **Miguel Wenceslao de Angulo** I found in the back of the title page of the 1844 edition of Don Quixote.

In the same Angulo family, I found other women named Sofia who could have written the letters and were also contemporary with Pedro Lindo and the One Thousand Days War, but soon I found they should be discarded as Federico's lover. Once again, I asked: who could have been the amazing woman who wrote the letters?

At what appeared to be a new dead end in my search for Sofia and Federico, I came upon a copy of the *Memorias*[3] of Rafael Reyes, a book that illuminated the events that took place in Popayán and Colombia in the 1800s during the decades before the One Thousand Days War.

Reyes, due to his family ties with the person that had signed the little book and his historical role during the period when the letters were written, provided a new focal point in my quest to identify the lovers. Sofia and Federico would have known him, or known of him and his family. In his *Memorias* he touched on many persons of great importance in the history of Colombia during the XIX century. He and his family left Popayán around 1885 when, bankrupt in the quinine and rubber businesses in the Putumayo and Amazon regions, Reyes started his military and political career that culminated when he became president of Colombia. He was an entrepreneur, an adventurer, a political leader, president and dictator. He was also a key figure in the diplomatic and business negotiations between Bogotá and Washington, London, and Paris that led to the end of the One Thousand Days War, the loss of the Panama Isthmus and the rights of Colombia to the Panama Canal. At this time Theodore Roosevelt[4], who supported the separation of Panama from Colombia, purchased the rights to the Canal from the French Canal Company and completed the Canal in 1914.

Amalgamating the *Memorias* of Rafael Reyes with other historical sources, I developed a broader image of the world in which Sofia and Federico had lived. This took me to the origins of Colombia[5] in the early nineteenth century and even to the dawn of the seventeenth century when don Miguel de Cervantes published the first edition of Don Quixote. I had the stage, the audience, and the libretto, and only the main actors were missing. *How was I to find them?*

The letters and the thread of the story had come from Popayán. I needed to keep following these hints to illuminate the lives of Sofia and Federico, which remained hidden but were very much alive between the lines of the text and in the veins of new generations.

For me it was marvelous to think that a little book had traveled from Spain across the ocean and along the tortuous mule paths of the Andes to arrive to Popayán in the office of the distinguished lawyer Miguel

Wenceslao de Angulo and then from the hands of a beautiful maiden, in love and full of passion, to the hands of a political prisoner, to end up, somehow, in an old bookstore in Cali and finally in my own hands.

I still didn't know who they were and knew little of their lives and struggles. But I had started in search of the *"yet to come"* again and was moving and learning from my failures. The first discoveries continued to propel me forward in slow motion. Since I was closer to retirement: soon I would have the freedom to explore the intriguing story that had come to my hands in my student days. *What would be my next step?*

I would have to start from the beginning, unafraid to mingle historical facts with the fruits of my imagination. That, I did. I continued, trusting I would find a happy end to the adventure I was involved in since I walked into the bookstore and found the 1844 edition of *Don Quixote*. I had started to write a novel.

PART TWO:

In the XIX Century

In America, the whole world is Popayán.

—Policarpo del Pando[6], Fiscal of the Spanish Crown, XVIII century

III: Encounter in Popayán

> But on a certain day, tired of that monotonous living,
> and the evening chats with that cunning friar...
> I sailed to America, that was the last opportunity,
> for the hopeless, as was then common saying...
> and arrived to Popayán, a welcoming and pacific place...
> He was buried at the south corner of the Plaza Mayor
> under the massive brick walls of a canonic tower...

—Rafael Maya, *Poesía (Don Quixote dies in Popayán)*[7]

POPAYÁN, 1889

On New Year's Day 1889, don Nicomedes Lemos, wearing his new Panama hat, left his bookstore—*El Libro*—after breakfast and walked two blocks down the street to meet with his circle of friends in the Plaza Mayor. His granddaughter, Mariana, was left in charge of the store. From the north corner of the Plaza he noticed with surprise that his old friend Dr. Juan Francisco Usuriaga had finally returned to the city. Dr. Usuriaga had seen him already, and was waiting under a splendid carbonero tree to tell him the news about his family. "Don Nicomedes! What a pleasure to see you again," said the old doctor, extending his hand in a warm greeting. They hadn't seen each other since 1885, when the Usuriaga family left Popayán to go to Ecuador looking for asylum, escaping the war of 1885.

Don Nicomedes embraced his old friend, welcoming him back to Popayán after such a long absence. They looked at each other without knowing where to start; they had so much to catch up with. The old bookseller was the first to speak. He had special news to share.

"Federico, my grandson, showed up at home on Christmas Eve without having told anyone he was coming. We hadn't seen him since 1882 when, as you probably remember, he went to Panama to work for the French Canal Company. They declared bankruptcy at the end of the year and Federico and many others were left without a job. It was a great adventure: he had dreamed of building that canal since he was a teenager, when he started civil engineering studies at the university, following the advice from General Mosquera. Federico came back home and this time, I believe, he came to stay for good. He has plenty to do in the years to come here in Popayán."

"Bien! I congratulate you and join you and your family in the celebration of this happy event. I will stop by the bookstore soon to greet him personally. I have had a special affection for Federico from the day I brought him into this world."

At that time, Colombia was enjoying relative prosperity. President Holguín had initiated the modernization of the country by installing the first telephones and electric lights in Bogotá and was improving transportation facilities by land and water along the most important rivers. The stability created by his government was a key incentive for the return of many families that had been in exile since the days of the war of 1885.

Dr. Usuriaga told don Nicomedes about his experiences during their exile in Ecuador and mainly talked about the problem that he and his wife, doña Julia Carrasco, had faced since a few months before leaving Quito to come back to Popayán. It had something to do with their beautiful daughter, Sofia, a teenager and their only child.

"What's wrong with her?"

"My poor daughter is suffering from a frightful sentimental crisis since her friend and admirer, Alberto Carrasco, departed for Bogotá to study jurisprudence. In Quito, where he completed his high school studies, he visited her daily. Now she doesn't know what to do without him. My poor girl has lost interest in everything. Her days go by waiting for a letter from Bogotá and the letters from Alberto take longer than the previous ones. She writes him ten-page letters and he replies with four lines, without bothering to answer the thousand questions she asks about his life, friends, and studies at the *Colegio del Rosario*. Julia is concerned about her and hopes they might soon formalize their relationship. She does not want her daughter to wait until she is forty to get married as she had done. I don't know which is worse off. Both have me concerned and are driving me insane."

Don Nicomedes, who knew from his own experiences with three granddaughters—almost daughters to him—of the pains of unrequited love, suggested that his friend obtain some romance novels for his daughter as an antidote for her nostalgia for the absent Romeo.

"Tell doña Julia to stop by the bookstore where my girls can help her find the novels that will take care of her depression. I will have a word with Mariana. Don't forget that *Don Quixote* is the best book to entertain the old and the young and provides wise advice for all kinds of pains, including depression."

Dr. Usuriaga took into account the recommendations of don Nicomedes and asked doña Julia to look for some pretext to bring Sofia to the bookstore. He preferred that they solve their own problems. He lacked the tact and patience needed to convince his daughter about what was good for her. She was a very stubborn person, just like her mother.

Doña Julia listened to her husband, and following her usual ways, ignored what he was asking her to do. She knew that the following day he wouldn't remember what he had asked for. However, when in the month of May the doctor asked her to stop by the bookstore to get a few books he had ordered, Sofia was then in the deepest depression ever and her mother decided it was time to do something about it.

Doña Julia showed up at the bookstore on a warm day, accompanied by Sofia who had just turned sixteen. Mariana, the oldest of the Nicomedes granddaughters, was by herself at the store that afternoon. When she saw doña Julia and her daughter, she said, "What a pleasure to see you here. I assume this is Sofia. She is a handsome woman now. The last time I saw her she was still a little girl. It's amazing how young women can change in a moment. How can I help you?"

"You are right, Mariana, Sofi has grown a lot and is going through the pains of adolescence. I came after some books that Federico has for my husband."

"Federico has been gone since yesterday. He went to survey a property near Calibío and should return any time. Would you like something to drink? The heat is unbearable."

"No, thank you, we had a drink just before coming. We'd better entertain ourselves by looking at some novels. Sofi just turned sixteen and I would like to give her a novel or two as a birthday present."

"Sofia, have you read *Don Quixote*?" Mariana asked the girl.

"No, but one of my friends in Quito was reading it and she loved it."

"We have it in a deluxe edition with a leather cover. I am sure you would love it. My sisters and I read it and we enjoyed every page."

Mariana's comment pleased Sofia. She wasn't being spoken to as a little girl as her parents did.

"Can you show me the book, please?"

Mariana smiled, noticing the insecurity of the young woman.

"My pleasure. Come here and I'll show you several books that you may like."

Sofia approached the bookshelves and Mariana showed her several editions of romantic novels, ideal for young women. When they were looking at the books, Federico arrived accompanied by Clodomiro, who was his assistant when they surveyed properties in the countryside. He couldn't miss any opportunity to use the spyglass that Federico had brought him from Panama. When she saw them, Mariana said, "Federico, you came just in time. Doña Julia is looking for some books that you have for the professor and I have no idea where they are. By the way, this is Sofia, their daughter who is sixteen now. Can you believe how much she has grown? I think the last time you saw her she wasn't even ten."

"Doña Julia, Sofia, good afternoon. Please, give me a moment to arrive, I need to wash up and I will return with the books. They are upstairs in my study."

Sofia already had heard her father mentioning Federico and had imagined him to be a man with thick spectacles and an altar boy's face. When seeing him and hearing the tone of his voice addressing doña Julia and her as well-known persons, her legs almost buckled and she almost dropped the book in her hands. Mariana observed her amusedly. It wasn't the first time that a female client had reacted like this upon seeing Federico.

Sofia selected *Don Quixote* in the deluxe edition, as a gift from her mother. Federico didn't take much time to return with the books for Dr. Usuriaga. In the meantime, Mariana noticed that doña Julia frowned at Sofia's nervousness and her interest in the detailed observations made by Federico about all the secrets hidden in Cervantes' book.

Federico's appearance, the tone of his voice, and his deep knowledge of the books captivated Sofia. He looked at her in a way that felt almost like a caress. She felt very womanly in his presence. She also felt a mysterious attraction between them. Mariana and doña Julia didn't miss the expression on her face.

Doña Julia's reaction wasn't rare at all. She couldn't imagine a descendant of don Juan de Argüello, one of the city founders, paying attention to a book merchant, a poor nobody. Alberto Carrasco, her favorite, was the chosen one for her daughter's wedding in the cathedral. There was no question about that. Not on her life.

From that day on, the nostalgia for Alberto's letters disappeared. Sofía became a voracious reader of novels and found new ways to visit the bookstore again and again. She even became friends with the Lemos sisters and Mariana became her confidante.

During one of those visits, Federico noticed that Mariana was chatting with doña Ana María, Sofía was discreetly looking at Federico while pretending to be browsing books. Federico was pleased with her interest and to get her attention asked her about her friend Alberto Carrasco who was in Bogotá.

"I don't know if you have recent news from Alberto Carrasco. I wonder how he is doing at the *Colegio del Rosario*. It's been a while since I've seen him."

Sofía, surprised by his question, said, "Just after he left he used to write to me often. But with the slow mail his letters take two months to get here and it has been weeks since I've heard from him. I think he has forgotten me."

Federico looked at her in a way that Sofía found flattering, and said, "Does it bother you to be ignored?"

"No, not anymore." She said while looking at him with a smirk that was almost a smile, wondering why he had asked that question.

Federico didn't need more hints to feel invited to continue the conversation. From that day on, her visits to the bookstore became more frequent. The books gifted by her relatives or borrowed from the Lemos sisters didn't last her a week. Doña Julia came dragging her feet, and for that reason most of the time Sofía came with her godmother Ana María. Mariana started to wonder which of the two women was more interested in Federico. They both wanted his attention and he flirted with them; perhaps he was curious or perhaps interested in one or the other, or both. Mariana thought about how alike men can be.

*   *   *

MARIANA HAD BEEN THROUGH THICK AND THIN since her adolescence. Life had forced her to grow up early. Her mother, doña Micaela
Beltrán, died of complications from a miscarriage at the beginning of
1868. Nothing could be done to save her life, not the special homeopathic treatments nor the daily visits of Dr. Juan Francisco Usuriaga,
nor Father Paredes and the servants endless prayers. In the end what
caused her death was puerperal fever. And so at fifteen Mariana became
mother *de facto* of Rosita, seven years old, and Lola, who was already
nine. Her brother Federico was eleven and was not at all useful. But he
did not ask for much and was very independent.

While delirious between life and death, doña Micaela asked Mariana, her first born, to be in charge of her children and of her husband,
Professor Gallardo Lemos. Men like him did not serve as mothers; they
could not even take care of themselves.

Professor Lemos, of unstable temperament since he had served in the
horrendous war of 1860 and had been wounded, had become a widower
and had traded his love for his beloved Micaela for drinking. Drained
by a severe depression after losing his only love, he started to drink fermented chicha (corn liquor) and aguardiente (anisette) at Delfina's Inn
until he lost the desire to eat, his memory, and in the end the will to live.
In one of his constant days of drunkenness he entered the chicken coop
and in the middle of a *delirium tremens* attack he raped Carlota, their
maid, thinking that she was his Micaela because she was wearing an old
dress inherited from her mistress. The professor violated Carlota over
broken chicken eggs, struggling with the rooster—known by the maids
as don Clodomiro—who was trying to defend his descendants. Carlota
managed to get away from him—too late—and blamed the broken eggs
on don Clodomiro who had scared her.

When Professor Lemos, in a moment of lucidity, discovered that

Carlota was pregnant and that he had confused her with his Micaela, he entered into a new state of depression closer to madness. He tortured his family and their neighbors for months by loudly reciting interminable poems in several languages under the sour orange tree on the patio. He also dictated philosophy classes and fragments of stories about the little that remained in his withered memory. On one occasion he was terrorized by hallucinations of enormous insects that chased him, he ran and ran around the orange tree slapping at them in the air until he fell down and was overtaken by a heart attack. Don Nicomedes found him on the ground with his clear blue eyes fully open looking at the midday sun, surrounded by putrid sour oranges. He had been rendered skeletal, left with only his bones, but he had a beatific smile on his face. He was probably looking at Micaela receiving him lovingly in the afterlife. That day don Nicomedes traded his role of grandfather to become a father to his grandchildren.

In December 1868, on the Day of the Holy Innocents, when the family was preparing for Professor Lemos' funeral, Carlota gave birth to a little baby boy with a large head, enormous hands, and the beady eyes of a rooster. The maids named him Clodomiro and he remained Clodomiro. Mama Pola, the eldest and wisest maid, claimed he was the son of the rooster don Clodomiro that had made love to Carlota thinking that she was a hen.

Carlota breastfed the baby until she discovered he was a dwarf. From that day on she ignored him completely and dedicated all her time to taking care of her performing parrots, who knew how to insult their visitors in several languages learned from listening to professor Gallardo Lemos when preparing his classes or reciting poetry while walking along the corridors around the patio. Rosita adopted the little dwarf as her baby doll and slept with him until she turned fifteen. Her favorite pastime was to read him children's books. Clodomiro the dwarf enjoyed the love and attention of his babysitter and one day, when he was not quite five years old they discovered that he had learned how to read by listening to Rosita. From that day Clodomiro spent his free time reading every book he managed to get in his large hands. He read like Rosita, pointing at the words with his index finger and eventually just moving his hand over paragraphs as he devoured them with his bulging eyes. They never sent him to school, but his erudition was incredible. In the same way he accumulated knowledge listening to everything happening in the bookstore. Nothing escaped his attention. Listening to foreign visitors, he became interested in other languages and trained Carlota's parrots to say more insults in new languages. His large head had room for everything written, seen, or heard. But only a few knew about it. He only shared his knowledge with special persons. At the bookstore he became best friends with Pedro Lindo, a young assistant hired by don Nicomedes to help in the bookstore after Federico's graduation as an engineer. Pedro Lindo, a local boy of humble origins, discovered that Clodomiro was the most intelligent and best-informed person in the bookstore, and the whole Lemos Beltrán family.

Pedro Lindo became an assiduous student of medical books in his free moments at the bookstore. He studied languages and accounting with Dr. Benjamin Lenguas who was a client of the bookstore. From 1881–1883 he studied at the university to perfect his knowledge in medicine working with local doctors so that he might become an expert surgeon, receiving a diploma in homeopathic medicine in 1898. Clodomiro accompanied Pedro to his language classes and they enjoyed employing foreign words to annoy the other members of the family, who didn't know much about exotic languages such as Greek or Sanskrit. Only the parrots were not irritated—on the contrary, they bent their heads so as to better hear what was being said. Perhaps remembering something they had heard from professor Gallardo Lemos.

When Federico came back from Panama, Pedro Lindo realized he was redundant at the bookstore and accepted an offer to work as an accountant for the governor, don Manuel Antonio Sanclemente, who later became president of Colombia (1898–1900) during the first part of the One Thousand Days War. Mariana took over the bookstore's accounting.

Clodomiro, when he wasn't occupied at the printing shop he managed with Rosita and Lola, helped at the bookstore by running errands, delivering orders, and visiting clients with overdue bills. Between jobs he enjoyed training the parrots he had inherited from his mother, teaching them new sentences in several languages. His dream was to figure out how parrots think to be able to truly communicate with them.

Federico, after assuming the bookstore's management, started to take part in secret meetings of the liberal opposition to the government along with his old professor, Dr. Cajiao, who had welcomed him back home as if he had never left Popayán.

As time went by, Federico started to take an interest in Sofia Usuriaga in spite of the large difference in their ages. He didn't miss any opportunity to coach her on her reading choices or to bring some books to her attention. Their relationship acquired a more complex flavor, mainly because of the constant opposition of her parents. Doña Julia wanted her to be with Alberto and Dr. Usuriaga just couldn't imagine Federico as her husband. The strong-willed Sofia wouldn't tolerate her parents trying to control her future. She managed to find other ways to meet with Federico. She was in love with him and her godmother supported her. Both admired Federico and he was interested in both of them.

*   *   *

ON JANUARY 10, 1894, Saint Nicomedes' Day, the man named after him celebrated his ninetieth birthday with his family. He sat in his armchair afterward with a glass of brandy in his hands. He wore the same black wool suit he had worn when he came from Galicia, which

Mariana had ironed that morning for the occasion. His plan was to take a siesta, but this time he did not wake up to open the bookstore. He fell into such a profound sleep, and with such a peaceful and tranquil appearance on his wrinkled face, that his grandchildren tried and failed for some time to wake him. He had died in peace with the living and the dead, fully dressed and ready to be buried after having celebrated his life with his family. Dr. Usuriaga, his lifelong friend, declared him dead and authorized the burial.

That night, don Nicomedes' soul pranced at will around the city streets, accompanied by his soul mate don Tomás Cipriano de Mosquera (1798–1878), who had come to welcome him to the world of the dead. Also at the Plaza Mayor was the soul of don Francisco José de Caldas, a famous scientist admired and visited in Popayán by Baron Alexander von Humboldt before the baron visited President Jefferson in the United States of America. Caldas explained his method for calculating the height of mountains by measuring the boiling point of water, as compared with a thermometer calibrated at sea level at Tumaco. Don Nicomedes' greatest surprise was to run into the souls of Don Quixote and Sancho accompanied by the soul of don Miguel de Cervantes, who was on vacation in the Indies because he couldn't stand the cold of Madrid in January. This initiation into the afterlife was the most interesting thing he had witnessed. At dawn, when the wandering souls started to take possession of the minds of the local citizens, he attended the wake of his own stiff body. It was very amusing. He had never heard so many lies in such a short time.

Dr. Usuriaga couldn't recover from the sadness of having lost his lifelong friend and bookseller. They had had so many things in common. The doctor couldn't live without books and missed talking about them with someone he loved and respected. Thus he decided to accompany his old friend. On July 24, 1894, he didn't wake up. In his dreams he had run into don Nicomedes doing his nightly ghost rounds. His friend had told him that to die, the best thing to do was to pretend one was dead until one was totally convinced. This turned out to be the best advice he had received in his eighty-four years in this world. Father Juan María Cadavid took care of authorizing his Christian burial in funeral ceremonies at San Agustín church, where he had attended Mass from the age of four. In simple numbers, he had managed to go to Mass at least once a day for about 30,000 days. As a prize for his devotion, he was authorized by Saint Peter to continue the investigations about the origins of dead languages that he had initiated in 1834. Since that 24th of July, his soul dedicated the time after a siesta in the afternoons to work in his office, where he had all the pertinent documents in his archives. Doña Julia continued to join the professor's ghost—busy at work in his office—after taking her aromatic water when she got up from her own siesta.

Her father's death gave Sofia some hope for her love life. She had one less opponent to worry about in her struggle to become Federico's wife. However, she still had to convince her mother that Federico was the chosen one, not Alberto. Don Emilio, her mother's only brother, joined the war against Federico.

*   *   *

THE DIFFICULT RELATIONSHIP between Sofia and Federico continued without any major change until Alberto Carrasco returned from Bogotá in 1896 as a Magistrate of the Judicial Court. He had decided to find the way to make Sofia his future wife, the woman who would bear his children. Alberto's visits, supported by doña Julia and Sofia's uncle don Emilio, alternated with her secret encounters with Federico at her godmother's house.

IV: The One Thousand Days War

> Our grandchildren... may find it difficult to understand the type of insanity that led us so many times to carnage between brothers... and why we are the last representatives of the political fanaticism, intransigency, and cruelty that lasted more than a thousand days and didn't leave anything standing.

—Rafael Uribe-Uribe[8]

"The war has started! The war has started!" shouted Constantino Zambrano, running out of the telegraph office into the Plaza Mayor to share the news with all of those present. It was the war all were expecting at any moment.

The news had traveled in stages, from telegraph clerk to telegraph clerk, over the broken lands of Colombia until it reached Popayán. From the Plaza Mayor it passed quickly from mouth to mouth heating—like the molten lava of the Puracé volcano—the blood of the younger generations of the two parties. The aroma of death and gunpowder—which the city of the national heroes well knew—floated once more in the air and the women and the old men felt the horrible and cold omens of another war: the cold of hunger and death. But nobody imagined that this war, just starting, would bathe the entire nation in blood and bring mourning to each family. It would be the longest and bloodiest of all the wars of the nineteenth century; the agony of the Colombians joined the agony of the century.

The new Constitution of 1886 divided the state powers into three branches: executive, legislative, and judicial. It abolished the federal state, and created a new state, The Republic of Colombia, now had a central government in charge of the social and economic administration. It defined the presidential term to last six years, declared the Catholic Church as the official religion and exempted the Church from taxation, and divided the national territory into departments.

These constitutional changes attacked the roots of the aspirations of the Liberal Party and were the seed of the war of 1895 and later of the One Thousand Days War (1899–1902) that consumed the lives and dreams of a whole generation of Colombians.

The "mortal telegram"[9] sent by the Liberal Directory to all its regional officers was ignored by the leaders of the revolution of the State of Santander. The boiling blood of the youngsters prevailed over the measured reasoning of the elders, who still had painful memories of their own wars and those of their parents and grandparents. On October 18, 1899, the war exploded in Santander and it changed everything.

Federico confirmed the news with Constantino, discussing the significance of the moment with him and realized privately that his relationship with Sofia Usuriaga would become from there on more difficult if not impossible. He had to see her. At once, he took the *Calle del Callejón* and headed to Sofia's home. She was waiting for him, standing by the window unaware of the gravity of the news about the war.

"What a look you have on your face!" she declared.

Federico grabbed the bars of the window and squeezed them until his knuckles turned white.

"The war has started in Santander!"

"What madness! Come in and tell us about it. My godmother is visiting with my mother."

"I am sorry, but I can't. I just wanted to share the news with you personally. I'll see you soon."

She was left wondering what would happen to them and their relationship. She had loved him with all her soul since the day she met him. In fact, Federico left suddenly because he didn't want to see the godmother, whose husband General Luis Enrique Zorilla had recently been named governor.

Sofia blew him a kiss from the window and in great sorrow followed him with her eyes until he arrived at the corner, when he turned around for an instant as if he had felt the kiss she had sent to him.

"Goodbye, my love," he said between his lips as he turned around to wave to her when he felt that she was still watching him. His mind was full of questions and fears that only time would resolve. She didn't perceive the whole meaning of the moment but with a woman's intuition she realized they were between the wall and the sword. She didn't know what to tell her mother and her godmother Ana María.

Her godmother had done her best to convince doña Julia that even though Federico was a liberal and of middle-class origin, he was well educated and could be a good husband for Sofia. Federico felt uncomfortable with the godmother, a complex woman, the wife of a military officer and political figure whose job frequently required him to leave her alone and forgotten. She was much younger than her husband and demanded more attention than he could give her. It was rumored that she was close to Antonio Ramos, a good friend of Federico and his sisters, whom he expected to see at the meeting of Radicals—nickname given to liberals—that night.

Federico knew that his situation was untenable and perhaps impossible; as a liberal he couldn't avoid being part of the conflict already in motion. As the suitor of Sofia—the daughter of doña Julia Carrasco

Argüello and the goddaughter of the new governor's wife—he would be fighting against the family of his future offspring.

Federico was expected at a meeting of the Radicals at the home of don José Dolores del Pando. Lost in his fears and concerns, he walked like a ghost along the *Calle de Santo Domingo* and then took the *Calle del Empedrado* to reach the home of don José Dolores del Pando. The group of Radicals included several key members of the Cauca Liberal Directory and some invitees friendly to their cause. His professor, Dr. Cajiao, would be in charge of the meeting. The liberals had to make critical decisions to recruit volunteers and allocate resources at once. The Godos—nickname for the conservatives—would not give them a break; they were at war. The government's heavy hand would impose new arbitrary taxes on the liberals to hang them by their own rope. Down the street, looking to the west, he could see red clouds bathing the sky in blood, announcing the horrors of the coming war. Soon it would be dark. The cool afternoon breeze forced him to button his vest and then he knocked on the door of the Pando family home while looking around to see if anyone had followed him and he waited for the door to open.

He found that the customary *tresillo*—Spanish card game—had been postponed indefinitely and all the attending folk were already involved in conversation about politics and the imminent impact of the war on their lives. They discussed the roles to be played by each one, either as combatants or members of the resistance. At midnight Federico left the meeting and took a different route to return home. The streets were empty and there was fear in the air. Mariana had stayed up waiting for him.

In the following days young men from the most distinguished liberal families departed from Popayán protected by the shadows of night to join the various groups that had started to assemble the liberal forces in the south.

*   *   *

As THE YOUNG LIBERALS DISAPPEARED to join the Radicals, several families also started leaving the city, taking asylum in Ecuador where they had the political and economic support of its President Eloy Alfaro and counted on relatives or friends to house them during the war. Many never returned to Colombia.

Some of the exiled Colombian citizens in Ecuador formed a support group for the liberal cause. When they heard the good news about the victories of the liberal forces in the battles in Santander, the exiled liberals realized it was time to act and organized an attempt to take over Popayán by surprise on Christmas of 1899.

The Popayán inhabitants—old Christians—accompanied by their families and servants, would be at church celebrating Christ's birth. There would be an open-air concert and fireworks at the Plaza Mayor. It would be the day of peace on earth to men of good will, the last Christmas of the nineteenth century, a day that offered a parenthesis of calm during the ongoing war. The Radicals never imagined what would be waiting for them.

The news of the magnitude of the liberal victories at the battles in Santander, at Peralonso and Terán[10], grew as it traveled from Cúcuta to Quito. The heroism of General Uribe at Peralonso and the impact of the defeat on General Villamizar ballooned over the distance. Each victim at Peralonso came accompanied by ten more in the news. The exiled liberals felt that victory appeared to be at their fingertips. It was the moment to take advantage of the confusion in the capital and the old warriors and with their sons and dependents agreed to attack Popayán. A growing pilgrimage of liberal patriarchs departed Ecuador about the middle of December, moving like a colored snake along the muddy paths of the mountains, engaging the youngsters and peons of the liberal landowners. The alcohol from the guarapo, the chicha and the aguardiente helped to kill the wet cold and made the loads lighter and the walk merrier toward the expected victory in Popayán.

Meanwhile, the government spies in the inns and the tobacconists of the small villages warned the prefect in Popayán about the menace approaching the city. The prefect and the governor summoned the City Council to a secret meeting at the Government House to prepare the defense of the city.

Colonel Pinto, a seasoned combatant, proposed to ambush the Radicals at about twenty kilometers south of the city. The soldiers of the Second Battalion of Timbío would lead the battle and their comrades of the Battalion Junín, headquartered in the city, would act as reservists to enter in combat if needed. To avert any suspicion, the Music Band of the Junín started to rehearse the music program for the festivities of Christmas Eve and Christmas. Everything was in order and an apparent normalcy prevailed.

Meanwhile, Colonel Pinto had left the city with a group of officers during the night of December 10 to organize the ambush. The day before Christmas Eve, his troops took positions on both sides of the road south of the village of Flautas. They selected a rocky terrain with abundant brush to hide the soldiers and protect them if there was a counterattack. A man was put every 30 feet, at three different levels, so that there were fifty men per level on each side of the road. The group closest to the enemy would be at about 300 feet, where the sharpshooters would not fail. The rest of the battalion, about one hundred more men, would be located closer to Flautas ready to finish off any Radicals who managed to escape in that direction or to contain the liberal advance if the ambush failed.

On the morning of the 25th, a gray and rainy day, the Radicals got up early to eat and warm up in preparation for battle. The dense morning fog appeared to favor them. They departed jogging gaily and thinking of arriving to the city by noon, just in time for the Christmas celebrations.

Innocent—like Herod's victims—they approached the trap set by Colonel Pinto where his soldiers were hidden holding their Mauser rifles tightly, anxious to finish off the enemy. The new Mauser rifles had a reach of hundreds of feet and their smoke-free powder wouldn't give away the location of the shooters. The air felt tense. The soldiers' hands were sweaty even though it was cold. They held their breath for the moment chosen by Colonel Pinto to start the attack.

The road gradually filled with the joyful Radical vanguard armed with spears, machetes, homemade shotguns, and Remington rifles. The rear-guard forces followed them at some distance. At the chosen moment, Colonel Pinto gave the attack order and the bugle call started the shooting. The sound of the bullets was thunderous: bullets from 300 rifles poured down like rain over the terrified pilgrims, hitting them from both sides of the road. The charges repeated without rest, each time more deadly. They busted chests, broke arms and legs, blew away heads; bullets bounced from the rocks creating further havoc. The wounded: agonized, impotent, tasted rage mixed with blood. The liberal officers fell from their mounts with the surprise of death painted on their faces. Other horses, scared by the shooting, threw their riders and ran out of control when feeling the bite of the bullets in their loins; they tried to escape by galloping without riders or dragging the wounded ones. There was no place to hide. The surprise was complete.

In a disorderly retreat—each one on his own—the Radicals scrambled for escape from an invisible enemy that killed anyone that moved. Of the 1200 Radicals only 600 survived with some of them wounded; others had not yet entered the ambush and they ran south to warn the rear-guard and their families or to look for a safe place in the jungle. The disorderly stampede saved them from total annihilation. Some of the leaders died without knowing why or when. Others got a *coup de grâce* or a machete blow that terminated their agony. Many others were simply shot summarily. The well-to-do prisoners' ransom would be expensive.

Not far away in the village of Flautas, the neighbors thought that the battle noise in the distance was Christmas fireworks. The governor and the prefect received the news of victory after noon and immediately initiated a roundup to capture those involved in the failed assault on Popayán. Believers and innocents continued celebrating Christmas in holy peace. Others ran for cover on hearing about the defeat.

On the Day of the Innocents, the citizens of Popayán received the troops from the Timbío Battalion with triumphal arches decorated with flowers and invited them to the market, where they were honored with an open-air banquet. Dozens of barefoot prisoners, humbled and humiliated and tied with leather ropes or chains, followed the victors. The Junín Battalion Band celebrated the victory with a concert in the Plaza Mayor. The bookstore *El Libro* didn't open that day. A sign on the door written on a small chalkboard said:

Closed until the next century.

V: Visiting the Godmother

> The idea about the letters was a suggestion from my
> godmother, as indirect advice.

> —Second Letter from Sofia to Federico

That Tuesday, early in the new century, as she always did, Sofia
went to visit her godmother, Ana María Carrasco, her mother's
favorite cousin. Before leaving her home she looked right and
then left as a precaution. There were refugees all over the city. They could
be found in the Plaza Mayor, in churches and schools and on the sidewalks, or they were staying with friends or relatives. Popayán didn't have
enough space to house the people displaced by the war. Food scarcity
was critical and even those of wealth in other times had just enough to
not succumb to hunger.

When she arrived at her godmother's she saw beggars coming after
her to ask for a coin. Amelia the maid saw her and opened the door in a
hurry to allow Sofia to come in, and she slammed the door to keep them
out of sight.

"They almost got to you!"

Sofia, once inside, took a deep breath and filled her lungs with the fresh air of the hallway. It smelled like peppermint. The simple act of breathing in that familiar aroma calmed her down.

"Is my godmother awake from her siesta?" she asked the maid.

"Yes, Niña Sofia, she is waiting for you on the patio."

Sofia walked into the patio, a rectangle with a stone fountain in the center. It was crowded with begonias, ferns, bougainvillea, multicolored orchids and fuchsias hanging from the beams along the corridors. Sofia found her godmother attentively embroidering a tablecloth intended as a future wedding present. Her godmother supported Sofia's relationship with Ferderico. whereas doña Julia only approved of Alberto for her daughter.

Her godmother was a small, slender woman, with good posture. Ana María was sturdy like all the Carrasco women. Her earrings matched the ring on her left hand, and the weight of the gold and the emeralds stretched the lobes of her small ears. Her fleshy and prominent lips gave away her dominant and sensual character and her some times flaring nostrils reflected her moods when they stretched for more oxygen. She ruled with her chocolate brown eyes: the eyes of a worldly woman who has seen everything. Sofia looked like her, although taller and with green eyes.

"Sit down, " the godmother said, without greeting her or making any comments about her dress or her looks as she usually did. Sofia sat next to her, and asked, "What's wrong?" but her godmother noticed that the maid was observing them with great curiosity from a corner of the patio and called out, "Amelia, go and make us a coffee."

The maid obeyed and feeling rejected, turned around to hide her disgust. Everything was a secret since the war started.

The godmother looked at Sofia with a sadness she was incapable of hiding.

"It's something very serious," she said, making her voice smaller and swallowing her saliva. "Luis told me in confidence when he came for lunch that the prefect, Saturnino Belalcázar, wants to put Federico behind bars. They suspect he was involved in the failed attack on the city."

"Federico compromised?" She couldn't say more and stared at her godmother with eyes full of tears and fear. Her lower lip trembled and she felt cold and disoriented; if she hadn't been sitting she would have fainted.

The godmother, noticing Sofia's reaction, got closer to her to place her goddaughter's cold hands between her own.

"You are freezing," she murmured.

Sofia looked at her, overwhelmed with an emotion new to her heart, and started sobbing. She felt like she was drowning and no words would come out of her mouth. Finally, babbling and unable to control her tears, she said, "It's the damned war!"

She had felt that Federico was into something. It was a feeling, a concern, an I-don't-know-what that had taken possession of her since the days before Christmas when he began disappearing without mentioning where he was going. She even feared that he could have been involved with some soulless woman. He wasn't the same person.

The godmother gave her a handkerchief and said, "Here, dry your tears! I smell coffee. Let me call Amelia."

Sofia received the handkerchief, which smelled of cologne, and dried her tears very slowly. She was full of suspicion and questions.

Amelia brought the coffee and asked, "Something else, Ma'am? What's wrong with the niña?" She couldn't bear to see her crying.

"Oh, it's nothing. Family things, none of your business," said the godmother, annoyed with the maid.

Amelia, looking at Sofia with a sad expression left the patio.

Sofia slowly sipped the coffee while enjoying the warmth of the cup in her hands. She felt her pulse come back again and her cheeks recovered their color.

Looking at her godmother, she said, "What can we do? I will do anything for him. I will not tolerate seeing him in jail or being treated as though he were a dog."

"Calm yourself," her godmother exclaimed.

Sofia obeyed her, taking longer and longer sips of the coffee. She was self-absorbed, looking for answers to a thousand questions that ran through her mind.

After a long pause, the godmother put her cup on the tray. She said, "The prefect and Luis are responsible for all of us. They don't know what to do with the requests for justice made by the families that lost their sons who were trying to defend the city. They are being petitioned by the relatives and by the friends of those involved in the battle at Flautas. The nuns in the convents were in fear of what those wild men could have done to them and the novices. Just imagine!"

Sofia looked as she waited for an answer to all her fears.

"Thank God, Colonel Pinto and his soldiers defeated them. Luis says they captured about sixty Radicals, some of them from well-known families. Antonio Ramos came barefoot and in chains and his girlfriend saw him on his way to prison. His own family doesn't know what to do. Those poor people, they relied on him for everything."

"Who else is in prison?" Sofia believed that her godmother knew the past and the future. She was like a town cryer. What she didn't know she guessed, almost always correctly.

Her godmother continued, "From what I know, they have Dr. Cajiao. The prefect had him jailed after the assault. It was logical, if you think about it: he is the chairman of the Liberal Committee. I heard he was interrogated for hours but refused to talk. Luis said that Dr. Cajiao is a tough one. They said he will not give away any information and has no fear of anybody. I think he would die before betraying any of his friends. To me it is horrible to see him in prison. Such a cultured man, so gentle and pleasant, not long ago he was the president of the university. He deserves better treatment. He is not a beast."

Sofia, thinking about Federico, said,"Do you know if they tortured him? It truly frightens me to imagine Federico in jail. He is very discreet and doesn't do anything without thinking about it very carefully and in my heart I know he is not involved but as ill as he has been, he could easily die in that pigsty. They don't even have the means to feed the poor men, they hardly can feed their own soldiers."

"Are you feeling better now?" asked the godmother, avoiding the question about torture. She couldn't share all of what Luis had told her. She also knew how to be discreet when it was necessary.

"Yes, I think so, thank you, but I have to see Federico at once to tell him the prefect intends to arrest him, to make sure they don't catch him by surprise."

"Yes, but tell him that all of this is highly confidential. It could cost Luis his own head. Tell him not to share this with anyone. Tell him to write directly to Luis if he wishes but not to go to the Government House. If he decides to write to Luis, you may bring me the letter and I will deliver it to Luis."

Sofia stood up and warmly embraced her godmother. She trusted her with all her heart more than anyone.

"Amelia!" shouted the godmother. She wanted the maid to accompany Sofia.

"I am going home. My mother will be waiting for me and I am afraid to go by myself. If I don't see you sooner, I'll be back on Tuesday." And Sofia left with Amelia.

"Don't cry any more, Niña, everything will turn out better," said Amelia, trying to start a conversation. Sofia nodded without comment. She didn't want to talk to anyone. She didn't trust anyone but her godmother, not even the Holy Father and certainly not Amelia.

The godmother tried to continue embroidering but could not concentrate on her project. She asked herself what would become of Sofia and of Federico if they locked him up, but she had no answer. She was not as wise or as much of a fortune-teller as Sofia thought, but she loved Sofia like the daughter she never had. It all was in the hands of the prefect and Luis. Frustrated, she folded the tablecloth and put it away in her sewing bag. She was concerned about Antonio Ramos. But she couldn't talk about her feelings with anyone, for no one knew that Antonio Ramos was her dear lover, that he was the man her husband Luis could only pretend to be. What would happen if Luis found out she and Antonio were lovers? But, what else could she do?

VI: Sofia in Federico's Home

Your sisters are thinking of talking with Pedro Lindo. What I
am telling you about, they don't know.

—Second Letter from Sofia to Federico

When she returned home, Sofia felt obligated to check on
her mother wondering how she was doing but fearing to
have to listen to her putting Federico down. Doña Julia
did not even try to accept Federico as the potential father of her grandchildren. "Lemos-Usuriaga" didn't sound right to her as their full family
name. Belonging to families like the Argüello, with four hundred years
of history in the city, where did Sofia come up with the idea of getting
involved with a newcomer? Don Nicomedes could have been an honest
Galician and a well-read man with many good local friends, but in Popayán he wasn't more than a poor bookseller: roots there, a newcomer.

Sofia walked into her father's studio and found her mother reading
on the sofa next to the desk where her father, the professor, had always
prepared his lectures or looked for the origin of a word in a language
forgotten for a thousand years.

"Hello Mother, how are you feeling?"

"I find it hard to describe how I am feeling. Every time I come here to read I cannot stop thinking about Juan Francisco. I can see him working at the desk, and I talk to him but he doesn't answer. He hasn't changed; when he was alive he didn't answer either."

"But Mother, you have lived for years without him and you continue with your visions. Let him rest in peace. If you decided to read seriously and stopped looking at the walls with the book in your hands, he would leave the desk and you wouldn't see him again. I promise you. Concentrate on your reading, please!"

"All right, dear. Tell Betsabé to bring me a cup of tea. She knows which one calms me and helps me to read in peace."

Sofia went to the kitchen and asked Betsabé to make a cup of tea.

"Betsabé should bring your tea soon," she said upon returning to her mother.

"Thank you, my dear. God bless you."

Sofia had no clue that Betsabé's tea was what made her mother envision the professor as though he were alive. Betsabé made it with fresh chamomile, coca leaves, and brown sugar. Sofia went to her room to change her blouse before going to visit with the Lemos sisters and to see Federico. She had to let him know what the governor had said about the prefect's plans to put him behind bars.

"Mother, I am going to visit with the Lemos to look for some books and return others. I will take Betsabé with me. Get comfortable and drink your tea. If you need anything, ring the bell to get Griselda's attention. She is doing the laundry. Ring hard, she likes to play deaf. I'll warn her to make sure she doesn't find any excuses."

Her mother nodded while sipping the tea again with the book open on her lap. The professor would appear anytime. Sofia blew her a kiss and with the same hand she waved goodbye. By the front door she found Betsabé sweeping the sidewalk to stay busy as she waited for Sofia.

"Stop what you are doing and come with me, please. It's about to rain any time. I feel water in the air. If we move fast enough we may get there without getting wet."

When they passed Santo Domingo Church, it started to rain and they had to hurry to avoid getting wet. Betsabé, laughing out loud, announced their arrival. From her desk Mariana saw them crossing the street, and was surprised by the bustle made by the maid and the unexpected arrival of Sofia.

"Come in, come in or you will get soaking wet!" said Mariana, standing up to greet Sofia. Betsabé left the books on the counter and ran to the kitchen to visit with Mariana's maids.

"Have a seat, please. What brings you here in such a hurry?" Mariana continued, leading Sofia toward the chair next to her desk.

"I came to check on Federico, and to return these novels and look for some books."

"I am concerned about his illness. He still has the chills. This morning he was feeling better and now he is reading upstairs in the study. As you know, Federico cannot stand noise when he is ill. He becomes an ogre. Lola and Rosita left because he didn't want to see them and complained they were too noisy. I expect them back at any time from visiting with friends. Why don't you go upstairs to see him? It will be a pleasant surprise, he misses you."

Sofia climbed the stairs nimbly and found Federico seated in the rocking chair with a wool blanket over his lap. He was reading *Two Treatises of Civil Government* by Locke. When she entered the room with her rosy cheeks he couldn't hide a smile of pleasure and surprise.

"The sound of your heels made me think that Lola and Rosita were back, they move like a storm. What a surprise to see you instead! Sit down, please. That wicker chair next to my desk is very comfortable."

"How are you feeling? Mariana just told me that you are better but you look pale. You have to take care of yourself," she said and got closer to him to kiss his forehead since nobody was around. Kissing him, she noticed he had a fever.

Federico looked at her tenderly without saying a word. She continued observing him and did not like his appearance. He smelled like a sick man. Then, she delivered her news.

"Early this morning I went to visit with my godmother and she gave me the darkest news. Luis has told her in confidence that the prefect is considering putting you behind bars because they suspect you were involved in the Flautas attack."

Federico did his best not to show any surprise, and said, "Someone who strongly dislikes me is making up stories. I am not involved with anyone. But if they want to put me in prison they will do it, with or without proof. The prefect is locking up everyone who is not a known Godo or a declared government partisan."

"My godmother suggested that you should write to Luis to ask if he can help you. She thinks he can help you. She offered to personally deliver your note to make sure nobody knows about it. She is terrified that Luis could be accused of treason or something else if it's known he is granting favors to the liberals."

"Give her my thanks and my regards, but let me think about it. This is not something I should do without weighing the consequences. I do not want to compromise the governor nor give the impression I am at fault."

Sofia put her hand over Federico's and looked at him with a mixture of tenderness and sorrow. Then she heard the noise of Lola and Rosita coming upstairs to greet her.

"I must go now. Send me a message with Clodomiro if you decide to write the letter. I will take it to my godmother at once. Please take care of yourself."

Sofia stood up to greet Lola and Rosita and they greeted and embraced her. Federico said goodbye to Sofia and wished her good luck with his sisters, making it clear he wanted to be alone. After the women left, Federico—concerned and drained by the news—put the book on the table and wondered who had betrayed him. It had to be someone very close to him, an enemy or a dishonorable friend.

Federico closed his eyes, moved the blanket up to his neck and got lost in his thoughts. The fever gave him a sensation of exhaustion and a warm feeling of wellbeing, a feeling that he enjoyed. Right there he decided he would write to the governor to ask for help to try to convince the prefect to change his mind. He had no other choice; he couldn't run away or abandon his sisters and Sofia in the middle of a war. Besides, he had an important role to play in the Liberal Party. But he was incapable of writing at that moment. Without realizing it he fell into a deep sleep.

VII: Federico Writes to the Governor

The Godos claim you don't have any disputes to be settled.

—First letter from Sofia to Federico

The next morning, Federico was up at an earlier than usual hour. Clearly, he hadn't slept well. He could feel it in his bones. The idea of writing to the governor, asking for his help to avoid being put behind bars by the prefect, made him nervous. He didn't have a good idea of what to say in his letter and wasn't sure if asking for his help was his best option. After a while, he asked for a cup of coffee and went to his study to clear his mind. He concluded he couldn't continue to live in fear and the only solution was to make a decision.

The strategy was to start the letter in order to defend his innocence and blame his enemies for accusing him of being part of the failed attempt to take over the city on Christmas Day. He also had to protect his pride and respect for the authorities regardless of the outcome of their decision. In brief, he was sick and needed a few days to recover. It was time to write.

He took a page of engineering paper that he had used in his surveying projects and wrote:

POPAYÁN, FEBRUARY 3, 1900

Don Luis Enrique Zorrilla.
Dear Sir and friend:

I thank you very much for the kindness you have shown in informing me about the determination made by the prefect to detain me for my supposed participation in the recent events of the assault on the city. I understand that this can only be due to intrigues by someone who strongly dislikes me and, I assume, wants to see me behind bars. Even though I cannot pretend to be an admirer of the government's ideology, as is known to those who know me well, I am convinced I have no disputes to be settled.

For this reason, I assume the freedom of begging you to plead with the prefect to grant me more time, until I recover from an illness that has me incapacitated. As a citizen, I respect the office of the Prefect of Popayán and I am willing to surrender to the authorities if they believe they are justified in moving forward with his determination.

I remain, in expectation of your orders,
your courteous friend.

Federico Lemos

Satisfied with his letter, Federico put it in a sealed envelope that he hid in his coat pocket. The decision to write the letter made him feel much better. Then Clodomiro came to check on him and Federico asked him to get closer.

"Do me a favor: go and tell Sofia that I want to see her as soon as possible." Clodomiro knew what Federico meant when he wanted something done 'as soon as possible.' He nodded and left at once, trotting hurriedly as fast as his short legs could take him.

"What's going on? This business of 'as soon as possible' is suspicious," he muttered to himself as, without losing a moment or looking around in the shops, he went directly to Sofia's home. She listened to Federico's request, grabbed a grapefruit from the fruit basket, and departed with Clodomiro, who had a hard time keeping up with her.

When they arrived at the bookstore, Sofia greeted Mariana and without further ado told her she wanted to check on Federico.

"I'm downhearted. It has been two weeks and he continues to have a fever. Go upstairs. Yesterday you made him feel better and he slept after your visit."

"I won't be long. I just want him to know I am thinking about him. I brought him a grapefruit, I'll give it to him and come right down."

"He is reading. Go ahead, he will happy to see you and he loves grapefruit."

Sofia climbed the stairs in a hurry and found Federico in his studio.

"I brought you a little present. You look renewed. You don't know how much I love to see you with good color."

"Yes, it is true I am feeling better. I can't wait to get rid of this illness. Thanks for the grapefruit," he said, while taking out the envelope to give to her.

"You know what it is about. Don't allow anybody to see it. Not even Mariana."

"I understand. Don't worry. God willing, Luis will help you."

Sofia put the envelope in her skirt pocket, got closer to Federico, said goodbye and kissed him on his forehead. He still had a fever and that distinctive smell of a sick person.

"I'll see you soon. Eat the grapefruit, please, it'll make you feel better."

She winked at him in a loving manner as she left the room and went downstairs to say goodbye to Mariana.

"He is improving and his color is better but he looks like he still has a fever. Oh, I wish I knew what was wrong with him! Make sure he eats the grapefruit. I would love to visit with you but I must go."

"Would you like Clodomiro to accompany you?"

"No, thanks. I prefer to go alone. I will get there faster." They understood each other. She didn't notice that Clodomiro had heard her and had made a face at her unkind comment.

*   *   *

SOFIA DIDN'T WASTE A MOMENT: she went directly to her godmother. Amelia opened the door and accompanied Sofia to the bedroom where Ana María was asleep. She was not a morning person. Sofia woke her up, kissing her on the forehead.

"Luis is at the farm, what brings you here at this hour?" said the woman as she sat up in bed and she stretched.

"I think you can guess. I saw Federico a few moments ago and he seems better but he still has a fever."

"Did he write something for Luis?"

"Yes, he did. That's why I came. Here is the letter. God willing, Luis may be able to help him. With all that I hear about the prisoners and those that have disappeared I have not been able to sleep after what you told me about the prefect's intentions. I was up all night."

Ana María took the letter from her hands, looked at the seal on the envelope and put it carefully under her pillow.

"I will deliver it to Luis as soon as he is back from the farm. He loves the countryside and I love when he goes away because I can sleep until late without feeling guilty. Tell Federico he can count on my help. I will find a way. Let us have a little coffee. Without my morning coffee, I am useless." She called Amelia to ask for coffee for both of them.

The maid came and left, wondering why Sofia was visiting so early. What was she looking for? What did she need?

VIII: The Governor and the Prefect

My uncle said that your sisters should go to see the prefect at two o'clock.

—Third letter from Sofia to Federico

D on Luis Enrique Zorrilla, the governor, returned from his farm on Saturday afternoon accompanied by Delfino Alegría, the army's payroll clerk and an old friend. They shared a love for rabbit hunting. Delfino was one of the few persons in Popayán who addressed the governor by his first name.

"I'll see you on Monday, Luis. I've been missing our hunting adventures. Now, I can't wait to have rabbit cacciatore. Thanks for everything," he said from the saddle of his horse, and continued toward the *Calle de la Moneda* where he lived. They had become close neighbors since Luis and Ana María moved to the Government House.

Ana María heard them arrive and spruced up to greet the men at the door. Luis was letting a servant put his horse away.

"How did you do at *La Floresta*? Did you manage to rest?"

"Yes dear, thank you. We had a great time. Every time I go to the farm I have less of a desire to come back to the city."

"Did you bring something for the week?"

"Delfino and I shot six rabbits, three for the Alegría family and three for us. I also brought you some lilies, a bag of fruit, and two bunches of plantains. The potatoes were not yet ready for harvesting. Gumersindo sent you a cheese that he had been aging and two chickens that had stopped laying eggs."

"He is a good man. Since we hired him the farm hasn't stopped producing. At least we know he is not eating everything."

"He asked for permission to help some relatives displaced by the war who wished to stay at the farm until they can return to their places. They should have enough to eat."

"I assume you gave him permission."

"Of course. It's the natural thing to do. We have to be human. There is so much tragedy in war. Nothing gives me more pleasure than helping someone in need."

"Speaking of need, Sofia came to visit and brought a letter from Federico Lemos. Do you want to read it now?" she said, and he nodded.

She handed him the envelope, which she had refrained from steaming open only by great effort of the will, and he proceeded to read looking up now and then to frown at his wife. The veins of his temples began to pulse, which she knew showed that he was irritated and he couldn't hide it.

"Damnation! We just defeated them and he comes up with his liberal pride and his opinions about the government, as if that would convince me to help him. If the prefect sees this letter he will put him in jail right away."

"But Luis, you are overreacting. You must help Federico. Sofia will die if they put him behind bars. He is not used to living among criminals. I know he is innocent," said Ana María, stressing her words to make sure Luis understood that this was between the two of them. He had to do something to save Federico.

Luis took a deep breath. "Calm yourself, my love!" he said. "I'll see what I can do. Tell Sofia that I cannot promise anything certain. This decision belongs to the prefect and he is not in the best mood to be helping someone like Federico, a known liberal. I will have to twist his arm." He folded the letter to put it away in the secret drawer of his desk. He thought it could be useful later on.

"I have an idea," Ana María said, to get his attention.

Luis turned around and leaned on the desk to listen to her. She observed him carefully looking at his body language.

"What's on your mind, Ana María?" he said, dragging the words. He was still aggravated and she knew it.

"Let's go to see the Belalcázars to take them some lilies and part of the cheese. They can't refuse our gift. We won't stay long. I promise. And, by the way, you can talk to the prefect to make sure he helps Federico. He is an old client of the bookstore and knows that the Lemos sisters don't have anybody. It would be a crime to leave them without Federico."

"But you know it is too late to go visiting anyone, much less the prefect who is not very amicable these days"

"If we wait the lilies will wither. Let us go right now. It is only two blocks away and I need a walk. I didn't even think of going out while you were away," she said, heading to the kitchen to get the presents. She knew how to manipulate him.

"Soldiers don't understand anything but orders," she muttered so he could not hear.

When she returned with the flowers and the cheese wrapped in plantain leaves, Luis was already waiting for her in the hallway. He was used to waiting. It was his fate.

"Here, hold these things for a moment while I put on my shawl. It is getting cold and I don't want to catch a cold."

A few minutes later she came back wearing her shawl. Luis gave her a satisfied look. She was a beautiful woman who knew how to control him with her little finger. She was the the governess of the governor.

*　　*　　*

THE PREFECT AND HIS WIFE MARISA received them cordially and asked them to come in. Marisa was happy with the flowers and even more pleased with the cheese.

"You don't know how grateful we are you haven't forgotten us. With the war we have lost our friends. People don't come to visit anymore, I do not know if it is because of fear or hatred. Come in, there is a chilling air out there tonight," said Marisa, while taking Ana María by her arm. "Saturnino, please offer something to Luis while we arrange the flowers in a vase."

The governor noticed that Marisa said 'please' to the prefect. Ana María never did that with him. She always told him what to do.

Luis thought, as he walked with the prefect to the parlor, that he could take advantage of their moment of privacy to bring attention to Federico's situation.

"To your health!" said the prefect, toasting Luis, who raised his glass and took a good sip with evident pleasure. The prefect joined him, carefully taking only a little sip and wondering about the reasons for the visit and the presents. He didn't have to wait long. The governor said, "I have something uncomfortable to share with you. I do not know if you know that Federico Lemos is courting Sofia Usuriaga, who is Ana María's goddaughter."

He responded, "No, I didn't know. I don't get involved with things like that. That's the business of matchmakers."

"Sofia says that he is quite ill. I would appreciate if you would give him a break until he recovers. It would be hard if you put him behind bars in good health but it could be fatal for Federico and even worse for Sofia if you put him away while he is still very sick."

"It is true. I always look at the human side of these issues. But as prefect I must apply the law to whomever it applies and when it is necessary, even more so now when the wounded who fought in Flautas are asking for justice."

"We both know he is a liberal—it's something he doesn't hide—but above all he is an honest gentleman who has served the city well and deserves to be treated as such."

"I will consider a truce after I verify how sick he is. The information I have in my hands forces me to proceed as I told you I would. Are we finished?" said the prefect, speaking low and quickly when he saw the ladies coming back with the vase of flowers. He finished his brandy in one gulp. He was completely annoyed.

"It is your decision and as such I will respect it," said the governor, setting his glass with the dregs of his drink on the table. Then, addressing his wife, he said, "Let's go, Ana María. It is getting darker and you promised that we would not stay late."

He shook hands with the prefect, looking at him in the eye, and said goodbye to Marisa, wishing them a good night. Ana María remained silent.

"Thank you for the cheese and the flowers and for coming to see us, even if it was only a short visit," said Marisa as they were leaving. There was an icy cold wind coming from the Puracé volcano. What was the prefect thinking? wondered Marisa.

IX: Federico Is Taken to Jail

> Don Quixote raised his eyes and saw that on the road he was
> following, about twelve men on foot were coming toward him,
> strung by the neck, like links on a long iron chain, all of them
> with shackles on their hands.

—*Don Quixote,* First Part, Chapter XXII

POPAYÁN, FEBRUARY 1900

Federico woke up to a luminous morning and felt somewhat recovered from his illness. His soul was back in his body. He had a good breakfast and went to the bookstore, where Mariana was dusting the bookshelves and putting papers in order. Clodomiro was reading an enormous book, engaged in the big task of attempting to memorize all the words in the Spanish dictionary.

"You don't know how happy I am to see you around here again," said Mariana.

She didn't like the looks of her brother. He was still very pale and the wrinkles on his forehead added ten years to his quixotic figure. Her clinical eye didn't fail: he was still sick and they had no idea what was ailing him.

"I miss the routine of the bookstore."

"Is it true that you feel better?" she said to find out what he would say.

He looked at her, evidently annoyed, and said, "Yes and no. The breakfast suited me well and I came to see if by doing something in the bookstore I might forget my illness. I still don't know what's wrong with me."

He moved the stool closer to the counter and sat down. It was his favorite spot, his throne. Mariana noticing that Clodomiro was spying on their conversation and, to get rid of him, asked him to find out from Mama Pola—the oldest maid, who had raised them—what was needed, to make a shopping list, and to go with her to the market.

Clodomiro left happily for the kitchen—he loved to go shopping and to taste everything in the market. Also, he was a master at bargaining.

As soon as he left to look for Mama Pola, Mariana said, "Since you have been sick I have no inner peace. I feel restless all the time. I don't know what is worse, war or fear." Federico listened thoughtfully before he answered.

"Don't worry. The liberal victory is imminent. This war is a business of months, if not weeks or even days."

"You say that and they just defeated you at Flautas."

"The first corn is for the parrots," said Federico, annoyed by her comment, and continued to browse the book he had on the counter as if she didn't exist. Frustrated, his sister shrugged her shoulders and continued with her duties. She didn't believe a word of what he was saying.

*   *   *

AROUND NINE, TWO OF FEDERICO'S OLD FRIENDS, Salustio Guzmán and Evaristo Rengifo, arrived to find out how he was doing.

"Good to see you on your feet again. How are you feeling?" said Salustio.

"Not as well as I would like, but it looks to me like I won't die from this one," Federico replied.

"I came to get back the book by Locke that I assume you have already read at least twice." said Evaristo.

"I am happy you fellows came," said Federico. "I have surprises for you both."

To Salustio he gave *La Mascota* and to Evaristo the *Deontology or Science of Morality* by Bentham and Locke's *Civil Government*, returning the loan.

"How did you like it?" Evaristo asked.

"It fits the moment. Without doubt, we are more than justified to rise in arms against an oppressive government that limits our constitutional freedoms and denies our most elemental rights as citizens."

"Look carefully at Bentham and you will see that, with Locke, they are the two ideological pillars of the Liberal Party. The differences between Bolívar and Santander about civil and penal legislation defined the ideologies of the conservative and liberal parties. For that reason, Bolívar prohibited Bentham's works by decree, in opposition to Santander, adopting a clerical and conservative position that is the foundation of the 1886 Constitution. These are the sources of the conflict we are living and the reasons to justify this war."

"Don Miguel Antonio Caro has these sources on his brain," said Evaristo sarcastically, thinking about the old conservative politician.

"I would prefer if you leave your political peroration for another day," said Mariana, fearing that somebody could hear them. Even the walls had ears.

Clodomiro, returning with the grocery list, heard Mariana and got intrigued by the unfamiliar word *peroration*.

"Don't worry, we only stopped for a moment to check on Federico's health and exchange books. Reading is one of the few freedoms we still have," said Evaristo, departing in animated conversation with Salustio.

"I'm glad they didn't stay long," said Mariana to Federico.

"I am glad they came. Friends who don't retreat when things get difficult are rare."

"Yes, it's true. But I would prefer if they came to buy books and not to loan them," said Mariana, raising her eyebrows to frame her commentary. Her brother was too much of an idealist and didn't realize that they had just enough to eat. He lived in another world.

At that moment she noticed that Clodomiro was patiently waiting with the grocery list in his hand. She gave him the money for the food they needed and sent him to the market with Mama Pola.

*   *   *

WHEN THE CHURCH BELLS RANG at noon, Mariana closed the bookstore. The aroma of tortilla soup was coming from the kitchen and she was hungry. They wouldn't go to the funeral Mass for the victims of the battle at Flautas. Federico's health was a good excuse to stay at home and she didn't feel like listening to sermons. Besides, she was hungry and the smell of tortilla soup was tempting.

*   *   *

AT TWO O'CLOCK, AFTER THE SIESTA, Federico and Mariana opened the bookstore again. Standing by the threshold she watched the people coming and going, looking for clients or familiar faces. Then she noticed a man in the entrance of the church of Santo Domingo who appeared to be spying on the bookstore. She had seen him going by during the week and even that very morning. He was a stranger, and why would he be loitering there if not to spy?

As if he could read her mind the man entered the church. She remained thoughtful and fearful but didn't say anything and went back into the bookstore. She had plenty to do.

It was a slow Friday and she sat by her desk and opened the accounting book with the reverence generally used by priests during Mass when they open the Gospel. She retrieved her pen from the velvet case and dipped it in a thick dark green glass inkwell. Then she let the pen drip off its excess and started to settle accounts in the columns labeled Payments and Receipts. There was not much to settle but routines put order in a person's life and Mariana couldn't live without it.

Writing was a pleasure. She loved her writing style, clean and clear, with rounded letters in the French style that she had learned at the *Colegio de María*. To write with a pen was like painting or playing a musical instrument. The pen converted her thoughts into words and numbers, the story of the business.

"Ink smells like the spirit of ideas," she muttered to herself. She stopped writing, and breathing in the ink vapors and lowering her eyelids, she stretched her neck with a sensual motion, like a swan. All that was missing was someone to appreciate her beauty. She was an attractive woman even if some thought of her as a spinster.

Next to her, by the well-used wooden counter, Federico killed time browsing through books. He appeared to be made of wax. The wrinkles on his forehead gave away the tension that was oppressing him. It was a matter of time. His clandestine position in the liberal resistance did not allow him to leave the bookstore. His only option was to live normally as long as he could. If they put him in prison they wouldn't be able to prove anything, he believed, but he couldn't concentrate right now. His mind jumped from one thing to another. It was the restlessness of his presentiments.

Mariana, who had known him since he was born, felt it too. Clodomiro was looking for something in the enormous dictionary of the Spanish language: *Diccionario de la Lengua Española* of don Ramón Joaquín Domínguez. He had just found the word *perorate* that he heard Mariana say. The dictionary said:

"*Perorate*: speech or reasoning, sentence or angry harangue, upsetting and untimely."

Then, in an *upsetting and untimely* way two officers in uniform entered the bookstore armed with regulation revolvers and sabers. They wore blue jackets with high collars and golden buttons. Both wore black riding boots. The younger one, Sergeant Orlando Barbosa, a young man with dark skin and a joyful face, wore a black plush hat. He looked more like a student disguised for the traditional student parties in southern Colombia than like a military officer. The other one, impeccable, tall and lean, was Lieutenant Froilán Bordón. He exhibited the vestiges of a recently shaved blue beard and a black French military hat with a gold ribbon that matched the buttons of his blue jacket, which reached only to his waist. He looked like a freshly painted little tin soldier.

"Good afternoon," said the tin soldier Bordón, raising his weak voice to be noticed. Mariana looked at him with contempt. Federico thought: *My time has come.* Mariana's face clearly showed her confusion: what were they there for? Clodomiro, the most astute, didn't have to ask any questions. He knew why they were there. He straightened his neck and stopped the rocking chair's sway.

"Don Federico, I have been ordered to arrest you and take you to prison," said Officer Bordón, showing him a document on official paper.

"The capture order from the prefect," he announced, shaking the paper. The announcement created a tense silence. Only Clodomiro's eyelids moved as he lifted his gaze from the book to the room and his bulging eyes captured the moment like a photographic plate in the dark chamber of a camera. He was all eyes and ears. Even the rocking chair, when it stopped moving, ceased ticking off demarcations of time.

"Capture order?" said Federico, looking at Lieutenant Bordón.

"Yes, sir," said the lieutenant, handling him the paper.

Federico read it and he froze. He had lost his freedom. He passed the paper to Mariana and closed the book. He approached the counter while looking coldly at the officer. His temples throbbed. He made a sideways glance toward Mariana, who had just finished reading the order, and found her eyes full of questions and sadness. The paper was fluttering in her shaking hands.

"Lieutenant, this is shameful, coming from the prefect or from the Pope," said Mariana, standing up with the paper in her hands.

"These are orders, ma'am, nothing personal," said the lieutenant with a small shrug and a voice that reflected his insecurity and nervousness. The handcuffs clipped to the young sergeant's belt jingled as he, too, shuffled abashedly.

Federico stretched out his hands and submitted to Sergeant Barbosa, who nervously handcuffed him while noticing Mariana's fury.

"With your permission," said Officer Bordón, while taking Federico by the arm to take him out to the street. Six soldiers were waiting on the sidewalk, all of them in blue and white uniforms and straw hats.

"Cowards!" shouted Mariana from the doorway, with all the impotence and fury that came with the arrest of her brother. It was painful to see her brother treated as a common criminal while he was still recovering from his illness.

Federico, very calm and self-aware, looked at her again and bowed as a sign of farewell before he departed with the officers without looking back toward the bookstore. He felt that somebody well known had betrayed him. They didn't have any proof to detain him.

When he moved into the street he didn't see how surprised Lola and Rosita were, observing him from the balcony. Mariana slammed the bookstore door furiously and went upstairs to look for her sisters.

"What did Federico do to be taken prisoner?" they asked in unison.

"Nothing, idiots, nothing! The Godos do what they damned well please." The sisters were bathed in their own tears and felt terrified to hear Mariana using vulgarities.

"But you are not a soldier or a whore to speak like that!" Lola said.

The maids, scared by the slamming and the sobs, came up to see what was happening. Mama Pola couldn't stop shaking her head and making the sign of the cross. "Holy Blessed Saint Barbara! What are we going to do without don Federico?" said the old maid. She had seen everything in half a century of wars and knew from her own experience that in the time of war those detained today are dead tomorrow.

"Don't be concerned," Mariana drew herself up. "Federico isn't guilty of anything. This is a ploy to get money we don't have. They put the innocent in jail and try to extort their families." But privately she wondered if she would see Federico alive again. Mama Pola just raised her eyebrows, looking at them through her wise eyes that gave her thoughts away.

*   *   *

FEDERICO, UNCOMFORTABLE WITH THE HANDCUFFS that hurt his wrists, tried to stay as calm as he could in his situation. The showy uniforms of the guards and the sight of Federico in handcuffs attracted the attention of neighbors, beggars, and bystanders. Some people who knew him said hello with dissimulation, hiding the fear they felt on seeing him as a prisoner. Several vagrants laughed to see a well-dressed man this way. For the first time, Federico felt the pains of the war in his own flesh and moved from a being a member of the liberal secret committee to a battlefield soldier. The same streets that had taken him from the bookstore to school were taking him to prison. He again felt the honest pride of those that put their life at risk to defend their ideals and rights. Going as a handcuffed prisoner, brought to mind the image of the *Ecce Homo* condemned by the local Pharisees. The group turned the corner following the *Calle del Empedrado* and continued to the jail by the *Calle de la Cárcel*.

Clodomiro, like the Holy Spirit, knew how to be everywhere. Mariana noticed neither that he stepped down from the rocking chair nor that he followed Federico; the guards did not notice his presence. The only one who saw him was Rosita, who didn't miss anything that her little dwarf did. Clodomiro examined everybody, each door and each window, to see who said hello and who insulted, and in the middle of his anguish and fear he enjoyed every moment. He felt like he was at the circus looking at the clowns, the tightrope walkers and the beasts taking part in the show: comedy and tragedy together this time as the tightrope walker fell from his rope. Scrutinizing the colorful military uniforms, he muttered to himself, "This may explain why the people in the military and the circus dress alike." Secretly, he loved their colorful attire. He had his own way of looking at the world. Everything was different looked at from the perspective he had as a tiny person. He was always below and the others above. But, in another way, he was always above, since only those we ridicule know firsthand the darkness of our hearts.

Federico alone saw the dwarf, and then Clodomiro reacted to Federico's look by moving his large head in a way that only they understood, a fraternal signal between those upstairs and those downstairs. They had a very intimate and mysterious connection. A look was enough. Federico looked at him once more and was escorted into the prison.

Crossing the threshold of the prison, Federico detected with disgust a humid mist, a mixture of the alcoholic stink of the guards and something even more disgusting. It smelled like a pigsty, of excrement. He couldn't breathe nor could he open his mouth. In the patio, Lieutenant Bordón transferred Federico to the guard in charge. That man took Federico to the dungeon, removed his belt, and took all he had in his pockets. With one single push he propelled him inside a dark room crowded with people and slammed the door. The smell was impossible. There were green flies everywhere. The prisoners looked at him in surprise, for he was so clean and well dressed. Federico saw a young man of distinguished bearing with a messy beard amid the human mass crowded in the room. He was looking at Antonio Ramos, dirty and almost unrecognizable, as Antonio said, "What brings you here?" He looked like a beggar dressed in rags, but Federico had relaxed a little to see a man he knew, and the prisoners' attitude changed when they saw the new arrival was Antonio's friend.

"They imprisoned me for my presumed collaboration with the attack on the city. I knew they brought you in chains from Flautas but I wasn't expecting to see you here," said Federico.

"I see that the defeat was inside and outside," said Antonio.

Federico asked, "Who accompanies you?" Antonio was chained to a tall, dark, and slender man.

"You idiot, it's Domingo Cervantes."

"Sorry, I didn't recognize you either. I heard about your comission from Constantino but didn't know you were a prisoner." Federico reached out to shake Domingo's hand. "How did you get here?"

"Colonel Pinto's troops escorted us to the city on the Day of the Innocents. The Godos brought us tied and barefoot from Flautas. We were three days without food. Since then, if we are lucky, we get a watery hogwash soup twice a day and coffee with a hard piece of dark bread in the morning." said Domingo.

"I was detained at the bookstore. I don't know who gave me away. It had to be someone known, a trusted person."

"Be careful whom you talk to and what you say in here," Antonio whispered. "People keep disappearing. The guards claim they were transferred to another prison or were set free, but when you look into it you find out they were shot. The Godos do what they want and then invent some story to fit their facts. They believe in their own lies."

*   *   *

CLODOMIRO HAD WATCHED FEDERICO disappear into the dark prison gate and then he slipped away in a hurry to tell Sofia what had happened. When he arrived at the Usuriaga home he waited for a few minutes before knocking on the door. He was out of breath. As he gasped he looked around: nobody had followed him. He used the door-knocker to make one loud sound followed by two rapid ones and three more to finish: tan, tan-tan, tan-tan-tan..

Betsabé recognized the code and went to open the door. Sofia saw the maid going by her bedroom after the knocking at the door; she called out to her, "Come here, Betsabé!"

The maid stopped. It was an order.

"It's Clodomiro," she said, whispering.

The knocking continued insistently. The maid looked at Sofia, raising her eyebrows to ask what to do.

"Open the door to find out what he wants."

Clodomiro, anxious for a reply, knocked once more: tan, tan-tan, tan-tan-tan. Sofia knew it must be something urgent.

Betsabé opened the door and saw him looking as red as a tomato.

"Hello, is Niña Sofi at home?"

"What's your hurry? What's going on?"

"The soldiers detained don Federico. Is Niña Sofi at home?"

"Take a deep breath or you are going to die," said the maid and allowed him to come in. Clodomiro followed her to the room where Sofia was waiting.

"Don Federico is in prison," said the dwarf when he saw her.

"Tell me what happened! Tell me!" said Sofia, and she told Betsabé, "Bring me a cup of tea and something for Clodomiro. He is as red as a beet."

"Some lemonade, if you have it."

The maid, proud or disgusted, raised her shoulders and went to the kitchen.

Clodomiro told Sofia all he had seen and heard without missing any detail.

She interrupted him constantly to ask more questions: What did Mariana say? Who detained him? Who insulted him? Who greeted him? And so on. Clodomiro replied to all her questions without hesitation. He had memorized every detail: the whole world could fit within his large head of 24 inches circumference.

While they drank the tea and the lemonade and Sofia questioned and Clodomiro commented, the maid lingered in a corner without saying a word. She couldn't believe what she was hearing. Her eyes moved constantly as she followed the conversation. It was her way of thinking. It had to be exhausting to think like that.

Sofia could take no more company. She thanked him for coming and asked that he tell Mariana she would come to see her soon. The dwarf took his last sip of lemonade and handed the cup to the maid.

Betsabé accompanied him to the door and followed him with her eyes until he got lost around the corner. He had not paid any attention to her. She slammed the door. He was not like that when they were alone.

Sofia was desolate and furious: with her godmother, with Luis and with the prefect. She locked herself in the bedroom and face-down on the bed holding her pillow with both hands cried until she ran out of tears.

"My God, what can I do?" she asked herself, looking for a way out of what fate had dealt her and her beloved Federico.

The first thing that came to mind, as always, was to go to see her godmother. Ana María knew everything and could find the direction at any crossroads. She called Betsabé and said, "I am going to visit with my godmother and then with the Lemos. I won't be late."

"Don't you want me to accompany you?" asked the maid.

"No, I am going by myself."

Betsabé noticed her mistress had been crying. That didn't look good. She was not the type that cries for no reason.

"I wonder what don Federico is involved in?" she asked herself, turning her eyes up toward the heavens for an answer. She looked and looked and nothing came to her. She would have to wait.

*   *   *

SOFIA FOUND HER GODMOTHER in the parlor dressed in mourning; she had not had time to change her clothes after the funeral Mass to honor the victims of the battle of Flautas. She knew Sofia would come to see her as soon as she found out about Federico and so Ana María wasn't surprised by her arrival.

At breakfast, Luis had informed her that the prefect's order to detain Federico, after the funeral Mass, was a done deal. He told her it was inevitable and that he couldn't do anything. The order was already in the hands of the officers in charge.

"Ana María, this time don't say a word to anyone," the governor had told her in a sharp tone, almost an order, just before going to the funeral Mass.

"I will never finish Sofia's trousseau tablecloth because this war is putting everything to an end," she murmured before Sofia's arrival interrupted her thoughts.

Without greeting her, Sofia said, "Clodomiro just told me that Federico is behind bars! That he was taken out of the bookstore in handcuffs and is in detention in the jail."

"Yes, dear, I already knew out about it," said the godmother, who had risen to embrace Sofia tenderly.

"You know everything even before it happens," the girl whispered in her ear. And then, more urgently: "Do you know what will happen to Federico?"

Then she felt her godmother's embrace and waited for an answer that would relieve her nervousness. But this time Ana María did not answer. She was thinking of all that could happen and she did not have the courage to tell Sofia. She simply held her tighter, the only thing she could do for the girl.

Finally, she tenderly pushed her away, and said, "I am not even able to think. I don't know what to tell you. Go and talk to Mariana. Ask her what happened at the bookstore. She must have been there when he was detained. What a horrible thing! What are they going to do without Federico? Women are being left alone. It is a tragedy. Even Antonio Ramos was brought in chains as though he was a criminal."

Sofia, seeing that her godmother was, if anything, in a worse state of mind than her own, decided to depart.

"I will leave you alone now," she said kindly. "Pardon me for bothering you with all my problems. My mother is incapable of helping me. She is living in another world." She couldn't wait until Mariana gave her all the details about Federico's capture.

Her godmother said, "Do as she does: consult with the spirits to see what you can find out, and then you tell me what they said."

Sofia looked at her, surprised, and kissed her on both cheeks and said good bye. She left for the bookstore thinking, *Consult with the spirits. . . is she going crazy, also?*

*   *   *

MARIANA, LOLA, AND ROSITA didn't know what to do. They had been humbled by the surprise arrest. Mariana had had the feeling that Federico was involved in something, but she didn't guess that he would be incarcerated. He had not even mentioned to her that the prefect was planning to detain him. Federico had his political activities, his business, and his family in separate compartments and Mariana, his confidante, knew about the business and the family. But secrecy was essential to protect himself, his political accomplices, and his sisters. His discretion was absolute. In communications with the National Liberal Directorate he used only his pseudonyms and even for that he was careful and he used two of them: *Lambda* and *Armodio*. Clodomiro was his private courier, for though the dwarf was extremely curious Federico knew he would never betray him.

When Sofia arrived at the bookstore she encountered the three sisters and Clodomiro, who pretended he was reading in his rocking chair in the corner. He thought in code, like parrots think, and that was his secret. He had learned from Leonardo da Vinci the importance of living in code.

"You finally came! We were waiting for you," Mariana exclaimed, rushing to embrace Sofia. The two women were Federico's allies and shared him in a relationship coated in mutual jealousy as they competed for his attention. But Mariana saw in Sofia her future sister-in-law. She considered Sofia as the only woman that really deserved to be Federico's wife. Mariana preferred to think that her role was to be Federico's best friend.

"I can't imagine how you are feeling," said Sofia to the Lemos sisters, corresponding to their embraces that felt more like condolences. She was frightened. Her premonitions, in particular, were terrifying her. Where did she come up with such dark ideas? Why did she have to imagine the worst that could happen?

"He was so animated after your visit. The grapefruit made him feel better. You don't know how much it helped him."

The expression in Sofia's face said it all; Marianna spoke of her brother as if he were already dead.

"Yes, and today they came to detain him. Isn't that strange?" said Rosita.

"This morning I saw a man on the stairs of Santo Domingo who was trying to hide his presence. I had seen him walking by and I felt insecure. I felt and suspected his intentions. He must have been a spy," said Mariana.

"You read too many novels. You think like a detective," Lola chided.

"I think Mariana is right," said Sofia, trembling. *They must be spying on me too.* "Didn't it occur to you to ask Federico about the spy?"

"No, it didn't cross my mind. But if I had thought about it I wouldn't have said anything. It would have been cruel, considering the condition he was in. He couldn't have faced more bad news."

"You are right. Now I understand," said Sofia, trying to apologize.

"It is five o'clock. Let us close the shop and have something to drink. Would you like a hot chocolate?" Mariana offered.

"I would love one, but I cannot stay long. I left my mother alone," said Sofia.

"Don't worry. I understand. My grandfather was like that. He forgot he was in this world. That is what happens to old people. They start to leave us little by little until they leave entirely," said Mariana, nostalgically thinking of don Nicomedes. But this time he was not there to comfort them. They were alone without anyone. And it was the war.

X: From the Jail to the Prison

They put me in chains, as a symbol of ransom, more than to
secure me. . . and they did this with many other gentlemen and
important people, labeled and held for ransom.

—*Don Quixote*, First Part, Chapter XI

Dawn. Federico was squatting against the wall under the
window facing the *Calle de la Cárcel*. He was thirsty and he
needed to relieve himself. His body ached all over. He tried to
stand up and was unable to do so. He looked over his knees, trying to
find a spot where he could urinate. A beam of light entered through a
crack between the wood panels and it split the space in the room. Thou-
sands of tiny particles floated in the heavy air of the dungeon, coming
and going into the light beam and getting lost again in the darkness.
He counted seventeen bodies in seventeen different positions. They
were puffing, snoring, and coughing. The bells rang to announce the
five o'clock Mass. He couldn't tell if the sound came from San José or
San Agustín. It was all the same to a sick man.

He felt like a mummy in a clay urn. He knelt with great effort and,
crawling like a spider, he crossed the room by feeling his way, trying not
to touch anyone. Somebody pulled at his trousers and pointed to a hole

in the adobe wall. He placed his forehead against the wall and peed into the hole. Some of the liquid got lost in the hole and some ran down the wall looking for cracks between the brick tiles on the floor. His socks felt wet. He was drained. He did not have enough energy to go back to his spot under the window. Defeated, he leaned against the door, allowing his body to slide down until he touched the tiles and the cold of the floor traversed the seat of his pants.

When the bells rang six, a guard opened the door and Federico had to stand up. He went out looking for fresh air and he felt the cold in the corridor. Several prisoners were drinking from the patio fountain. He approached them and waited for his turn. Desperately he drank the cold water until he couldn't hold any more. Then somebody called his name.

"Federico!" It was Dr. Cajiao. "I had no idea you also were detained by the godos. When did you get here?"

"I came in yesterday. They accuse me of being involved or somehow compromised in the attack at Flautas," said Federico.

"We are in the same boat. Are you still ill?" the doctor asked.

"I was improving until yesterday but today I feel lousy," said Federico.

Dr. Cajiao put his hand on Federico's forehead and found he had a high fever. He said, "Drink plenty of water and eat whatever they give us, even if you can't stand it. Breakfast is coming soon. Lunch will be at ten and dinner at five in the afternoon. If you are lucky, they may allow you to get food from outside but do not count on anything for at least a week. You have to ask for permission and pay a fee."

Breakfast was a piece of hard dark bread, along with hot water sweetened with brown sugar. For lunch they got a watery boiled corn soup with a piece of plantain, two potatoes, and a little piece of meat of uncertain origin. Dinner was a couple of boiled potatoes and coffee with a little sugar. It was a starvation diet. Some of the prisoners from Flautas had been there about a month and were already skin-and-bones. The meager diet converted the strongest into an invalid who barely had enough energy to walk across the room. It was a diabolical system, designed to reduce the prisoners to puppets who only moved when the puppeteers pulled the strings to play with them. In such conditions, being sick was as close as you can get to a death sentence.

*   *   *

AFTER A WEEK, FEDERICO HAD his first visitors. Sofia and Mariana came to see him, bringing clean clothes, something to eat, and a poetry book, *Ritos* by Guillermo Valencia, who was a great poet and friend of the bookstore. They were allowed to visit for fifteen minutes.

Federico felt ashamed. He was filthy and smelled like a wet dog. He kept a prudent distance so they couldn't smell him.

Sofia didn't know whether to laugh or cry about what she felt.

"That beard looks good on you."

"With my diet soon it will turn white or yellow."

Mariana told him that the bookstore had opened daily and sales had improved with visits from friends who came to ask about him and his health.

"Give them my best greetings. God willing they will continue coming and buying."

"Whether they come or not, we will be here every week at the same time. We have paid for a month. Take off those dirty clothes and we can wash and mend them," said Mariana, handing him a fresh pair of pants, shirt and socks.

Federico changed his clothes behind a door as the two women turned around more from pity than discretion. There was no place to hide. Mariana received the bundle of dirty clothes and gave him a towel with a toothbrush wrapped in it, a bar of soap, and a hemp bag with something to eat, and the book. When she gave him the hemp bag she whispered, "Clodomiro says that a hemp line is good for fishing. He put a hook in the back of the book." Federico listened in silence.

They had hardly spoken any words when the guard told them to hurry up. The fifteen minutes were almost over.

"Goodbye, brother," said Mariana looking at him with sad eyes.

"Goodbye, my love. Give my greetings to Domingo," said Sofia.

"Goodbye, my Dulcinea," said Federico.

"Is there anything you want us to bring next week?" Mariana asked.

"Bring me a set of cards, some wool socks, and any food you can bring. Give hugs to Rosita and Lola, and my best to Clodomiro and the maids."

Fig. 3—Early 1900's view of the Military Jail (left of the image, with two towers, already demolished) and part of the front arches of what is now the Hotel Monasterio, the only part of the original monastery that has been preserved. Photo obtained from professor Tomás Castrillón Valencia, Universidad del Cauca.

"Clodomiro is the one who misses you the most. You can't imagine how much he has helped at the bookstore."

"Give him a special greeting and my thanks for following me all the way to the prison, and for thinking about fishing."

"We'll do as you say. Eat what we brought for you," said Mariana.

The guard gave them a new signal that it was time to say goodbye and checked the hemp bag. Then he looked at the book and shook it to see if anything would fall out. He said nothing about the soap, the towel, and the toothbrush.

"Would you like to taste anything, Officer?" asked Federico, thinking that the guard could be of help some day.

"The cheese looks good."

Federico gave him the cheese and the guard broke off a chunk to taste it.

"May I go?" asked Federico politely.

"Go ahead, there are others waiting," said the guard.

Before leaving, Federico opened the bag and put as much food as he could in the pockets of his pants and coat. He left the rest in the bag to share with his cellmates. They either lived or died together.

*   *   *

MARIANA ACCOMPANIED SOFIA HOME. On the way they only talked about Federico: his beard, his pallor, the bad smell, and the dirty clothes. But they were happy to have seen him and sorry not to be able to see him for longer.

They never imagined he would be in prison for months. The visits continued, week after week. Luckily, Federico's health improved, but at every visit he looked thinner and thinner. From February to July, he must have lost thirty pounds. He was careful not to let them see him without his shirt; his ribs were visible like those of a poor man's horse.

*   *   *

EARLY IN JULY, THE GOVERNMENT spies informed the authorities that the liberals in the prison were in permanent contact with the Radicals. There were rumors of a new attack on the city and the governor ordered that the leaders of the political prisoners be transferred to the military jail (Fig. 3), down the street from the Church of San Francisco, where they would be incommunicado. The visits with Federico stopped at once when he was transferred along with Doctor Cajiao, Antonio Ramos, Domingo Cervantes and Hernandes. Federico had to share the same cell in the second floor of the military jail with Domingo, who was very ill.

*   *   *

POPAYÁN, AUGUST 1900

Sofia didn't wait long to ask for help from her godmother to find a way to communicate with Federico. The godmother already knew of his fate from the best source and expected her visit anytime.

"I was waiting for you. I had the feeling you would come to ask for a way to keep in touch with Federico."

"Tell me what to do, please. I am dying to find out how he is and what he may need. "

"Listen, Sergeant Llaves, one of the military jail guards, is the son of Filomena, who was one of the maids at my home when I was a child. Yesterday, I talked with him to assure that he can help you. But, you must be careful not to put him in a compromising position. I told him it would be a matter of passing Federico a book or something extra to eat. Just like you and Mariana did in the jail at the Calle de la Cárcel."

Sofia embraced her, amazed at her ability to come up with the solution to her problems and the answers to her questions even before she arrived at her home. The godmother held her tightly and proceeded to give her advice.

"Tomorrow, I have to visit with Domingo Cervantes, who I've been told is in the same cell with Federico. I promised Zoila, his wife, to bring Domingo some medicines for his ailments. I got permission from Luis to allow me to enter the prison to see him. I'll be happy to give Federico a note, to let him know what you are going to do to make sure there are no surprises when the Sergeant shows up with something for him."

Sofia wrote a note for Federico and gave it to her godmother. She delivered it to Federico when she came to see Domingo. He read it and was informed that she had a plan to use the book of Don Quixote to exchange letters with him. While the godmother helped Domingo with his medicines, Federico replied to Sofia on the same paper. The godmother was discreet and didn't read it, suspecting it was a message between lovers.

In the note, Federico gave Sofia instructions to get in touch with his sisters to ask them to visit with Delfina, who was the owner of the inn next to the prison. He was asking them to request Delfina's help to get Hernandes out of jail by placing a ladder against the prison wall to allow him to escape.

*   *   *

XI: Delfina

Don Quixote, taking the innkeeper's wife by the hand, said:
I only tell you, that I will keep eternally imprinted in my
memory the service you have rendered me.

—*Don Quixote*, First Part, Chapter XVI

After the battle of Flautas, the barracks building—headquarters of the Junín Battalion—was converted to a prison to accommodate the growing population of political detainees. The jail for ordinary criminals on the *Calle de la Cárcel*, where Federico was first incarcerated, didn't have room for so many men and the nature of the prisoners was different.

Delfina Bocanegra Beltrán was the owner of *Las Delicias,* a one-story inn next door to the Junín Battalion headquarters along the *Calle de la Moneda.* She sold food, supplies, chicha—fermented maize beer—and aguardiente. She had two billiard tables and half a dozen gambling tables for playing cards and dominoes. In the corridor, along the inner patio, there were six tables with benches on both sides where the customers ate their meals.

After the attack at Flautas the schools were ordered to close and thus, almost ruined Delfina's business. She was saved by the decision taken by the prefect and the governor to convert part of the barracks into a prison, with room for about 200 prisoners and their guards on the lower floor. Officers and important political prisoners occupied the upper floor. The towers on the corners of the building allowed the guards to keep an eye on the streets, the patios, and the roof of the building.

Delfina wasn't initially happy with having prisoners living next door to her inn, but in the long term she got the benefit of new customers who came to visit relatives in prison. Her best clients were the card players, some serious gamblers and others who were just old neighbors with nothing else to do. Between shots of hard liquor and smoking cigars they cheated each other and laughed, loudly slamming the tables when they won a trick. From what she heard from the gamblers and visitors that came in and out of the inn, Delfina was up to date about what was happening or was going to happen in the city, the neighboring towns, and in the bedrooms of the neighbors. She was the best-informed person in town.

Her lover, Martín Cienfuegos, the prison's sheriff, told her in bed that Federico Lemos, the owner of the bookstore *El Libro*, had been transferred to one of the high-security cells on the second floor of the prison. Delfina had known Federico since he was a boy. Professor Gallardo Lemos, his father, was a great pool player who liked to have a few drinks at her inn. After the death of his wife, Micaela, who was distantly related to Delfina, she often had to send the professor home with one of the maids because he was so drunk he didn't know how to go home or even who he was. She felt sorry for his family, who seemed to live from one tragedy to the next. First it was Micaela, then the professor, followed by don Nicomedes, and now Federico. She shuddered to think what else could happen to them.

It was several days after Federico's transfer to the prison when she noticed the arrival of Mariana, Rosita, and Lola. She thought she already knew why they had come. She asked them to come in and wait for her in the inner patio. But then Mariana explained to her what Federico was asking for and offered to pay Delfina something for her help. Delfina reddened with fury. These half-relatives that had scarcely looked at her since the professor's death—as if it had been her fault for having sold him the liquor—now had the nerve come to ask her to help a criminal— some stranger named Hernandes—to escape from prison at Federico's request. And they wanted to pay her for it as if she were their servant! She would have helped Federico to escape but to help somebody else—a stranger and a criminal—she could not even think about it.

But the sisters pleaded with her, reasoned with her, explained that this was what Federico wanted. When she managed to calm down and was able to talk again she told Mariana she wouldn't help a stranger in anything and that she would not provide a ladder. However, she offered to leave the hallway door unlocked to allow him to go out to the street if he jumped down from the prison's roof.

"Tell Federico that if there is a light on, it cannot be done. He can do whatever he wants but in the dark. Now, it's better if you go away before some officer finds out I've been talking to you." And so the sisters hustled away.

"That damned old woman knows only about drunkards and how to clean out their pockets. She doesn't give a damn about Federico. It's all about money," said Mariana to Lola and Rosita while they walked toward Sofia's home. She would be waiting for them, anxious to hear about their meeting with Delfina.

XII: *Alberto*

Alberto came today. He told me he was going to take an
interest in your case.

—First letter from Sofia to Federico

Sofia's hands used the needle with enviable skill. A gold thimble,
inherited from her grandmother, shielded her finger. She was
embroidering a pair of goatskin slippers for Federico. The needle
entered into the leather just as easily as the able spear of Don Quixote's
cut through the bodies of the enchanted giants. Each stitch was like a
love song: she wanted to surprise him on his Saint's Day. Her image,
reflected in her dressing mirror, imitated her movements with amazing
fidelity. Between stitches she dreamed of Federico and of the pleasure
of walking arm-in-arm with him in the Plaza Mayor. She was stylish
and elegant and enjoyed imagining the impression they would make as
a married couple. While embroidering the slippers, she could also envision Federico sitting on the floor in the prison with his back against a
wall, feeling hungry and humiliated with his idle hands over his knees.
Turning to her labor she relished the memory of those brief moments of
passion in the parlor or at a back corner of the bookstore when they'd
managed to be alone.

Between one memory and the next somebody knocked at the front door. Betsabé went to open it and from the door she called out, "It is don Alberto."

Sofia, surprised that the magistrate would come to visit so early in the day, replied, "Let him in and invite him to the parlor. I'll be there in a minute. I am going to spruce up a little. You can offer him a coffee in the meantime."

His unexpected visit could be used to help Federico. She knew she could get whatever she wished from Alberto. She had known how to manage him since they were in love in Quito during their years in exile. Alberto continued to hope to attract her again. With Federico in prison since February, perhaps he felt he had a new opportunity to make his intentions known. From the time he was a teenager he had dreamed of the celebration of their wedding at the cathedral in the presence of all the town notables.

Alberto Carrasco y Maisterrena firmly believed he came from no-ble ancestors and wasn't used to the idea of being defeated by people he considered to be of lesser lineage. One way or another he would get what he wanted, and he wanted Sofia with a force more possessive than sentimental.

While Alberto drank his coffee, Sofia powdered her face, put lipstick on, and added a couple of touches of perfume on her wrists and behind her ears. She approved of what she saw looking in the mirror. Her two-piece brown dress with a pleated skirt and a high-collared short jacket highlighted her beauty. The gold earrings proportioned to her beautiful ears were her only jewelry. She had arranged her hair in a high bun sim-ilar to Mariana's.

Sofia entered the parlor room showing confidence and approached Alberto to greet him. He stood up and admired her with pleasure, con-templating her beauty with a playful look, and taking her by the hands, said, "Little dove, what a pleasure to see you again."

Sofia couldn't stand to be called 'little dove' or to be taken by the hands like that. She was intimidated by his hawk-like-face so close to hers. Skillfully she escaped from his claws and, making a great effort to hide her annoyance, said, "Please, take a seat and forget about your nonsense. Our home is not a dove's nest."

He looked at her defiantly with a mocking and sensual smile and sat down. He enjoyed challenging women. Sofia sat on the woven straw sofa next to his chair where she could better accommodate her pleated skirt and remained thoughtful for a moment as she prepared her strategy for the visit. Alberto drank his coffee in small sips, gazing over the rim of his cup at her with a lascivious look.

He was elegant and distinguished-looking. His gray eyes shone over his prominent nose. He walked with a posture beyond vertical, taking long steps and looking from his bird of prey eyes as if searching for a dove to satiate his appetite. Everybody knew of his claims to ancestral relations with the Spanish nobility and all in Popayán were informed about his private audience with the Pope, his Holiness Leo XIII. They knew he shared a certain resemblance to the Pope from the little prints he brought from Vatican City, along with dozens of rosaries made with authentic wood from the Mount of Olives, to give to his friends and acquaintances.

Sofia, trying to control her feelings of hatred and rage, looked at him seriously and in a measured voice said, "It is almost a miracle you have come here. I was thinking of asking you for a favor and your visit saves me the trouble of going out."

"And what is it about? What can I do for you, my dear?" Alberto interrupted in a serious tone, scooting closer to her as if trying to hear her better. Sofia, nervous and under the pressure of his inquisitive look from less than a few feet from her face, blushed a little, bit her lip and said, "It has to do with Federico, as you can imagine. I am scared to death about what could happen to him in prison. The government is shooting people for any reason and just a suspicion is enough. To make things worse, and this is very confidential, Federico is trying to help one of his cellmates to escape from prison. I am afraid he may end up being shot for trying to be a Good Samaritan."

"That can be either very dangerous or very useful," Alberto replied, looking at her with a bothersome insistence that almost made her cry. "If somebody finds out that Federico is involved with the escape plan, he could end up against the wall, but the same information well managed could help to get him out of prison. And speaking of the prison, who is the detainee who Federico is trying to help?"

Sofia's heart started to palpitate out of control. She blushed carnation-red and without thinking she said, "Hernandes is his name. I understand they want to get him out of the prison through Delfina's Inn."

Alberto, getting so close to Sofia she could feel his breath on her face, looked at her with a spark of complicity and spoke with a voice both mellifluous and confidential.

"I cannot deny what you ask of me. I am going to take an interest in his case and I believe that if I say something about Hernandes, I will be able to get Federico out. Of course, I cannot guarantee anything and I fear everything could turn upside down if they suspect Federico is compromised and is trying to save his skin. I will think about it carefully. This thing about Hernandes is a double-edged knife."

"Do all that you can without compromising Federico. He is incapable of betraying anyone. If something happened to him, I could never forgive you."

Alberto, feeling he had lost the hand, turned to a defensive attitude to recover Sofia's favor: he proceeded to inform her of the seriousness of the situation and the danger that he would assume if he tried to help his friend Federico. He gave her the darkest reports he had heard about the prisoners. Since the leaders had declared war to the death, no prisoner could count on his life. She listened to him, very worried, but she was in control of herself by the time she replied.

"To avoid any misunderstanding, I will inform Federico of your intentions to help in whatever way you can and I will inform him of your idea of talking about Hernandes." She punctuated her speech with a captivating smile that left Alberto in ecstasy and more determined than ever to make her the woman that he had dreamed would share his bed and give birth to his children.

Betsabé showed up at that moment, as if she had been summoned to take away the coffee tray, and Sofia took advantage of her arrival to say goodbye to Alberto and accompany him to the door. She knew how to be coquettish when needed.

"I expect you will bring me good news soon," she said, and she started to close the door slowly to force him to go. Confused, feeling defeated by Sofia's composure, Alberto adjusted his frock coat, stood taller, and departed, stepping carefully in his shiny boots to avoid the fecal offerings that outsiders and locals had left as souvenirs of their satisfied needs along the sidewalks.

"Pigs!" he said to himself as he sidestepped.

PART THREE:

THE LETTERS

Walking along it with Don Quixote and Sancho, we arrive
at the understanding that all things share two origins. One is
our perception of things, "their meaning", what they are when
we interpret them. The other is their "material nature', their
actual substance, which constitutes them before and above any
interpretation.

—José Ortega y Gasset, *Meditations on Quixote*

XIII: Before the First Letter

Where I saw her for the first time, when I took her the letter
with the news of the insanities and stupidities your grace was
doing in the heart of the Sierra Morena.

—*Don Quixote*, Second Part, Chapter VIII

POPAYÁN, JULY–AUGUST 1900

It wasn't just hot, it was the hottest summer day. Sofia was making a doily for her nightstand to keep herself busy. While crocheting she could forget all her worries; it felt like being at church. Each stitch was a new prayer. Between stitches she looked at the hummingbirds hovering in the air around the fuchsias on the patio.

But then she began to think about Federico, to be tortured by her imagination.

When will he be out? Without him, I won't be able to continue living. What will I do if he contracts some horrible disease or if they kill him? Has he eaten today? I don't know what kind of political intrigues involve him. His secrets and his messages make my nerves go out of control. What in the devil could they be plotting?

She took a break, raising her eyes to look at the hydrangeas that Federico had planted next to the pond. For an instant, a smile between sweet and contemplative floated on her lips. In another instant she frowned. She was worried and anxious. She had waited and waited and didn't know how to wait any more.

Federico had been in prison for more than five months and they couldn't find a way to get him out. Early in July, he had been transferred from the civil jail to the military prison, next to the Government House. Now, she could neither see him nor talk with him. Recently, her godmother had suggested that she write to Federico in *Don Quixote's* book, using a secret code. Federico was her Knight Errant and this time she would write the first letter in code, and even better, in double code. She had an idea for a new secret code that she wouldn't share with anyone, not even with her godmother. She and Federico could read each other's minds. Secrets were impossible between them.

It was about two o'clock. She was waiting for the Lemos sisters, who were visiting with Delfina. Suddenly, Betsabé showed up with a refreshing glass of *masato**. The maid was a magician, foreseeing her needs, reading her mind, knowing Sofia was thirsty and worried about something.

"Niña Sofi," she said in a playful voice, "please drink the *masato*, I made it with cinnamon and orange leaves. And do not do so much needlework or you are going to go blind before you get old."

Sofia slowly drank the thick *masato* not knowing what she was doing. The maid noticed that her eyes were not there; she was looking at something else. Betsabé waited patiently and to rescue her from her stupor, she tried to start a conversation.

"The Lemos sisters should be back any time. Ña Mariana said they wouldn't be late and that was after don Alberto left this morning."

Sofia looked at the maid without saying a word and handled her the empty glass. Far from a mind reader, Betsabé couldn't understand her mistress. She had days when she wouldn't stop talking and days when

---

*Masato: a fermented rice and brown sugar drink.

she hardly said a word. The girl ignored her maid as if she didn't exist apart from her function, but Betsabé knew why.

Betsabé was a charming person—full of good habits, bad habits and funny expressions—and Sofia loved her as a sister. Nobody could laugh more often and with more joy. They had grown up together and were connected by a pact stronger than friendship. Sofia overlooked her tricks and antics and sometimes she treated Betsabé as an ally and companion more than as a maid. She was the mirror that talked back. But they could never become true friends. It was impossible. She was the Niña and Betsabé was the maid, a barrier that was part of her traditions. Betsabé had to accept them and obey them without question.

Sofia, animated by the *masato*, stood up and took her sewing kit with her to put it away in the cedar chest in the hallway. She loved the smell of the cedar when she opened the trunk. On the way, she stuck her index finger in the dirt of the begonias' pots to check if Betsabé had watered them. Satisfied, she cleaned her finger on her skirt and continued to her room. Without knowing why, she decided to powder her face in front of the dressing mirror. She was vain and smiled approvingly at her looks. Then she smoothed the organza skirt with her hands and tucked her long-sleeved blouse under the belt. She would write to Federico as soon as she had fresh news from his sisters. When she was still in front of the mirror, she heard somebody knocking at the front door and felt that the Lemos were back. She looked in the mirror once more and went to open the door.

The three sisters came in, happy to escape from the outside heat. The dust, the flies, and the smell of horse manure made the streets unbearable. To come into the house was like moving from barbarism to civilization. The Lemos were overheated after walking from Delfina's inn and were anxious to talk with Sofia. They shared that mysterious similarity in Federico's family, a mixture of goodness and distinction. It had something to do with living around books, and it set them apart from other people. Sofia greeted them warmly and took them into the parlor where they sat very straight in the wicker chairs. The shiny mosaics on the floor reflected their skirts' edges. An image of the Sacred Heart of Jesus and a framed photo of don Juan Francisco Usuriaga with General Mosquera taken at the Puente del Humilladero[11] were the only ornaments in the parlor. Doña Julia, the widow, was taking her siesta. Sofia did her best to keep her mother away from anything related to Federico, since Julia couldn't tolerate him and always used abusive language when talking about him. When they sat, Betsabé, more curious than genuinely hospitable, arrived with three glasses of refreshing *masato* for the visitors. Sofia guessed her intentions and sent her to the kitchen to grind corn and get it ready to make tamales.

"If you don't grind it now we won't have tamales for dinner," said Sofia, pointing her index finger at the maid. Betsabé left for the kitchen disgusted, grumbling as she walked away, "The hell with corn-grinding and tamale-making!"

Sofia heard the maid cursing, rolled her eyes, and said, "She has no cure."

The Lemos sisters looked at each other and smiled at the same time.

"Maids are by nature curious. They have to know everything. They know more than mirrors and confessors," said Mariana, drying her forehead with a white linen handkerchief that had her initials embroidered on it with her own hair. Then she put the handkerchief away and drank her *masato*. It was delicious, one of Betsabé's secret recipes.

"Now, tell me about Delfina," said Sofia when Mariana had finished drinking the *masato*. Mariana thought for a moment and said, "When Delfina saw us she became very nervous, moving around like a chicken ready to lay an egg. As you can imagine, she already knew about Federico's transfer to the prison. I came to the point and told her that Federico needed her collaboration in order to help Hernandes escape. First, she became very pale and then all her blood went to her head, her moles disappeared, she was furious. 'Do you want me to be shot?' she said loudly, with her hands on her hips. Finally she calmed herself and said she would help but refused to set up a ladder. She said that Hernandes could jump down from the roof. That if he broke his legs, that was his problem, not hers. That he didn't know the city nor where to go, and a thousand other things. The only thing she agreed to do was to leave the hallway door open. Then she said, 'If there is a light on, it is not possible because the maids are still up or the gamblers are still playing *tresillo* and I am not going to ask them to go to help this bandit to commit more crimes'."

During this recitation, Lola and Rosita stayed mute. In important matters, Mariana generally spoke for all of them. They murmured to each other about what Sofia was wearing. They told her they loved her silk shirt. Theirs were less fancy, made by Mariana with cotton cloth and embroidered with little flowers: Lola's always blue and Rosita's green to tell them apart. Clothes were the only thing they fought about and it was a sorrow to them that Mariana's clothes didn't fit them.

When they left after a short visit, before three, Sofia was more nervous than ever and thinking of all the ways the plan could go wrong. *Lord, deliver us from Federico's fury!* Betsabé came back from the kitchen to pick up the glasses, followed by the sweet smell of freshly ground corn and molasses. She took the tray with her and spoke to Sofia over her shoulder as she left.

"Niña, don't worry. Who knows what God wants? He will decide what is needed." And she returned to making the tamales to make sure they were ready before dinner.

Sofia also left the parlor and checked that her mother was still in deep sleep; every year since the professor's death, Julia added more time to her siestas. Satisfied, Sofia entered her own room and locked the door to make sure nobody would bother her. She took the little book of *Don Quixote* from the nightstand, grabbed a pencil from the drawer, sharpened it and started to write sitting at the windowsill overlooking the street. A woman with a tray on her head passed by selling papayas. The afternoon sun projected the shadows of the windows' grilles onto the floor and illuminated the book she had in her hands. Her prodigious memory took her to the exact page where she wanted to start her first letter in code. She had planned everything she wanted to say for hours. She opened the book to Chapter VIII:

> Where it is told what happened to Don Quixote, when he was on his way to see his lady, Dulcinea del Toboso

It said: *Blessed be the Almighty Allah!* Sofia gave thanks to God instead and turned to the point in Chapter VIII where Sancho says to Don Quixote:

"Where I saw her for the first time, when I took her the letter with the news of the insanities and stupidities your grace was doing in the heart of the Sierra Morena."

Sofia smiled coquettishly amused at how surprised Federico would be when he read her letter. She got the tip of the pencil wet with saliva and put a dot under the a of *primera* (*first*), another dot under the m of *merced* (*grace*), one more under the o of *haciendo* (*doing*), and then one more under the r of *corazón*

98
vez primera, cuando le llevé la carta donde iban las nuevas de las sandeces y locuras que vuesa merced quedaba haciendo en el corazon de Sierra Morena. ¿ Bardas de corral se te antojaron aquellas, Sancho, dijo don Quijote, adonde ó por donde viste aquella jamas bastantemente alabada gentileza y hermosura ? No debian de ser sino galerías ó corredores ó lonjas, ó como las llaman, de ricos y reales palacios. Todo pudo ser, respondió Sancho; pero á mi bardas me parecieron, si no es que soy falto de memoria. Con todo eso vamos allá, Sancho, replicó don Quijote, que como yo la vea, eso se me da que sea por bardas que por ventanas, ó por resquicios ó verjas de jardines, que cualquier rayo que del sol de su belleza llegue á mis ojos, alumbrará mi entendimiento y fortalecerá mi corazon de modo que quede único y sin igual en la discrecion y en la valentía. Pues en verdad, señor, respondió Sancho, que cuando yo vi ese sol de la señora Dulcinea del Toboso, que no estaba tan claro que pudiese echar de sí rayos algunos; y debió de ser que como su merced estaba ahechando aquel trigo que dije, el mucho polvo que sacaba se le puso como nube ante el rostro y se le escureció. ¡Qué todavía das, Sancho, dijo don Quijote, en decir, en pensar, en creer y

Fig. 4—Beginning of Sofia's first letter, page 98, Tome III, 1844 Spanish edition of *Don Quixote*.

(*heart*). Then, her eyes joined the four letters and read *amor* (*love*) and she felt happy. It was her first word in code: *amor* (Fig. 4). A Mona Lisa smile appeared on her lips. She stopped for a moment, thought about Federico again, and blew him a long kiss while looking tenderly at his portrait on the nightstand.

At that very moment in the prison, Federico felt as though Sofia had just kissed him on the forehead. It was the magic of love that can enter through locked doors.

After the kiss she continued composing the letter. She told Federico about his sister's conversation with Delfina and about Alberto's visit to her home. For a moment she hesitated about mentioning Alberto, fearing awakening Federico's jealousy, but decided that it was more important to give him hope.

She wrote the whole letter in one sitting and didn't stop until placing the last pencil dot under the *o* of *caballero* (*knight*) close to the end of chapter X. At that moment she had the shadow of a new smile on her face, imagining Federico's surprise while reading her letter in code. Then she looked at the etching—on the opposite page—that was titled: *Don Quixote kneels down in front of the supposed Dulcinea* and her face was filled with a new light. She wasn't any *supposed Dulcinea*. She expected to see Federico on his knees one day asking for her hand in the same manner so gallantly shown by Don Quixote kneeling in front of the peasant maiden he imagined was Dulcinea. She was pleased at seeing how well the story in the text complemented what she had said with the pencil dots under the letters. She couldn't wait one more minute to deliver the letter to Federico. His surprise would be unforgettable. She didn't know how to thank her godmother for having spoken with Sergeant Llaves to take care of delivering the book to Federico.

Sofia used Volume III, where the Second Part of *Don Quixote* starts with a dedication from don Miguel de Cervantes to his friend and mentor, the Count de Lemos. She couldn't have found a better place to write her secret letter to Federico Lemos, her "Count" and lover.

It was close to sunset. She put the little book containing her first letter in her bag and slowly opened the door of her room to avoid disturbing her mother's sleep. She asked Betsabé to wake her up from the nap around six and to have dinner ready for six-thirty or seven. She told her maid she was going to pray the rosary at San Francisco. Sofia took a one-pound cheese and a few corn tamales, put them in her bag, said goodbye and left. Betsabé looked at her from the window, wondering what she was up to, since she knew very well that you do not need cheese to pray the rosary.

In the aisle of San Francisco, the smell of the votive candles filled Sofia with peace. She knelt down and looked at the image of the Immaculate Virgin Mary, who implored with her eyes. Sofia put her trust in her as she made the sign of the cross by instinct. In two more minutes she left the church using a side door. The sunlight forced her to cover her eyes with her lace mantilla as she walked toward the prison. Before arriving she pinched her cheeks and licked her lips. Then she approached one of the guards at the entrance.

"Good afternoon. Can you please ask Sergeant Llaves to come to the door? Tell him it is Señorita Sofia."

"Just wait here, Señorita, said the guard, and soon returned with Sergeant Llaves, who was wiping his hands on his pants to clean them.

"How can I be of service to you, Ña Sofia?"

"Sergeant how is Filomena? My godmother mentioned that she is not well. Poor dear!" The sergeant understood what she was talking about when she mentioned the governor's wife and his own mother.

"She is better, much better. Thank you," he said.

"Thank God! Can I ask you a favor, Sergeant? Could you take this little book, this cheese, and these tamales to don Federico?"

The Sergeant looked at her slanted green eyes, her pink cheeks, and her red lips and, spellbound, he said, "With the greatest pleasure, Ña Sofia."

"May God reward you, Sergeant."

Having accomplished her mission, Sofia returned to the church to give thanks to God for her godmother's help. The rosary was already well underway when she looked around and saw María de Lindo, Pedro Lindo's wife, who smiled at her. She was as charitable and pleasant as her husband. Sofia waited until the priest said the last Hail Mary, playing with her rosary and thinking about Federico's surprise. Then she gave thanks to the Virgin and joined the ladies who were going home for dinner. María greeted her graciously and asked about Federico and her mother as they walked together toward her house. There they said their goodbyes and María continued toward her own home feeling sorry for Sofia. Betsabé already had tamales and corn soup with fried plantains ready for dinner; there was no meat. Her mother was reading in her father's study, her empty teacup on the table. Sofia greeted her.

"I thought about waking you up before I went to pray the rosary, but decided it was better for you to take your nap. In any case, I prayed for you. María de Lindo asked me to say hello. She is crazy about her little boy." Her mother listened to her without paying any attention to her words. She wasn't there; she already lived in the other world. Sofia wondered what her mother was mumbling about and walked away.

At dinner, as was their custom, there were three place settings. One for her mother, one for Sofia, and the last for the late don Juan Francisco who according to doña Julia didn't miss a single dinner. It was true that all that was served on his plates by Betsabé somehow disappeared from night to morning.

"Something about the spirits," she said. What doña Julia didn't know was that after dinner, Betsabé would put the plates under the orange tree on the patio to feed the ghosts of her ancestors. Her "ancestors" made sure the plates were clean by sunrise.

*   *   *

Betsabé's great-grandfather whose family name was Balanta had been a gold trader—the Kangaba's business for generations along the Guinea coast—lost his freedom when he was cheated by slave traders. Ironically, he was sold to a noble family from Popayán—the Angulo—who owned rich gold mines in the Barbacoas region on the Colombian Pacific coast. The Balanta family made a living mining gold with the sweat of their brows, trading freedom for food for their children, feeling at home in the middle of the tropical jungles. Since then, they became the favorite family among the workers of their gold mines and haciendas due to their energy, their distinguished poise, their cheerfulness, and honesty: *Noblesse oblige.*

From her grandma Malinka she had learned the singsong of her ancestral origins that was transmitted to Betsabé in the original Mandé, the language of the Kangaba. Thus, Betsabé was the person whose roots came from the oldest nobility found in Popayán, older than the Spanish and the Inca. The Kangaba had been kings eight centuries before the arrival of Columbus to the New World. The nursery rhyme learned by Betsabé from her grandmother was a tale about the names and feats of the sixty kings of Kangaba. Betsabé repeated it when she thought about her grandmother. The harmony of the rhyme—both African and Arab—gave her a special feeling of inner peace uniting her with her ancestry, even if she didn't understand a word of what she was saying; something similar to what she experienced when repeating with the congregation the songs in Latin they had learned from Father Paredes in church.

After dinner, Sofia went into her room. She couldn't stop thinking about how Federico would react when reading her letter. She had to tell her godmother about how Sergeant Llaves had looked at her when she gave him the book. *Would they find her letter in code? Would Federico have the book already? Could they kill him?* After this last question, she decided she had to stop thinking about that possibility.

XIV: Sofia's First Letter to Federico

Write it down two or three times in the book your grace, and give it to me, that I'll have it well kept.

—*Don Quixote*, First Part Chapter XXV

My love, owner of my heart, I have the pleasure of writing to you again. They talked with Delfina. They say that it is very difficult, either because the maids, at the slightest noise, become suspect of the prisoners, or because the card players are there. That she will not help that man in anything. That, if he wants, he can climb to the tile roof between the hours of seven and eight thirty. If there is light, he should climb down because it is a sign that the maids are there and it is not possible. However, if it is dark, he can jump from the roof without making noise. That if he gets killed she doesn't care. That she will leave the passageway open but she will not come out. She wonders where this man will go without knowing where to go. That they will capture him, she said.

Now, listen to me. Since you told me about this I have something in my heart. I have the feeling that this man by asking for your help is trying to trick you. The same thing happened to your sisters. I beg you my love not to help him. He is the most infamous being. I know it from trusted and reliable sources. The Godos say that you don't have any compromise that could be proved. I do not question that this man is trying to trick you and perhaps somebody is behind it. Do not get involved my dearest by helping this man. If you want you can tell him what this lady said, but if you don't, avoid him by all means.

Alberto came today. He told me that he would take an interest in your cause. That perhaps they will listen to him if he says something about Hernandes. He gave me the darkest news. He said he knew that the Godos praised him too much and that he suspected that kind of praise. Do not get involved, my little love. Your Sofia begs you. If he escapes, he will let them capture him and will say that you helped him.

I will come to see you soon. Believe me always to be your trustful lover.

I embrace and kiss you, my love.

*   *   *

FEDERICO LOOKED AT THE LITTLE BOOK, fascinated by Sofia's ability to get it into his hands. She knew how to make good use of her contacts and her charm. He anxiously looked for the pencil dots signaling the beginning of the letter. He found the first four dots, in Chapter VIII. His face was invaded by a broad smile when he found the first pencil dots that said: *Love* (*Amor*) and started to tie letter with letter to find words, sentences, and eventually her first letter in code. He was annoyed by Delfina's refusal to help with the ladder. But he couldn't blame her. She could lose her business and even more. What hurt him the most was to find that Alberto had visited Sofia's home making offers to betray Hernandes. He couldn't stand Alberto. He knew what the man was after and knew that betraying Hernandes or "his dear friend" Federico amounted to the same thing.

But there was something else in her letter—that she didn't write with pencil dots—something related to the story Sancho and Don Quixote were involved with. In

116
luz del sol de hermosura que vas á buscar. ¡Dichoso tú sobre todos los escuderos del mundo! Ten memoria, y no se te pasé della cómo te recibe, si muda las colores el tiempo que la estuvieres dando mi embajada, si se desasosiega y turba oyendo mi nombre, si no cabe en la almohada si acaso la hallas sentada en el estrado rico de su autoridad, y si está en pie mírala si se pone ahora sobre el uno, ahora sobre el otro pie, si te repite la respuesta que te diere dos ó tres veces, si la muda de blanda en áspera, de aceda en amorosa, si levanta la mano al cabello para componerle aunque no esté desordenado: finalmente, hijo, mira todas sus acciones y movimientos, porque si tú me los relatares como ellos fueron, sacaré yo lo que ella tiene escondido en lo secreto de su corazon acerca de lo que al fecho de mis amores toca: que has de saber, Sancho, si no lo sabes, que entre los amantes las acciones y movimientos exteriores que muestran cuando de sus amores se trata, son certísimos correos que traen las nuevas de lo que allá en lo interior del alma pasa. Ve, amigo, y guíete otra mejor ventura que la mia, y vuélvate otro mejor suceso del que yo quedo temiendo y esperando en esta amarga soledad en que me dejas. Yo iré y vol-

Fig. 5—Photocopy of page 116, Tome III, 1844 edition of *Don Quixote*. Notice the *b* on the left margin and the pencil dots under the <u>er</u> of the word int<u>er</u>ior where Sofia is asking Federico to see (ber) what the text is saying: *concerning their love are faithful · messages and reliable accounts of what in the interior of their souls is happening... I fear and expect in this bleak solitude I am left.*

Chapter VIII, Federico found the section where the first pencil dots were and read:

> "Where I saw her for the first time, when I took her the letter with the news of the insanities and stupidities your grace was doing in the heart of the Sierra Morena."

These words added a new dimension to Sofia's letter, something pertaining to them only. It wasn't an accident either that she had used Volume III of the Second Part of *Don Quixote* where Cervantes wrote a dedication to his friend and mentor, the Count of Lemos. He realized that Sofia was writing to him "her first letter" in code exactly where Don Quixote had written "his first letter" to Dulcinea in Chapter VIII. There was a connection between Sofia's letter and *Don Quixote's* story. Two letters in one! What a surprise it was. How did she come up with such a great idea? She was a genius and from that point on he would have a double task: to read between the lines, what she said with dots, and within the text, what she said using the words of Sancho and Don Quixote.

As he continued reading her letter Federico came upon the place where Don Quixote says:

> "...that as soon as I see her, I don't care whether it is through a thatch or a window, or through the crevice of a door or through a garden's iron railings, that any ray from the sun of her beauty that may reach my eyes will illuminate my mind and strengthen my heart,"

Sofia had imagined him in the prison trying to see her from a window, *to illuminate his mind and strengthen his heart,* when she walked by the prison, along the Calle de Pandigüando.

On page 116 of volume III of the Spanish edition (Fig. 5) Sofia had added a *b* in the margin, followed by two dots under the word *inter_ior,* apparently asking him to look (*ber,* a Spanish misspelling of *ver*: to see) at the text and to pay attention to what Don Quixote says to Sancho:

> "My son, observe all her actions and every movement, because if you describe them as they were, I will find what she is hiding in the most secret place of her heart"

> "Sancho, if you don't know it already, that between lovers the external actions and movements concerning their love are faithful messages and reliable accounts of what in the interior of their souls is happening."

These phrases enforced the need to pay attention to not only what she said with dots in the letters but also to what Sancho and Don Quixote said in the text.

Immediately after, Sofia used more words from *Don Quixote* to describe the precarious situation Federico had left her in when he was taken to prison:

123

bradoras sobre tres borricos. Ahora me libre Dios del diablo, respondió Sancho; ¿y es posible que tres hacaneas, ó como se llaman, blancas como el ampo de la nieve, le parezcan á vuesa merced borricos? Vive el señor, que me pele estas barbas si tal fuese verdad. Pues yo te digo, Sancho amigo, dijo don Quijote, que es tan verdad que son borricos ó borricas, como yo soy don Quijote, y tú Sancho Panza: á lo menos á mí tales me parecen. Calle, señor, dijo Sancho, no diga la tal palabra, sino despavile esos ojos, y venga á hacer reverencia á la señora de sus pensamientos, que ya llega cerca: y diciendo esto se adelantó á recebir á las tres aldeanas, y apeándose del rucio tuvo del cabestro al jumento de una de las tres labradoras, y hincando ambas rodillas en el suelo, dijo: reina y princesa y duquesa de la hermosura, vuestra altivez y grandeza sea servida de recebir en su gracia y buen talante al cautivo caballero vuestro, que allí está hecho piedra mármol, todo turbado y sin pulsos de verse ante vuesa magnífica presencia. Yo soy Sancho Panza su escudero, y él es el asendereado caballero don Quijote de la Mancha, llamado por otro nombre *el caballero de la Triste Figura.* A esta sazon ya se había puesto don Qui-

Fig. 6—Photocopy of page 123, volume III, 1844 edition of *Don Quixote* where Sofia's first letters ends. Notice her signature, *S,* under the words '*despavile esos*', to the right of the *f* she wrote with pencil on the left margin of the page. Also notice the *o* that is part of the word *caballero* in the eighth line from the bottom up where her letter ends, when she says *amor mio* (my love) and the *o* of *caballero* is the same o of *mio*.

> "Go, my friend, and be your guide a better fortune than mine,
> and find a happier outcome than that which I fear and expect in
> this bleak solitude I am left."

Sofia felt lonely. She said she was *"in this bleak solitude."* She was full of fear, like Don Quixote was in the Sierra Morena when Sancho left him to go to deliver his letter to Dulcinea, and she was afraid that Hernandes would betray him. She feared that Federico would have the same fate his sisters had had. She feared *'the bleak solitude'* of war and the vacuum left by her absent love. Federico saw her situation and understood that he was not alone when he experienced the *bleak solitude* of prison in his cell.

When he came close to the end of her letter (Fig. 6) he found that Sofia had finished it by using the *o̰* in at the end of *cautivo caballero̰* to highlight his condition as *'captive knight'* or political prisoner. Moreover, the *o̰* in *cautivo caballero̰* was the last letter of her last phrase in the letter, when she says: I embrace and kiss you my love (*'Te abrazo y te beso amor mio̰'*). The captive knight (*'cautivo caballero̰'*) and my love (*'amor mio̰'*) were the same person and they shared the same *o̰* that Sofia selected, putting a dot underneath it. Each note of her symphony was there for a reason; nothing was superfluous, nothing was missing. Mozart couldn't have done a better job. He reflected.

This is marvelous. She is a genius. But he also couldn't stop worrying about Alberto.

XV: Federico Answers Sofia's First Letter

The day before yesterday, I had the greatest joy of my life, the most pleasant surprise, by reading your sweet little letter, which reveals the goodness of your soul, the tenderness of your heart.

—Federico's Second Letter to Sofia

The morning fog still floated over the patios when Federico woke up, hearing noises at Delfina's inn. He smelled the smoke coming from the inn's kitchen. His bones hurt and he needed to pee. After he emptied his bladder in a bucket, he returned to his mat where he lay down. Everything itched. He could smell the coffee next door. Domingo struggled with somebody in his dreams. Federico was thirsty and took a sip of water from his gourd while dreaming about a good breakfast. *How much wouldn't I give for a large cup of hot coffee or hot cocoa foaming with bubbles all the colors of the rainbow?*

The bells at San Francisco rang, calling to Mass, and a faint light entered through the cracks in the cell's door. Federico got closer to the light and opened the book to read Sofia's letter once more. He browsed anxiously until he found the first dot again. Three more dots and he read *amor* (*love*) and he felt *love* and became filled with it. *Love in four graphite dots.* This was an unforgettable moment of their love story.

It was the first time she had sent him a letter written in code. He could feel Sofia next to him. He could smell her when turning each page. He imagined her writing the letter and was full of tenderness knowing what she thought and did for him.

"And Delfina! That Hernandes should jump from the roof if there wasn't light. Is she crazy? How hard is it for her to help? Dumb ass! And what the hell is Alberto doing in Sofia's home?" he said to himself.

He didn't trust Alberto, who was and wasn't his friend. He knew they had been in love and he was jealous. He continued talking to himself.

"Sofia with Alberto and it has been months since I have given her a kiss. If he betrays Hernandes we are screwed. He is an imbecile. She doesn't get that he is using her. I don't mean shit to him. Son of a bitch!"

About the same time Federico had just finished reading the letter a second time, Domingo woke up. Federico shared the news from Sofia with him but the poor sick man was in no mood to hear anything. He interrupted his cellmate:

"Give me some water, please." He was nauseated and didn't give a damn if Hernandes escaped. It was past six when the guard opened the door, time to go to the patio.

They walked into the hallway. Federico was carrying the smelly bucket in his hand and the gourds for water over his shoulder, walking under the vigilant eyes of the guards. They shared a mutual hate for each other. The prisoners stood in line to empty the buckets, take a drink, wash their faces, and fill the gourds with fresh water.

For breakfast they got a tin cup of water with molasses and a piece of dark bread. No more food until dinner at three in the afternoon. Luckily Federico had eaten the tamales and the cheese that Sofia had sent with Sergeant Llaves.

Federico looked for Hernandes and Dr. Cajiao at breakfast and told them about Delfina's reaction to his request for help. It would be suicidal to try to escape without a ladder. Hernandes wasn't ready to jump from the roof; the man hoped to live a complete life after the war, to return to work on his father's farm and teach at the town's school. He would return to his town, El Socorro, Santander, alive or dead, but before that he had to deliver the arms to General Bustamante. But first he had to escape from prison.

Federico repeated Sofia's concerns to Dr. Cajiao, who said, "Those are women's issues. Tell her to convince that old gossiping witch to help, and don't forget to ask Sofia to keep an eye on Arcila. He should already have the guns that President Alfaro sent us. Regarding Hernandes, it is imperative that he gets out of here as soon as possible. I am afraid for his life if he stays here for too long."

Shortly after, Federico ran into Antonio and told him about Delfina and her reticence to help Hernandes. Antonio, who had been a regular client at Delfina's inn where he played card games like *tute* and *tresillo* and also billiards, said, "Delfina is Martín's lover and I wouldn't be surprised if she already told him in bed about what Federico's sisters asked her to do. Have you noticed that since the day before yesterday they reinforced the guards? We have to look for other options. I will talk to Dr. Cajiao about it. I don't believe Delfina is going to help us in anything. She is not stupid."

At noon Federico shared the last of his cheese with Domingo. Then he read the letter once more, wondering how she had come up with the idea of using Don Quixote's text as part of the letter. He marveled at Sofia's talent and imagination and decided he would imitate her in his reply letter. But he would not mention anything about Alberto.

Once he had the plan for his letter, he looked for a spot in the text to imitate her marvelous game and chose the passage in Chapter XI where the text says:

"About the strange adventure that happened to the brave Don
Quixote when he ran into the cart or wagon of the Courts of
Death."

It was the ideal text for his plans. He sharpened the pencil he carried
hidden in his coat and, with great care he proceeded to write the first
dots of his first letter in code using the first words of Chapter XI. He
wrote the first dot under the _m_ of _adem_ás. He hardly could see it in the
penumbra of the room. The next two dots he placed under the word _iba_
and applied more pressure to the pencil to see them better. He continued adding dots, jumping from one line into the next to avoid many dots
in the same line, until he managed to write the first phrases of his letter:

*Little love. My goodness.
My charm.*

He wrote well. It had been a while since he had written her a letter. It
was a pleasure to do it again and it gave him the sensation of feeling free.
When he read in the text that _Don Quixote went on his way,_ he became
the _Knight of the Sorrow Figure._ It was his turn to mock the enchanters
and haters to return to his beloved Dulcinea. He would be with her in
the intimacy of the letters. By the very hands of the officer and under his
nose the book and his messages would go to Sofia's hands and through
her _green and slanted eyes_ they would make a triumphant entrance into
her mind and her soul.

He read what Rocinante was doing: _"Feeling the liberty he was given
stopped at every step to graze the green grass that was abundant in those
fields"_ and realized he was free again, even to eat grass. He never had
imagined being a horse.

Federico was still playing the role of Rocinante when Sancho woke
him up from his enchanted dreams by saying:

"Sir, sorrows weren't made for beasts, but for men; but if men let their sorrows take over, they turn into beasts: thus, take charge your grace, wake up from your dreams and pick up Rocinante's reins, be alert and awake, and show the gallantry that Knights Errant should have."

At that moment Federico rediscovered his gallantry and wrote:

How much pleasure you have given to me with your words of love and consolation and how much I am grateful for them.

He was like a true Knight Errant, listening to the wise words of his faithful squire, and continued writing the letter dot-by-dot, gravitating between the text of Don Quixote and his own thoughts, connecting Don Quixote's mad ideas to the coded letter that soon would depart in the hands of Sergeant Llaves.

The power of love woke him up from his prostration and reminded him that he was a prisoner not because the Godos feared his weapons but because they feared his liberal ideas based on the equality of all men before God and the Law.

While Federico was lost in these thoughts, Domingo woke up and asked for help to get the tin bucket he needed and didn't have the energy to reach.

He had diarrhea with blood and he also vomited the cheese. Federico, alarmed by Domingo's situation, called the guard to ask for Sergeant Llaves. When he came, they gave Domingo water with brown sugar, cinnamon, and salt.

"This should get him better between today and tomorrow. If not, we will determine what to do," said Sergeant Llaves.

"Excuse me, Sergeant. I would like to ask you the favor to hand this little book to Señorita Sofia. If we get lucky she may bring us another cheese."

The Sergeant received the book and hid it in the coat of his uniform. He would do anything to see her again.

"I'll take it to her tomorrow. Now I must go, they should be serving dinner any time."

When the guards called for dinner, Federico stood up, put on his best face, and went downstairs filled with *the gallantry that Knights Errant should have* under any circumstances. It was the book's magic. Just by touching it he had become again a Knight Errant. He had returned to being Federico Lemos. Domingo snored. He imagined Sofia's face while reading his letter. What would she think about it?

XVI: Federico's First Letter to Sofia

There is no friend for a friend.

—*Don Quixote*, Second Part, Chapter XII

POPAYÁN, JULY–AUGUST 1900

Little love. My goodness. My charm. How much pleasure you have given me with your words of love and comfort and how much I appreciate them. I believe it's impossible that you will forget me just like I will never forget you, but each day I will love you more and more, because you will also love me with the same affection, with the same resolution.

Do not worry about the Hernandes issue. Even though we all have a bad feeling about him here, with the exception of Dr. Cajiao, I don't believe he is capable of doing what you fear, and it is impossible for him to trick me. I'm telling you this for a good reason. Besides, it would be convenient for him to go away. What concerns me is that since the day before yesterday the guards have been more vigilant. They have put guards all over and in places where there were none before. I am afraid that Delfina has said something. It would have been better if she had refused to help than to ask him to jump from the roof and to be checking on whether there is light or not. Do your best to get her cooperation but make sure she is not going to betray us. Tell me, if you know, whether Arcila is still there and tell anything else you know.

I send you my heart full of love for you.

Goodbye my queen.
Your

Ji

*   *   *

SERGEANT LLAVES DELIVERED THE LETTER TO SOFIA early in the morning the next day. He had shaved carefully, trimmed his moustache, and combed his hair with sugar water to make it brighter. Sofia opened the door to him with her best smile and gave him a tip sufficient to buy a few cigars. He made an obsequious bow.

"At your service, Señorita Sofia," he said. "Anything you need! Just let me know."

When he left, Sofia ran to her room to read Federico's letter with great expectations. She was delighted with his expressions of love but she could feel his insecurity through his words, always thinking that she could forget him. She also was happy about his comments related to Hernandes and in particular what Dr. Cajiao had said about him.

Federico's observations about the guards being omnipresent suggested that either Delfina or Alberto must have said something. It surprised her that he was asking again for Delfina's help. Perhaps, Federico had thought that it was Alberto who had betrayed them—but he hadn't said a word about the man, probably because he was jealous and didn't want her to know it. Of course they couldn't trust Alberto.

She felt it was very dangerous to ask her to go and find out if Aniceto Arcila was still at the brickyard where they hid the weapons. She was as compromised as Federico, but she was free to move around without suspicion. Most likely, her relationship with her godmother had something to do with her privilege, but it could also be that the Godos wanted to follow her to find out what she was doing, where, and with whom. She had to be aware of spies.

Sofia was delighted when she read about Federico sending her '*his heart full of love for her*' and also that he called her *my queen*. He signed only with his initial *F*. Clearly, he was more cautious than she was. Then, she realized he had imitated her by starting his letter in Chapter XI where the title said:

> "About the strange adventure that happened to the brave Don Quixote when he ran into the cart or wagon of the Courts of Death."

The selection wasn't accidental. Federico was in prison by orders from the *Courts of Death* and he couldn't have found better words to define his situation as a political prisoner.

On the same page he appeared to do a self-analysis of his mental situation by using the words of Sancho to Don Quixote at the Sierra Morena in reference to his self-absorption and his depression.

> "Sir, sorrows weren't made for beasts, but for men; but if men let their sorrows take over, they turn into beasts: thus, take charge, wake up from your dreams and pick up Rocinante's reins, be alert and awake, and show the gallantry that Knights Errant should have."

Federico was telling her of his pains and sorrows and his quixotic struggle with them. He wanted to ride Rocinante again and return to his life as a gallant knight. He wanted to be free as only Don Quixote could be, as only ideas can be. To achieve this, he would wake up: he had to be alert and awake to escape his depression. This wasn't a surprise. She had been in love with him for more than ten years.

Next, Federico had written a *p* in the margin, to call her attention to the text in Chapter XI, that he wanted to share with her:

> "What in the devil is this? What languishing is this? Are we here or in France?"

It was not hard for her to interpret. *Federico doesn't know what afflicts him. He doesn't understand the desperation that fills him and robs him of his drive. He wonders if he is in Popayán or in France waiting for the guillotine. But he is struggling and looking for a way to be the gallant knight he was before. No, he is not finished, he still wants to win."*

As she continued reading, she came upon two penciled letters in the margin of the text, a *p* and a *b*, that pointed to a phrase where he assumed responsibility for all her sorrows and pains. The text said:

> "Shut up, Sancho, replied Don Quixote lowering his voice; shut up,
> I say, and do not utter blasphemies against that enchanted lady, of
> her disgraces and misfortunes I am the only one to blame: her sad
> situation is all due to the envy that the wicked ones bear me."

Then she noticed that Federico also put an *X* in pencil on the right margin of the same page, where the text refers to Don Quixote's image of Dulcinea in contrast with the one proposed by Sancho, as the book said:

"Her eyes must be like green emeralds, slanted with two rainbows for eyebrows."

This phrase about her eyes and her eyebrows left Sofia enchanted, knowing how much he valued her physical beauty. Her intellectual beauty he didn't have to imagine. Of course he knew her well but sometimes he had his doubts about her. For example, he was jealous of Alberto.

Ahead, in Chapter XII, Federico wrote a letter *b* in the margin followed by a *g*. These two letters bracketed the words of Don Quixote that Federico used to offer her, *his queen*, the gold crown of the empress and Cupid's wings, where the text says:

> "If you, Sancho, had allowed me to attack as I wanted, you would
> have received the empress's gold crown and Cupid's colored
> wings...Never are the scepters and crowns of fake emperors made
> of pure gold, but of tin or tinsel, said Sancho."

The crown Federico offered to Sofia was of pure gold and not like the fake ones used by bureaucrats who sell themselves to obtain fancy titles such as governor or prefect. She felt like a queen then and momentarily considered going to the mirror to see if she was wearing the crown Federico had given her.

Federico came to the end of his letter in Chapter XII where he signed with a faint letter F in pencil at the end of the verse that said:

"There is no friend for a friend." *F*

The letter *F* in Federico's own handwriting and its location was a finger pointing at somebody: *'Angulo el Malo'* or the members of the company of actors dressed like governors, prefects, military officers, wicked men and the like, who had put Federico in prison. Sofia understood he was warning her not to trust Alberto and told her: *There is no friend for a friend,* and had put his signature next to it to make sure she knew what he was talking about. Knowing what that implied, she became furious with him.

How dare he question my feelings and loyalty? I will take care of that in my next letter. I know how to use a knife with a double edge. I've learned something from Alberto.

Sofia spent the entire day composing her response. She had never felt so deeply about anything she had written in the past. What she wrote she felt in her soul. This was a critical moment for their relationship. She couldn't stop believing that Alberto could betray them.

XVII: Sofia's Second Letter to Federico

Against that ruse I know another one, replied Sancho, to counter it with: I'll grab a club, and before your mercy has a chance to wake up *my anger* I'll make yours go to sleep...

—*Don Quixote*, Second Part, Chapter XIV

POPAYÁN, AUGUST–SEPTEMBER 1900

My beloved Federico, my lovely master, my only love and only goodness; you cannot imagine, my dear, that I would allow the immense burning and pure love I feel for you to become lukewarm or die and do not think, my good, that I could ever forget it. My love for you is immortal. It will never die. I swear on the most sacred thing for me and repeat what I have said to you so many times: that in any circumstance I'll prove to you my passion. Do not believe, my love that I would suffer from the demands you say, you make. Do not say that, even in jest. I went to see you because I love you with delirium, because it is my duty. If I didn't do it before, you already know why. Besides, I thought of surprising you on your Saint's Day. But believe me, my love, that I was delirious to see you. I would go anywhere to see you. I am yours, and I am ready to suffer anything and to prove my love to you in any circumstance. I love you with all my heart, with all the tenderness of my soul. You are my only illusion. My happiness would be to call you my spouse and love you and adore you in that dreamed home where all my happiness will be to love you, serve you, and sacrifice myself if it be necessary to make you happy, because that is what true love is. Your love is my life. Your caresses, your tenderness are my only ambition. With your love, I am the happiest person. I do not want more, nor desire more. Be totally convinced, my beloved master, that I am always the same for you. The same woman that so many times embraced you. The same, my little love, I am the same. I haven't changed and will never change. You cannot imagine how much I have suffered with our separation. I have not gone anywhere. Each day I miss you more. When I am sad, I grab your portrait and kiss it. This is my consolation. The flowers you planted for me are beautiful. I love them so much! I wanted to see you with anxiety on Monday. How much I would have given to give you a kiss! At night I dreamed that you were free and we were going to be together in three days. I wish my dreams would come true. Even though they punished the officer who was so good to me, if they do not release you, I'll be back.

However, I have some hope. Alberto told me he knew that Carbajal was coming next week and that the intention was to keep those that are compromised in prison. He talked to Martín and he said that it was the prefect's business. He told me to tell you he was very interested in your case. That if you wanted, you could write to some Godo who is your friend. That writing to someone would help, my good. Why don't you write to Delfino Alegría or Pedro Lindo. Pardon me, my love, for trying to give you advice. Forgive me because I do it out of love, because I cannot wait for the hour when they will let you go. If I could, I would go to ask for your freedom, even if I had to beg on my knees. I cannot live far from you, my only goodness.

The idea about the letters was a suggestion from my godmother, as indirect advice. Goodbye, my love. My dear, believe me always to be yours and receive my soul in a kiss I send to you. Yours eternally,

I ordered the slippers and adorned them for you myself. Tell Domingo that, if he wants, I can order some for him also or talk to Zoila. Your sisters are planning to

> talk to Pedro Lindo. They don't know these things I am telling you. I'll tell you what happens. Perhaps he can get you out. They assure me they will shoot the soldier today. You haven't answered in the book I sent you on Monday.

*   *   *

FEDERICO FOUND SOFIA'S LETTER to be an amazing outpouring of her feelings and was startled by her letter revealing his name, that she wrote "My beloved Federico." Her passionate words were like the visceral call of a drum whose force still shakes us more than a hundred years later. She offered herself freely, climbing on the altar of love, calling him to visit her to feel her passion under any circumstances. It was the love of wartime, humanity and divinity, life and death, without conditions. Sofia's letter used all the means at her disposal to convince him that his love was her only love, her immortal love.

He suspected the words he had used to end his first letter, "*There is no friend for a friend*," were behind Sofia's love storm. She knew of his insecurity and his state of depression, victim of the madness of war or jealousy, upon knowing Alberto was visiting her frequently. Reflecting on the letter, Federico wondered what other messages she included hidden in *Don Quixote's* text, just as she had done in her first letter.

He immediately noticed that she had started this letter using the *m* in *mercy* (*merced* in Spanish) to write her first sentence: "*My beloved Federico*." These words were within the sentence in which Sancho says to the squire of the Knight of the Forest:

"And before your mercy can come to wake up my anger, I'll put yours to sleep, with the blows of a cudgel, so soundly it won't wake up except in another world, where it is known I am a man that allows anybody to lay hands on my face."

The selection of this section—from Chapter XIV—to start her letter provided an explosive and overwhelming aperture to justify her love storm and to vent her anger. Sofia had used the words of Sancho to let Federico know that she didn't want to be angry but was ready to kill his own anger with the blows of a cudgel before allowing him to wake up her own feelings of frustration with him. Sofia was telling him she had guts. The sound of her voice was like the snap of a whip in a dark room. The one who was angry or jealous was Federico, not her. She added that nobody could lay hands on her face. Yes, she would kiss and more than that, as she clearly was telling him, but only when she wanted. She rejected forcefully any doubt Federico might have had about her behavior in his absence, be it with Alberto or with anybody else.

Federico felt she wanted to make sure he got her point and had put an *f* in pencil on the same page asking him to read the text that said:

"And let each man take care of himself, though the best would be to allow each one's anger to be asleep because nobody knows another man's soul."

That *f* she had written with pencil on the margin was also the first letter she used to write his name, *F*ederico. It was a message for him! She didn't deny being angry—just as he was—but she looked for peace and for all the means imaginable to show him her feelings and let him know he had no right to question her love or her passion because *nobody knows another man's*—or woman's—*soul*.

Next, she had found a few lines in the text to offer peace to Federico, using God as a referee to help them. The text said:

> "And God blessed peace and cursed fights. Thus, I inform your grace, Señor Squire, that from now on all harm and damage resulting from our quarrel will be on your account."

Using Sancho's words again, Sofia proposed to bring to an end the misunderstanding between them and challenged Federico to accept peace or assume responsibility for any further harm or damage in their relationship. She wanted no more fights. It was clear that there was a fight at some point between the letters, and also who had started it, and who had tried to avoid it. He could not question it.

Federico saw that Sofia had finished her letter close to the end of Chapter XVII, where she wrote her initial, *S*, between two key words in the text, namely: *Quixote and Sancho*. This was a very intriguing signal. She had put herself between the Knight and the Squire. She was the center of a marvelous trinity, a trinity where one cannot distinguish the members. It was a trinity where Sofia was sometimes herself, other times Sancho, and suddenly Don Quixote. This illuminated her duality and also Federico's. The two characters—*F* and *S*—were the authors of the letters that shared their identities in an amorous game where they were either Don Quixote or Sancho. Such behavior is the source of the quixotism of Sancho and the sanchism of Don Quixote.

Coming to the end of her letter, she had added a postscript that continued until Chapter XVIII. Before ending the letter, she had written the letter *h* twice, in Chapter XVII, to highlight the text that said:

> "It is a finer sight, I say, to see a knight-errant succoring a widow in some deserted site, than to see a knight-courtier flirting with a damsel in the city."

The allusion to the two knights—the errant and the courtier—made clear to Federico that she preferred the knight-errant Federico to the knight-courtier Alberto.

Federico was enchanted by Sofia's letter, both the part with pencil dots, and the part hidden in Don Quixote's text. After reading it, he felt terrible guilt over his doubts about her feelings. As soon as he was able to find a quiet moment in the prison, he wrote to her to tell her they were at peace with each other. No more fights. No more doubts. Ever.

In fact, that same night he sent the letter in an envelope with Clodomiro, by dropping it from the cell window. He used a line made from the hemp bag and the hook Clodomiro had hidden in the poetry book that Sofia had delivered to him while visiting the prison.

Clodomiro was dying to open the letter and read it, but he wasn't capable of betraying Federico. He was honest. Anyway, it wasn't his business to know what Federico and his girlfriend were talking about.

XVIII: Federico's Second Letter to Sofía

O my cousin Montesinos! I told you in my last request:
That after I was dead and my soul had left my breast,
you could cut my heart out of my chest with a knife or a dagger
to take it to Belermas's nest as my last gift to her.

—*Don Quixote*, Second Part, Chapter XXIII

POPAYÁN, AUGUST–SEPTEMBER 1900

My love. My good. The day before yesterday, I had the happiest moment of my life and its most delightful surprise when reading your sweet letter, which reveals the goodness of your soul and the tenderness of your heart. My charm, thanks for all the good you've done with it. Yesterday, I sent the other book to you and I don't know if you've received it yet. I ask you there if the written envelope I sent with Clodomiro was or was not written in my handwriting, and I was afraid he might have opened it out of curiosity. You haven't answered me nor told me what is new. Do me the favor of giving my regards to everyone in your home and to my sisters, and tell them to do me the favor of getting the book *La Mascota* from Evaristo Rengifo, and from Salustio Guzmán a volume of the *Deontology; or, Science of Morality* by Bentham. Goodbye, my little love, don't forget me, and receive my soul and my whole heart in a passionate kiss that I send to you filled with enthusiasm and tenderness for you.

Hugs to you from here; your unforgettable

F.

*   *   *

SOFIA WAS OVERWHELMED by the kindness shown by Federico in this letter. They were at peace. His letter confirmed what the lovely letter he had sent with Clodomiro had said.

Sofia noticed Federico had started this letter on the last page of Chapter XXIII. She started right away to look for any hidden messages in the text.

In the last paragraph of the initial page Federico had put two letters in pencil, a *v* and an *f*, where Don Quixote said:

"Because you love me well, Sancho, you speak in such a way, said Don Quixote: and because you don't have experience in the affairs of the world, all things that may appear difficult seem to you impossible; but time will go on, as I said before, and I will tell you about some of those I've seen down there, that will make you believe in the ones I've told you about, whose veracity doesn't admit argument or dispute."

On reading the text, Sofia's reaction was instantaneous: she became furious at the attitude of her lover. How could he adopt a tone of superiority, telling her she didn't have enough experience in *the affairs of the world* and that any difficult thing seemed impossible to her. He also claimed not to admit argument or dispute from her side. His truth was unquestionable? What arrogance! He also said '*but time will go on*' and in the future '*I will tell you about some of those I've seen down there*' but he didn't say what or when. It was something he couldn't talk about, a war secret that remains secret until now; another of the many secrets that soldiers take home from war, which eventually drive them insane or to suicide. She almost pitched the book across the room. *What was he thinking about? That she was ignorant?*

However, in the same letter, Federico included a little verse in Chapter XXIV that apparently was not accidental. It said:

"Necessity carries me to war; if I was a rich man, truly, I wouldn't go."

He had used these words of Don Quixote to let Sofia know some of the reasons why he had joined the liberal resistance against the conservative government. He confirmed it by putting two letters—a *v* and an *f*—on the left margin to highlight the phrase that said:

"To what the lad responded: being scantily clad is forced by heat and poverty."

He was poor and had joined the war by necessity. He was an honest man of scarce means and had no qualms about saying it. Reading these words that showed his humility Sofia forgot her annoyance about him calling her ignorant. He was a humble man, something she always admired about him and that she only gained for herself much later in her life. To make sure there was no question about his feelings toward her, he wrote in the letter with pencil dots the following words:

Don't forget me and receive my soul and my whole heart in a passionate kiss that I send you filled with enthusiasm and tenderness for you.

This gesture reminded Sofia of the opening of Chapter XXIII, where Durandarte says:

"O my cousin Montesinos! I told you in my last request:
That after I was dead and my soul had left my breast,
You could cut my heart out of my chest,
with a knife or a dagger to take it to Belermas's nest"

Federico was sending his heart on the wings of a passionate kiss, full of enthusiasm and tenderness for her. He couldn't have done less after her marvelous second letter.

She continued reading in Chapter XXIII, where she found another interesting phrase from Don Quixote:

"All comparison is odious, hence we shouldn't compare anyone to anyone. The unique Dulcinea is who she is and Lady Belerma is who she is and who she has been. And leave it at that!"

With this phrase from Cervantes the misunderstanding between the lovers came to an end: *and leave it at that!* There were no more reasons for dispute.

Finally, in Chapter XXV, Federico had signed his letter with an *F* that he places under the middle of the phrase of text that says:

"And so thin that it was a pity to look at"
$\mathscr{F}$

He had placed his signature *F* under the word *was* to make sure there was no question that he was *so thin* like the skinny donkey in the story in Don Quixote. He was referring to the situation of the liberal prisoners during the One Thousand Days War. In Popayán in 1900, during the Holy Week religious celebrations, the society women organized visits to bring food to the prisoners who were starving to death.

That night Sofia reviewed Federico's words over and over again in her mind. His thinness tormented her. She never had experienced hunger and could not imagine the feeling of being reduced to a walking corpse. She had to find a way to get him out of there. She had to talk to her uncle don Emilio, to somehow get Federico out of prison.

XIX: Sofia's Third Letter to Federico

Brayed not in vain our mayors twain.

—*Don Quixote*, Second Part, Chapter XXVII

My love. My good. Today your sisters went to see the prefect. He received them graciously and said he would release you if you provide a certificate from a doctor and pay for one month. Mariana said there would be no problem doing this. I've just talked to my uncle Emilio who is the doctor. I told him that you had written saying you continued to be ill with dyspepsia and with symptoms of dysentery and that you had had a bad night, so please give that same information. Pretend to be sick, tie a handkerchief on your head. My uncle said that he would be there tomorrow after twelve and that your sisters should go to see the prefect at two o'clock. God willing, you will be out, my little love.

Goodbye my dear love, receive a hug from your

S

Pretend to be real sick. My uncle will see you tomorrow.

*   *   *

THE FIRST THING THAT FEDERICO NOTICED when reading this
letter was that Sofia had started it by imitating the first two sentences
of his previous one: *My love. My good.* She corresponded from equal to
equal, measure by measure. She said, immediately after, that his sisters
had gone to visit the prefect. There was a little tension in her words;
she was all business. He realized that she had selected a very interesting
spot to start her letter. Evidently, she wanted to make a few things clear
before closing their dispute.

Reading the text close to the end of Chapter XVII, just a few lines
before Sofia's first pencil dot where Don Quixote discussed the reasons
to go to war:

"No, no, may God neither allow nor wish. For prudent men, and
well-organized republics there are four reasons to take up arms,
and draw their swords and put their persons, their lives and their
possessions at risk: the first, to defend the Catholic faith; the
second, to defend their lives, that is natural and divine law; the
third, to defend their honor, their families and their properties;

the fourth, to serve their king in a just war; and if we would like
to add the fifth reason (which could count as second), to defend
their motherland."

Sofia had started her letter—exactly at the point where the text said:
"and if we would like to add the fifth..."—by writing the first dot when
the fifth reason is named: *"to defend the motherland."* She wanted to
make clear to Federico what the reasons were to initiate a war. She had
waited until the fifth one to make her point.

With these words from Don Quixote, Sofia replied to Federico's arrogance in his previous letter to let him know that she was well informed
about world issues and that he had no reason to treat her as an ignora-
mus, as he had done. And she didn't stop there. She wanted to give him
another lecture that is where Don Quixote says:

"To these five causes, the most important, one could add a few
others that should be just and reasonable and would oblige us to
take up arms; but to take them for childish squabbles, and for
causes that make us laugh or joke rather than to take offense, sug-
gest that those that take them up are not rational: especially when
taking unjust revenge (since no revenge can be just) which goes
directly against the Holy Law we profess, which orders us to do
good to our enemies and love those that hate us: a commandment
that, although it may seem difficult to comply with, it is so only for
those who have less of God in them than of the world, and more of
flesh than of soul: because Jesus Christ, true God and true man,
that never lied, nor could or can lie, giving us his law, said that
his yoke was soft and his burden light; and thus, wouldn't give us
a law that was impossible to comply with. Thus, my Sirs, you are
obliged, by divine and human laws, to quiet down."

This was Sofia's call to peace. She spoke from Don Quixote's mouth and eviscerated the causes of many wars as children's issues that make you laugh and that lack any reasonable foundation. She condemned revenge and quoted Jesus Christ and the commandments we must comply with, which tell us to do good to our enemies and to love those who hate us. What a great piece of advice for opposing political factions. In particular for those claiming to be followers of Christ! What a message to remind him and all the combatants of a thousand unjust wars quiet down because the divine laws demand it. Period!

When he continued reading the text in Chapter XXVII, Federico found that Sofia had also included in her letter the wise words of Sancho who says:

> "May the devil take me, said Sancho to himself, if my master isn't a theologian, and if he is not, he looks like one, as one egg to another. Don Quixote paused to take a breath, and noticing they still waited in silence, he wanted to continue with his discourse, as he would have done if the quick Sancho hadn't intervened, and seeing his master was taking a break, took his place and said: my master Don Quixote de la Mancha, who in other days was known as the Knight of the Sad Semblance, and is now called the Knight of the Lions, is a discreet hidalgo who knows Latin and Spanish romance like a Bachelor; and in what he does and advises acts like a good soldier, and knows all the laws and ordinances of what is known as dueling, to a T, and thus there is nothing to do but follow what he says, and if you are wrong, be it my fault, especially because it is said that it's foolish to lose your temper just by listening to somebody braying, that I remember when I was a boy I used to bray when and where I felt like it, without anybody stopping me, and with such style and perfection, that when I brayed all the donkeys in the village brayed, and that didn't stop me from being

my parents' son, who were very honorable fellows, even though
I was envied for this skill by more than four stuck-up fellows in
the village."

Sofia compared Federico to Don Quixote as painted by Sancho: *"discreet hidalgo who knows Latin and Spanish romance, etc... and in what he
does and advises acts like a good soldier."* She also referred to the masses of
the political parties and *"the four stuck-up fellows in the village,"* who on
hearing a donkey bray they feel they have to do the same.

Federico broke into a sweat after reading these words admiring the
intelligence of his lover. Sofia's whip provided some very good reasons
for the donkeys to bray and kick, and they continue to bray and kick; it
is part of their nature.

She couldn't have finished this letter without adding a resounding
touch at the end. In Chapter XXVIII, Don Quixote's words, said:

> "Turn your donkey's reins and go back home, because you will
> not ever take another step with me. O unconsumed bread! O
> promises misplaced! O man, more a beast than a person! Now,
> when I was thinking to raise you to a position, where, despite your
> wife, you will be addressed as Your Lordship, now, you dismiss
> yourself? And now, you depart, when I had the firm and binding
> intention to make you Lord of the best island in the world? Well,
> as you have often said, honey was not...etc. You are a jackass, and
> a jackass you will be, and will end your life as a jackass, and I
> believe that your life will come to an end before you realize and
> accept that you are a beast."

This was a violent moment in the relationship between Don Quixote
and Sancho and by extension between Sofia and Federico. Sancho's humiliation was such that tears came to his eyes and he confessed that in

order to be a jackass all he was missing was the tail and he invited Don Quixote—if he wished—to put one on him and promised to serve him as a jackass for the rest of his days. Touched and magnanimous, Don Quixote forgave Sancho and invited him to mend his ways, and to take heart and to wait for his promises to be fulfilled, since justice may be delayed but always arrives.

It was the perfect moment to end Sofia's letter and offer Federico the pardon that she hoped he would be waiting for. Her nobility was admirable and she didn't put a tail on him even if that was all he needed to be a true jackass. This was an amazing proof of both her strong character and her unique nobility.

Federico hoped that don Emilio would help him to get out of the prison. He thought about ways to show his frailty and appear weak and sick. But he wondered if the old bastard would help him.

XX: Federico's Third Letter to Sofia

> Wicked and ill-advised scoundrels, set free and in free will, the
> person you are keeping as a prisoner in that fortress or prison
> of yours, whether of low or high rank, or of whatever class or
> quality, I am Don Quixote de la Mancha, also known as the
> Knight of the Lions, for whom, by order of the high heavens,
> the happy ending of this adventure has been reserved.
>
> —*Don Quixote*, Second Part, Chapter XXIX

POPAYÁN, AUGUST–SEPTEMBER 1900

My love. My life. Don Emilio came yesterday to see
Domingo and said he was ill and that he had to be
transferred to the other prison. He saw me and told
me I looked well. That Martín had said that no one
was sick and no one will get out. That he was going to
report that Domingo is ill but I am well. Tell Mariana
not to pay a cent, because they will do what they did
the other day. I only wish they would transfer me to the
other prison. Tell Constantino that my pseudonyms

are Lambda and Armodio. I assume the books I left in the other house are already in your hands. I felt pain in the center of my heart not to be able to reply to your greeting the day you walked by the prison. I waited for your return, because the officer offered to allow me to greet you from the window, but I didn't see you walking by again. There—in the other prison—at least I had the hope of consolation and the pleasure of seeing and hearing you, the only desire left in my heart that is all yours. Goodbye my queen.

Do not ever forget me and receive all my love in a kiss I send you, your

F.

* * *

WHEN SOFIA RECEIVED FEDERICO'S LETTER, she already knew that don Emilio, her uncle, had betrayed them. He had come to inform doña Julia and Sofia that Domingo would be allowed to leave the prison, because he was ill, but that Federico was well, according to Martín, he claimed.

"At the prison, Martín is in charge, not I," said don Emilio to Sofia.

"Sure. You always come up with the same story," Sofia replied. "You just don't want to get your hands dirty. I don't comprehend why you asked Mariana to go to see the prefect at two o'clock. That was the worst thing you could have done. My dear friends are desolate and humiliated. Can you not imagine how they are feeling?"

Doña Julia listened to her without saying a word. She already knew that neither her brother nor Alberto would allow Federico to get out of prison. Their relationship was not approved by anyone in the family; they didn't care how much Sofia loved him.

After reading the letter and being aware of Federico's feelings, Sofia decided she needed to pay attention to whatever Federico had included in the other messages, hidden within the text in the length of his letter.

First, Federico had started this in Chapter XXIX dealing with the adventure of the enchanted boat. The text said:

> "Wicked and ill-advised scoundrels, set free and in free will, the person you are keeping as a prisoner in that fortress or prison of yours, whether of low or high rank, or of whatever class or quality, I am Don Quixote de la Mancha, also known as the Knight of the Lions, for whom, by order of the high heavens, the happy ending of this adventure has been reserved."

"Wicked and ill-advised scoundrels" said Don Quixote, raising his sword to the heavens, and Federico, in two brush strokes, painted his opinion of the nature of the bureaucrats enthroned in power during the One Thousand Days War. From his prison cell Federico said: *"set free and in free will, the person you are keeping as a prisoner in that fortress or prison of yours."*

Federico declared himself to be the *Knight of the Lions* and announced with great optimism that the high heavens had chosen him to give a happy ending to his adventure; just what Sofia and his sisters were expecting if don Emilio had not spoiled Federico's dream.

What struck Sofia the most was how Federico had finished his third letter. In Chapter XXXI, he had put his signature *F* between the words *not to you*, in the phrase that was part of the conversation Sancho had with the housekeeper of the Counts—doña Rodríguez de Grijalba—who said to Sancho:

> "You bastard, said the Dueña, burning with anger, whether I am old or not, I'll answer to God, and not to you, garlic-stuffed knave."

The selection by Federico of this enigmatic phrase to end his letter was at first a mystery. *Who was the Dueña he was talking about?* Why did Federico put his signature under *"not to you"* next to *"garlic-stuffed knave"*?

Apparently, Federico had put his signature in a very precise point to make sure that Sofia would see that the *"Dueña"* referred to him as *"garlic-stuffed knave, the bastard."* The *"Dueña"* reported only to God, and for that reason she referred to Sancho as: *"You bastard."* So Federico was telling Sofia that he knew her mother referred to him many times as the *"bastard"*. This could explain why don Emilio had changed his mind at the last moment after he had talked to Sofia about his visit to the prison at noon. He even asked her to tell Federico's sisters to see the prefect at two in the afternoon. *What did*

383

eed me la hiciese de salir á la puerta del castillo, donde hallará un asno rucio mio: vuesa merced sea servida de mandarle poner ó ponerle en la caballeriza, porque el pobrecito es un poco medroso, y no se hallará á estar solo en ninguna de las maneras. Si tan discreto es el amo como el mozo, respondió la dueña, medradas estamos. Andad, hermano, mucho de enhoramala para vos y para quien acá os trujo, tened cuenta con vuestro jumento, que las dueñas desta casa no estamos acostumbradas á semejantes haciendas. Pues en verdad, respondió Sancho, que he oido decir á mi señor, que es zahori de las historias, contando aquella de Lanzarote cuando de Bretaña vino, *que damas curaban dél, y dueñas del su rocino ;* y que en el particular de mi asno, que no le trocara yo con el rocin del señor Lanzarote. Hermano, si sois juglar, replicó la dueña, guardad vuestras gracias para donde lo parezcan y se os paguen, que de mí no podreis llevar sino una higa. Aun bien, respondió Sancho, que será bien madura, pues no perderá vuesa merced la quínola de sus años por punto menos. Hijo de puta, dijo la dueña, toda ya encendida en cólera, si soy vieja ó no, á Dios daré la cuenta, que no á vos, bellaco, harto de ajos: y esto dijo en voz

Fig. 7—Photocopy of page 383, Chapter XXIX in *Don Quixote* 1844. Notice Federico's signature (*F*) between and under *que no,* in the second row up close to the right side.

don Emilio know? Why did he betray his niece? Perhaps he had lied to Sofia and had done it on purpose. He had planned everything from the beginning. Simply put Sofia's family did want to get rid of Federico.

PART FOUR:

In Search of
Immortal Love

My love for you is immortal

—Sofia's second letter to Federico

XXI: The Escape

Don't worry about Hernandes. Even though we all have a bad feeling about him here, except for Dr. Cajiao, I don't believe he is capable of doing what you fear, and it is impossible for him to trick me. I'm telling you this for a good reason. Besides, it is convenient that he go away.

—Federico's first letter to Sofia

POPAYÁN, END OF SEPTEMBER 1900

The six guards aimed their French Gras rifles at the hooded soldier, who was tied to a pylon against the wall of the patio. Just before the shots were fired, the victim defiantly shouted: "Long live the Liberal Party!" When the bullets had penetrated their target, the young recruits contemplated the morbid scene they had created; it was by order of the prison's sheriff, Martín Cienfuegos. The blue smoke from the gunfire floated indecisively in the air as though awaiting the departure of the young soldier's soul from his body. Perhaps his soul would go to the liberals' heaven to be seated at the left hand of God the Father. The smell of gunpowder—the incense of war—invaded the hallways and the prison cells where his cellmates, who'd been startled by the discharge, wondered what had happened.

Martín, the prison sheriff, had noticed the fear in the faces of the young recruits who'd just fired.

"We'll have the same fate if we don't get rid of them first," he said.

When the church bells rang for the early Mass, the prisoners emerged from their cells, ready to stretch their legs and have something for breakfast. It was then that they discovered the bloody corpse bent over at the waist. Already simmering with resentment at their confinement, now they boiled over with rage and hatred at the untethered power of their jailers and of their superiors in the government.

Federico, Hernandes and Antonio talked with Dr. Cajiao about the execution of the soldier.

"His name was Justo Patriota, " the doctor said. "Do you know why they killed him?"

"No, I don't have a single idea," said Federico.

"Nor do I," Antonio said.

"He admitted to being a spy but refused to say what he knew. He didn't betray us," said Dr. Cajiao. "Now listen. General Pablo Emilio Bustamante is on his way with two thousand men to attack the city from the north early in October. Antonio, somehow we have to get Hernandes out of here."

"I'll do what I can," said Antonio. "Where do we have to deliver the rifles and the ammunition?"

"They should be at the *Hacienda Las Mercedes*, near Totoró, in less than two weeks. Bustamante is expected to cross the *Serranía de las Minas* and rest his men until we can deliver the arms. His plan is to attack Popayán as soon as they get the weapons. That's why you both must escape as soon as possible."

Hernandes had taken a long look at the dead soldier before he joined the group. No, he wouldn't give Martín the pleasure of blowing his head apart inside of a hemp bag. He would escape somehow.

"Do you fellows know about the convent's tunnel?" Antonio asked.

"Would that be another of your famous stories?" said Dr. Cajiao.

"No, doctor, I am serious. But I'm not sure if the exit into the church of San Francisco still exists. The last time I was in the tunnel I was fifteen years old," said Antonio.

"And what does San Francisco have to do with all of this?" asked Hernandes.

"Let me explain," Antonio replied. "What I propose is that we escape via the prison sewer that drains into the Río Molino. That drainage used to connect with a tunnel that went from the convent where this prison is now to the church of San Francisco. There used to be an exit by the sacristy of the church. The only person than can tell us with certainty if that exit is open is don Adolfo Dueñas. He knows the city, in and out, by heart."

"Escaping through the tunnel would certainly be better than jumping from the roof into Delfina's inn," said Hernandes.

"What makes you think the exit is still there?" Dr. Cajiao asked.

Antonio replied, "Have you noticed the bats coming out of the latrines in the evening? They must come from this very tunnel. And we can use the same route to get out by the church of San Francisco. But if we went through the sewer all the way to the river, we would have to crawl along it and I would prefer to be shot rather than to drown in that mess."

"I'm ready to get out one way or another," Hernandes said. "I must deliver the arms before Martín has me shot. He knows I came from Santander, where we defeated the Godos, and he wants to get even."

"It is decided, then," said Dr. Cajiao. "Antonio will help you to get out and will put you in touch with Arcila and Constantino to organize the delivery of weapons and ammunition to general Bustamante."

After agreeing on the escape plan, they decided that the following Sunday, September 30, would be the ideal day. Federico would write to Sofia at once to coordinate with Arcila and Constantino: it would be their job to get horses for the escapees to leave the city and they would also ask don Adolfo Dueñas if the exit into the church is still there and about how get out from the tunnel at the church of San Francisco. They also needed a contact to help them with the details of how to open the exit and what to wear to exit without being noticed.

*   *   *

LATE IN THE AFTERNOON, don Higinio the gravedigger came to pick up Patriota's corpse. He used a cart led by a half-starved old horse. With help from a couple of recruits, he loaded the corpse on board. The old animal, sensing the weight of the load and its smell, perked up its ears and by instinct departed for the graveyard. Don Higinio, sitting on the coachman's bench, was smoking a cheap cigar to keep away the flies that followed them.

*   *   *

ON FRIDAY NIGHT, Clodomiro, dispatched by Sofia, delivered to Federico a sealed envelope containing a letter from don Adolfo Dueñas that explained the details of the tunnel and the exit. Arcila would be waiting for the prisoners in the sacristy in the church of San Francisco and Constantino would have fresh clothes and saddled horses in the field close to the hospital across from the Río Molino.

*   *   *

ON SATURDAY, Martín noticed an unusual number of prisoners whispering to each other, and became suspicious. He doubled the vigilance. He also ordered a surprise general search to be done on Sunday at dawn before breakfast. If they hadn't had enough with seeing one soldier executed, he would have ten more shot to death.

*   *   *

ON SUNDAY, a cold and foggy day, the bugle gave the alert at dawn to start the inspection. Such a sharp sound at that early hour woke up the prisoners involved in the plot, and they wondered what had gone wrong.

Federico had spent the whole night helping Domingo, who continued to suffer from fever and vomiting. Both were exhausted. Domingo would not be transferred out of the prison for several days yet.

"What's going on?" asked the terrified Domingo.

"I have no idea," said Federico, "but it doesn't sound like an invitation to a party."

Dr. Cajiao wondered if Hernandes and Antonio would be able to escape. Had there been a betrayal by someone in their group or was there a spy among them?

Martín, wearing his black cape, with his .44 caliber Kerr on his belt, walked imperiously around the hallways yelling at the guards to hurry up, to wake the prisoners and get them out of their cells, to start the search.

The guards, emboldened by the tension of the moment, started to force the prisoners out of their cells and into the patio with curses and by pushing them and striking them with the butts of their rifles.

Hernandes ran into Antonio in the patio.

"Arcila and Constantino will be waiting forever," he whispered.

"Don't even think about it. We'll take advantage of this confusion to get out right now," said Antonio.

Meanwhile, Federico was on his way to the patio supporting Domingo by his arm. The poor man didn't have enough energy to walk by himself. He was as pale as death. A guard by the steps saw them coming downstairs and shouted at Federico.

"Let him walk by himself!" As he said this, the guard pushed and hit them with his rifle butt. Federico, enraged by the guard's abuses of a man so clearly ill, turned on him shouting, "Coward! Insolent!"

The guard slammed Federico's chin with the rifle butt.

Federico started bleeding from the mouth, but he grabbed Domingo—about to fall down the stairs and shouted, "Coward! Scoundrel!" and kicked the guard.

This time, the guard flipped his rifle around and he shot.

Domingo gasped, wounded, and said: "this damned Godo has killed me!" He crashed into Federico's arms pushing him off balance.

The guard shot his rifle again and the bullet went through Domingo and then hit Federico in the left leg above the knee.

The two friends rolled down the steps holding onto each other. Federico fell backwards, hit his head on the stone floor, Domingo fell on top of him. The two bodies lay immobile at the bottom of the stairs and blood dripped down the steps. They were entangled in an awkward posture. Their limbs were twisted. They appeared to be dead.

Martín noticed that Domingo was still alive and was looking at him with eyes full of hatred and terror, choking on his own blood. Martín aimed at his temple and put him out of his misery with the Kerr.44. That was the end of Domingo Cervantes.

Martín looked at Federico and didn't bother wasting another shot. The man was immobile, his face disfigured, wounded in the head with his body bathed in blood that was both his and Domingo's.

So began the revolt of September 30, 1900. The other prisoners, enraged at seeing their comrades in a pool of blood, grabbed the paving stones of the patio and attacked the guards. The guards shot at them, and knocked their heads with rifle butts.[12] Martín, his revolver in hand, cursed the prisoners and the guards as he tried to reestablish order. The hair on his head stood on end, his jacket was half torn off, his face was red and covered with sweat and he looked like a madman.

Hernandes and Antonio, veterans of other battles, knew exactly what to do and dropped to the ground when the shooting started.

"Let's go the tunnel," Hernandes said to Antonio. Crawling and rolling, they dodged the fighting and made their way to the latrines. They took advantage of the screaming, the confusion, and the rattling of the firearms. They lifted the iron grid of a latrine and dropped down into the sewer. Groping around, Antonio looked for the exit toward the tunnel, opposite to the water flow into the Río Molino. When Antonio found the hole above the wall of the well, he whispered urgently, "Help me!"

Hernandes leaned against the wall and Antonio, with the agility of a scared cat, climbed on his back to reach the cave leading to the tunnel. Then, he stuck his hand down toward Hernandes and in one pull lifted him up. Once inside the cave, a narrow muddy passage where they had to be on their bellies, they lit the tallow candle Hernandez had brought and crawled toward the tunnel.

"Here it is," said Antonio.

When Hernandes reached the tunnel and was able to stand up, he noticed that on the opposite wall there were several tombstones with dates in Roman numerals.

"Antonio, this is a catacomb."

"We need to keep going! Arcila and Constantino must have heard the shots. I wonder if they have already left."

They hustled through the tunnel toward the church, struggling with spider webs and bat guano that reached halfway to their knees, crouching low to avoid the brick arches of the tunnel. Even though they only had to cover about five hundred feet to reach the church, it seemed an eternity. At each noise they looked back in fear, waiting for any signs of life, to check if they had been followed.

Meanwhile, Arcila, wearing a monk's cassock as a disguise, waited impatiently in the sacristy with a pair of similar cassocks for the escapees. The day before he had bribed the sacristan to loosen the stone slab that covered the entrance to the tunnel behind the sanctuary in the sacristy room next to the main altar.

When they saw the light around the exit, Hernandes and Antonio climbed the moldy steps leading to the sacristy and knocked once. Arcila responded with two knocks, signaling to move forward. They pushed the stone between the two of them, and Antonio poked out his face, looking for Arcila, who was ready to help him out. Hernandes followed. They stunk.

Arcila handed them the cassocks.

"I heard the shots and the screams. What's going on?" he asked as they dressed.

"All hell broke loose at the prison. Get us out of here!" said Antonio, covering his head with the cassock's hood to hide his face.

"Let's go," said Arcila.

The three monks left the sanctuary and entered the church with their hands hidden inside the cassock's sleeves and their heads bent so the hoods fell over their eyes. The Immaculate Virgin looked on them from the High Altar with her hand raised as if to give her blessing. Once out of the church, they turned left and walked toward the Río Molino.

Some devout old ladies praying to the Virgin saw them leaving the church and one of them said to the others, "They smell awful. If they weren't monks I would say they came from hell itself."

Constantino was hiding behind a thicket of blueberry bushes, smoking a little cigar to stay warm. The horses were tied to a guava tree and their warm breath produced little clouds of vapor. When he saw the monks across the river coming his way, he felt great relief. He had been expecting the worst after hearing the shots.

The smelly monks yanked off their cassocks and their filthy clothing, then jumped into the cold river to get the stench off themselves. Shivering, they climbed naked onto the other shore, where Constantino handed them fresh cotton clothes, straw hats, and hemp espadrilles. Once dressed as peasants, they departed with Constantino on horseback, following the banks of the Río Molino.

When they left, Arcila put their cassocks in a burlap sack and returned to his home on the *Calle de la Compañía*. He changed clothes, had breakfast, and walked nonchalantly toward the Plaza Mayor. The locals were already talking about the revolt, the shootings, the screaming, and the slaughter. But nobody knew exactly what had happened.

*   *   *

CONSTANTINO AND HIS COMPANIONS followed the *Calle de Orinoco* toward the Ejido grounds and waded the small stream, the Río los Sauces, to climb toward the farmhouse of Víctor and Felisa, members of the Liberal Resistance. Their two immense dogs, Caronte and Calibán, approached the group to greet Constantino and sniff the visitors.

Víctor worked as a butcher and was in the cattle business in partnership with Constantino. He was an enormous man of immense strength, able to handle cattle and hogs that were challenging their slaughter. In spite of his looks, he was a friendly and peaceful person, incapable of hurting anyone. During the Holy Week Processions he played the role of a Roman soldier, wearing an armored suit custom-made to his measurements by don Toríbio Maya, a local smith. The town children knew him as The Gladiator. Felisa, his wife, was the expert in herbs at the public market.

She greeted the visitors amiably and offered them a breakfast consisting of hot coffee, roasted plantains, and fried pork. They ate with great gusto and voracious appetites. Like all the prisoners, Hernandes and Antonio had been slowly starving. After having eaten their fill, they celebrated their freedom with a shot of aguardiente. After their toast, Constantino returned to Popayán. On Sundays, he opened the telegraph office after the noon Mass.

On arriving at his office, he found an envoy from the prison waiting for him. He had orders to send an urgent wire to the government in Bogotá. Constantino read the message slowly as he transmitted it.

> POPAYÁN, SUNDAY SEPTEMBER 30, 1900: 12.30 P.M.
>
> TO: MINISTER OF WAR BOGOTÁ
>
> PRISONERS REVOLT JUNÍN'S BATTALION PRISON. SEVERAL
> DEAD, MANY WOUNDED. ORDER RESTORED.
>
> SIGNED: SHERIFF MARTÍN CIENFUEGOS

*   *   *

As soon as the officer left the telegraphic office, Constantino sent a second telegram:

> POPAYÁN, SUNDAY SEPTEMBER 30, 1900: 12.45 P.M.
>
> LIBERAL DIRECTORY BOGOTÁ
>
> TOOLS UNDERWAY
>
> SIGNED: ARMODIO

After he had signed the telegram using Federico' pseudonym (Armodio), Constantino wondered if Federico was still alive. *Would he see him alive again?*

XXII: Revolt at the Prison

Pedro was always ready to be of service to others, without
expecting compensation and without fear of being
contaminated. One of his charity patients infected him with a
disease that took him to the grave on March 8, 1907, before his
39th birthday.

—Gustavo Arboleda on Pedro Lindo, *Diccionario biográfico y
genealógico del Antiguo Departamento del Cauca*, 1926.

POPAYÁN, SEPTEMBER 30, 1900

The first shot fired after Federico and Domingo were attacked
came when another prisoner grabbed a rifle from one of the
guards and shot the culprit to death, right on the steps. His
vengeance cost him his life: Martín killed him on the spot. The weak-
ened and starving prisoners attacked the guards with whatever they
could pick up from the ground but the shooting was violent and brief
and the prisoners surrendered, because the guards were shooting to kill.
Humiliated and impotent, they were lined up against the wall with
their hands raised above their heads.

Martín, revolver in hand, shouted, "The first bastard who dares to
move will die."

Once the prisoners were subdued, Martín called the roll. He sent them to the cells, one by one, after each was accounted for. Two guards and six prisoners were dead, including Domingo and Federico, and eighteen were wounded, excluding those with minor cuts or lacerations. Ninety-six more had surrendered. Antonio and Hernandes were missing, of course: they couldn't be found anywhere.

The wounded victims leaned against the walls in agony and in pain, waiting for help from the prison's doctor.

Sofia's uncle don Emilio Carrasco had already been notified to report to the prison immediately. Don Emilio got ready in two minutes, grabbed his briefcase, and departed for the prison at once, walking as rapidly as his old legs could carry him. As he passed by Pedro Lindo's home, he saw lights on and stopped to ask for his help. Pedro, always ready to be of service, grabbed his doctor's briefcase and accompanied don Emilio. They had no idea what was waiting for them after the revolt.

The bodies of the dead had been left around the water fountain, in the center of the main patio. Pedro recognized Federico and Domingo among them. He felt great pain for his friends, and more for their families. He thought of Federico's sisters who had come to ask for his help, and of Zoila, Domingo's wife. They had lost a son in Flautas, and Domingo was her only support, another widow without hope.

While attending to the wounded, Pedro asked don Emilio if he had seen that Federico Lemos was one of the dead.

"Yes, and good riddance," said don Emilio while holding the needle in his left hand, shrugging to show he didn't care, and continued suturing a gash on the neck of the prisoner.

Pedro, always an honest man, was shocked by don Emilio's answer. Federico and Pedro had grown up together at don Nicomedes' bookstore and were close friends. He couldn't make sense of the old doctor's answer.

Martín approached the doctors to observe their work. When don

Emilio finished stitching the fellow with the gash on his neck, Martín asked, "Anything deadly?"

"Nothing to worry about." Don Emilio raised his arms as though saying why should I care. "In a week they will all be well. There are only a few with bullet wounds, and that's just a matter of cauterizing, putting a few stitches, and letting nature take its course. Pedrito is the expert in that front. We shouldn't pay too much attention to these bandits; if they die, they deserve it. What worries me the most is the number of dead and the impact Federico and Domingo's deaths may have on the public opinion. They are well-known persons and their families are related to very distinguished people."

"Don Emilio, what should we do?" asked Martín.

The old doctor took him aside and walked him away from Pedro, whispering, "It's easy. We just report some of the dead as missing."

Martín, smiling maliciously, gave him a slap on the back and said, "Great idea, doctor! What about if we burn them to make sure there are no footprints?"

Don Emilio listened to Martín's proposal, showing no emotion whatsoever.

"Domingo, the guard that shot him, and the unidentified prisoners will be reported as dead, and the others we can burn to ashes," said don Emilio.

"And Federico?" asked Martín.

"We will burn him also and report him as missing, along with Hernandes and Antonio."

"Did you say burn him?" asked Martín.

"Of course, that way he will disappear once and for all."

Meanwhile Pedro, seeing that Martín and don Emilio were away, approached the fountain to take a closer look at the dead. He noticed don Nicomedes' ring on Federico's hand and decided to remove it before anyone could steal it. When he grabbed the wrist to take the ring off, he detected a weak pulse.

He stood up and put the ring in his pocket. He had just done that when Martín and don Emilio approached him. Pedro wondered if they had seen him putting the ring away.

The old doctor said to Pedro, "I need to talk with you about something serious. We need to help Martín to get rid of these dead bodies. We plan to report that Domingo, two guards, and two prisoners died during the revolt. Martín will inform their kin to come to identify them and take away their bodies. I wonder if you mind taking the corpses of Federico, and the other four—who have no kin—to the cemetery. Don Higinio, the gravedigger, can be persuaded to dispose of the bodies by burning them. You just have to give him a bottle of aguardiente and a can of petroleum. Make sure he doesn't mix them up. If he is too drunk he may end up drinking the petroleum."

Pedro, astonished by the evil proposal, which by nature he would have refused, realized this was his opportunity to save Federico from a horrible death.

"Yes, I think this is a good solution to the problem. The dead don't care what we do with them. If you agree, I'll take their corpses away right now. This is the moment to take advantage of the confusion," said Pedro.

"Thanks, Pedrito. Martín will make sure they are put in hemp sacks. You don't know how much I appreciate your collaboration." And don Emilio shook hands with him to seal their deal. The problem had been solved.

"Don't worry about a thing, don Emilio," said Pedro.

Said and done. The guards loaded the five corpses in hemp sacks in the wagon of the horse carriage and covered them with an oilcloth. Pedro left the prison using the back door facing the *Calle de la Legislatura* and allowed the poor horse to set its own pace. Seated on the coachman's bench he headed to his office to find a way to save Federico's life.

*   *   *

AT ABOUT THE SAME TIME, Arcila, satisfied with his errands at the Plaza Mayor, decided to head toward Delfina's inn to look for fresh news about the revolt. The old witch was the best source of gossip in town. When he was walking along the *Calle de la Compañía*, he saw that Pedro Lindo was coming down the street in a carriage. Pedro also saw Arcila and gently made the horse stop to talk to his friend.

"Aniceto Arcila, what are you up to around here? What an incredible coincidence! I needed help and you have showed up out of nowhere. Join me, please."

Arcila climbed onto the coachman's bench, sat next to Pedro and asked what was happening at the prison.

"Let's go to my office first and there I'll tell you the whole story. We need to move as fast as we can without raising suspicion" said Pedro.

He parked the carriage behind a wall, out of sight from the street facing his office, and showed Arcila what was in the carriage's cart. He described his conversation with don Emilio and explained the situation in the prison as they took Federico's body into Pedro's office. Arcila noticed that Federico's body was very cold. He wondered if he was still alive.

"It's a miracle that he is alive. He has lost a lot of blood. I will do what I can to save his life," said Pedro.

They removed Federico's clothing and Pedro opened the shutters for light so he could better see the head wounds. They were messy, but not critical. Federico's swollen mouth was a mess and his nose looked like a piece of blood sausage, but the cranium was in one piece. Pedro found a bullet hole on the right side of the left thigh above the knee. There was no exit. The femur did not appear to be fractured by the bullet. Then, Pedro lifted Federico's eyelids to observe the reaction of his pupils to the light. The man appeared to have a cerebral injury complicated by the loss of blood. Pedro took some ammonia salts from his first aid kit and applied them to Federico's nostrils. Federico coughed several times and he opened his eyes. He is alive! Arcila took a deep breath of relief. They sat Federico upright to help him cough. He looked at them with empty eyes and no signs of having recognized his friends.

"I am, I am thirsty," he managed to say.

It hurt to talk. His mouth was full of blood clots and his face was swollen. Pedro poured water into a glass and helped Federico to drink. He swallowed with difficulty, spat out some blood, but he slowly drank the whole glass of water sip by sip. He had been completely dehydrated.

"Thank you," he said, releasing a deep sigh. Pedro and Arcila looked at him as if he had been resurrected from the dead.

"Where am I? What happened?" Federico asked.

"You were saved by the grace of God," said Pedro.

"And who are you?" asked Federico, disoriented.

"It's better if you don't talk." said Arcila.

Pedro cleaned the wounds of his patient with a cloth soaked in alcohol and applied a provisional bandage made from a sheet he ripped apart and soaked in Alibour water. He used the same sheet to make bandages for Federico's leg to stop the blood loss. Finally, they set him on a chair with the wounded leg supported on a stool. When they lifted his leg Federico screamed out in pain. "Ayyyyyy!"

"Pedrito!" he said next, recognizing his old friend.

María, Pedro's wife, came into the office alarmed by Federico's scream.

"My God! What has happened to don Federico? Holy Saint Barbara! I am going to tell Mariana and his sisters."

"Wait! Do not even think of telling anyone," said Pedro, and taking her by the arm he left to fill María in on what was happening. Then he told María to keep everything to herself as though their life depended on it. They would be in great danger if it were discovered he had saved Federico's life. He couldn't let him die, and he couldn't tell anyone he was alive. That was his dilemma.

After talking with his wife, Pedro returned to the office.

"Give me Federico's boots," he told Arcila. "I am going to put them on one corpse that is totally disfigured. This way don Higinio may think that the man wearing the boots is Federico if he recognizes the boots."

"I like it," said Arcila.

Pedro went to the cemetery with the other four bodies, one wearing Federico's boots, and left Federico with Arcila and María. He also carried with him a bottle of aguardiente and a can of the petroleum María used for their lamps. His plan was to get don Higinio very drunk before incinerating the corpses. This way perhaps he wouldn't remember if there were four or five, or who they were.

In the meantime, María returned with sweetened coffee for Federico and Arcila. She couldn't conceal the horror she felt, and made the sign of the cross several times, thanking God that he was still alive.

Arcila took his coffee and offered the other to Federico. "Don't choke on it."

Federico took little sips with visible pleasure though pausing between sips to cough. His mouth burned. He had swallowed the blood draining from his nose and his mouth. Arcila helped him by holding the cup and asking him to sip slowly.

*   *   *

BECAUSE IT WAS SUNDAY, don Higinio was walking around the tombs making brief visits to his ghost friends in his constant dialogue with the dead. Suddenly, he heard the squeaky wheels of a wagon and looked toward the gate to see who was coming.

Pedro got closer to him and pulled on the reins to stop the horse.

"Dear doctor, what a surprise! I didn't expect any visitors today. What brings you here so early?"

"Good day, don Higinio. I have a little job for you and some petroleum that Martín Cienfuegos sent you," said Pedro, pointing at the load he was carrying in the wagon.

"Now I understand," said don Higinio, getting closer to Pedro.

"What else did don Martín send me?" he asked.

Pedro understood what he was looking for and handed him the bottle of aguardiente.

"Refresh your throat and ask God to have mercy on these poor devils."

Don Higinio, just as Pedro expected, took a long drink of the strong liquor and smacked his lips to show his approval. Then he raised his eyes as though asking for permission and took another shot. He didn't offer any to Pedro because he knew Pedro didn't drink alcohol. He knew better.

"I needed this drink," he said. Pedro smiled. Everyone knew the old man couldn't resist a full bottle of liquor.

"Take another one, don Higinio." said Pedro.

This time the old gravedigger raised the bottle to drink to his own pleasure. He hadn't had breakfast yet. Satisfied with the aguardiente, he took hold of the horse's reins and led it toward the common pit to dump the corpses.

Don Higinio stumbled on the way and Pedro saw he was already half drunk. Three of those long sips were enough.

"Let me help you," said Pedro, grabbing him by the arm.

Between the two of them they managed to dump the burlap sacks into the pit. The old man looked at them with glassy eyes, shaking his head.

"Thank you, don Higinio. From now on it is your business. I need to return the wagon." And Pedro climbed into the carriage.

Don Higinio took two more drinks watching him leave and waited until he lost sight of the wagon. Then he put the bottle in his pocket and opened the sacks to search the pockets of the dead. It was then that he noticed the yellow leather boots. He had seen them before but didn't remember where. He removed them from the corpse and tried them on. They fit like a glove. His old shoes had worn-down heels and the left one had a hole in it.

Happily he tested the boots by walking around and pushing the bodies with his heel deeper into the pit and then he soaked them with petroleum. He took out his matches and set the bodies on fire. While taking another sip he looked at the blue flame over the corpses, which smelled like roasted pig and burned rags. He moved away from the fire and recalled that the deer leather boots he had on his feet belonged to don Federico.

"Dammit! Don Federico was one of the dead; may God hold him in His glory."

*   *   *

Pedro Lindo returned to the city to deliver the wagon to the prison. Martín heard the wagon driving into the yard and came to greet him. Don Emilio had already informed the prefect that the dead numbered five—including Domingo—and the wounded eighteen. Federico, Antonio Ramos, and Hernandes had been reported as missing.

After chatting with Martín for a while about the success of his mission, Pedro excused himself and returned home to keep tending Federico's wounds. He had to find a way to get him out of sight.

*   *   *

BETWEEN HALF-AWAKE AND ASLEEP Federico opened and closed his eyes. His whole body hurt. He felt an insatiable thirst. Each time he swallowed something, he felt a contraction along his head wound, as if someone was viciously grabbing him by the hair.

As soon as Pedro returned to the office he told Arcila that they needed to get Federico out of Popayán at once. Arcila suggested they could take him to Victor's farmhouse, an isolated place that was near enough to the city that would allow Pedro to visit without raising suspicion. Pedro approved of the idea; he was a good friend of Felisa and they shared a common knowledge of the use of medicinal herbs.

When María became aware of Pedro's return, she brought three cups of hot chicken broth. Federico drank his with a desperate appetite: for months he hadn't tasted anything so delicious. Pedro also drank his broth with gusto: he had been in motion for hours without any food and was exhausted.

The color was returning to Federico's semblance. "A sick man who eats will not die," said Arcila, enjoying his own cup of broth.

His swollen nose and mouth were messy looking but they were not as serious as they appeared to be. The real work would be removing the bullet from his leg and stitching up the head wound. María lit the little charcoal grill and started heating the cauterizing irons. Meanwhile, Pedro shaved around Federico's head wound and cleaned his leg to remove the dried blood and the dirt.

When Federico noticed Pedro checking the color of the hot irons he felt he was going to faint. He knew what was coming.

"You won't even feel the irons. It will happen very quickly," said Pedro and Federico grinned, doubting his words. He had seen cattle being branded.

Arcila left Pedro and María in charge and went to borrow Constantino's landau to carry Federico to Victor's farmhouse. His idea was that anyone seeing two figures in Constantino's sporty carriage would think they were delivering a wire to a customer.

Pedro stitched the head wound and washed it with a solution of potassium permanganate. Federico felt like his wound was boiling and he struggled to remain conscious. He had never in his life felt pain like this. His whole head throbbed as though his heart was beating inside his cranium.

Pedro, noticing the efforts the man made to hide his pain, knew he wouldn't take the irons well. So he gave him a long drink of aguardiente and asked him to bite on a cloth soaked in the same liquor.

"Take this drink and bite this cloth and do not move. Do we agree?"

"Yes, go ahead," said Federico. Pedro put the cloth in his mouth and started to work on the leg. He cleaned the wound with alcohol and, using a set of long-tipped pliers, grabbed the bullet and pulled it out of the wound. This time Federico's reaction was spectacular: he screamed like a stuck pig and fainted instantly. Pedro took advantage of the moment and applied the red-hot iron to the leg wound. Federico didn't move. Then Pedro closed the wound. María helped him to put a bamboo splint on the leg and they tied it with strips taken from the same cotton sheet they'd used for the bandages. Federico's body over the chair looked like a naked and forgotten mannequin. Pedro put away his tools in his shop and looked for the ammonia salts in his kit.

Just like he had done earlier in the day, he placed the salts under Federico's nose and the patient came back to life. Federico continued to feel the pulsing in his head and an intense pain in his leg, but he couldn't move it. Pedro gave Federico the bottle of aguardiente and he drank anxiously, looking for relief from his pain. María brought a pair of Pedro's old pajamas and they got Federico dressed. He was exhausted from the loss of blood, the pain of his wounds, and from the fall on the prison steps. For a moment he felt like Christ on the cross on Mount Calvary.

They had to wait a long time for Arcila to come back with the landau and a monk's cassock for Federico. They put the cassock on Federico and tied his torso to the back of the landau's seat with a leather strap. Outside, a chilling rain gave the afternoon a sinister feeling. The smell of death was in the air.

"I'll see you soon," said Arcila and departed for the Ejido to deliver his "wire" accompanied by the inebriated monk sitting next to him. The lively sorrel gained a speedy trot and quickly they were out of sight.

Pedro felt relief when they left. María embraced him tenderly. He had taken an immense risk and he still feared for Federico's future.

"I am famished," he said to his wife.

"Yes, you need eat something and take a nap," said Maria.

"I will do that later. Now I have to go back to the prison to check on the wounded. If I don't go, Martín may let them die."

"How awful!" said María, blessing herself three times, and then three more times.

Pedro's mind was full of concerns including how much doubt he had around Federico's survival and recovery. He could not get the cruelty of don Emilio out of his thoughts. They were a band of murderers.

XXIII: Federico's Convalescence

Oh no, don't die, your grace, my Master! Replied Sancho,
sobbing. Better, take my advice and live for many years, because
the greatest madness a man can do in this life is to let himself
die for no reason, without anyone killing him, nor any other
hands finishing him than those of melancholy.

—*Don Quixote*, Second Part, Chapter LXXIV

Arcila guided the landau away from Pedro Lindo's home and
followed the *Calle de Marcos Campo* heading to the Río los
Sauces. At each bump, he heard Federico's moaning mixed
with the sound of the carriage's squeaky wheels. Federico, wrapped in
his wool cassock, trembled from cold. His leg was itching and the pain
left him breathless and, eventually, he fainted when the carriage ran over
a very large hole in the road.

On arriving to the slow and shallow Río los Sauces, Arcila allowed
the horse to find the best route to cross it by instinct. On the other side,
the horse climbed the hill toward the farmhouse with the gabled roof
covered by moldy tiles. The house was almost invisible between the
achiote bushes, the bougainvillea, and the willow trees next to it. The
dogs came running toward the landau and barked, announcing the ar-

rival of the guests. Felisa calmed the dogs and opened the gate to let the landau in, and Víctor waited in the hallway with a shotgun under his arm. Hernandes and Antonio heard the voices outside and wondered who had come. Arcila smelled a mixture of brewing coffee and smoke in the air as he parked the landau under the roof overhang.

"May I give you a hand?" asked Víctor. They were all surprised to see the hooded monk that appeared to be dead.

"Be careful, because he is in a very delicate condition. Do you have a hammock where he can be comfortable?" asked Arcila, removing the straps from Federico's torso.

Víctor assented, and went to look for the hammock. When he returned, he laid the hammock on the hallway floor and placed the monk on it gently as if he were weightless. Antonio and Hernandes were terrified when they saw that the monk was actually Federico. With Victor's help, they carried their friend, wrapped in the hammock, into the kitchen.

"Is he really alive?" asked Felisa, doubt painted on her face.

"Yes, but he is badly wounded and has lost a lot of blood," said Arcila.

The dogs, attracted by the smell of fresh blood, got close to sniff the hammock and Felisa chased them away hissing, "Hush! Hush! Calm down! Be Quiet!"

When his friends placed the hammock on the kitchen floor, Federico came back into his own self, murmuring, "I am thirsty."

He was alive! They all celebrated his arrival and were happy to hear him speak. Then, Víctor slung the hammock's rope ends over the kitchen's wooden beams and they lifted it up to place Federico closer to the fire. Felisa brought him a cup of coffee and helped him to drink it. The warmth of the fire and the coffee helped Federico to recover consciousness. He looked around the room, wonder visible on his face, and said, "Where am I?"

His comrades looked at him with pity. His face was swollen and bruised from the abuse he had received. He looked like a true martyr.

The Franciscan cassock he was wearing helped to accentuate his tragic appearance.

"We are in a farmhouse, outside of the city," said Arcila. The others observed him with concern for his life.

Federico drank another couple of sips of coffee and felt nauseous. He was exhausted. Felisa took the cup from his hands while he looked at all of them with tired eyes and suddenly he lost consciousness again.

Víctor tried to make him more comfortable in the hammock and Felisa found a wool blanket to keep him warm. Then she sat in a rocking chair next to the fire to keep an eye on him. The dogs lay by her feet, keeping her company. Motioning with her fingers toward the door, she signaled to the men to leave the room. Outside, the rain continued to fall gently.

Hernandes and Antonio listened with fascination to Arcila, as he told them about Federico's incredible adventure and about the tender and miraculous care provided by Pedro Lindo and his wife.

"Pedro is a true saint. He is as good as bread," said Antonio.

As the three friends shared a few drinks and discussed the details of the arms delivery to General Bustamante, Felisa rose and fixed them dinner and prepared additional food for their trip to *Las Delicias* to deliver the weapons. Later in the evening, Federico woke up and Felisa fed him some soup from the iron pot she kept over the fire. He wondered who this woman was, who was treating him as if he were her own son. The smell of food and Federico's voice attracted the guests back to the kitchen.

"Antonio, where am I? Who brought me here?" Federico asked.

Antonio and Arcila told him about his odyssey from the moment he was shot on the steps at the prison until he arrived at the farmhouse, but he had no memory of any of it. They told him that some people would assume he was dead and others would think he had escaped and was hiding somewhere.

"You owe your life to Pedro Lindo," said Arcila. "Any other Godo would have let you burn alive. We need to tell your sisters and Sofía that you are alive; it would be a crime to keep them in such uncertainty. I will tell them that you are alive but they must not know where you are. Any mistake by any of them could cost us all our lives."

"I don't want Sofía or my sisters to know I am wounded, and would prefer not to see them until I can take care of myself. They would die from worrying if they saw me as I am now." After having said this, Federico couldn't keep his eyes open and after a few minutes he fell back into a deep sleep.

Arcila needed to be back in Popayán and, taking advantage of the rain and the darkness, he left to return the landau to Constantino. In town, Arcila gave Constantino an update about Federico's situation and described their adventure. Then it was time to rest; that day had been the longest one of his life. Once at home, he put his head on his pillow and fell into a deep sleep. He didn't have any energy left in his body, not even to dream.

* * *

FELISA, FINALLY ALONE, found the best position in her chair and, keeping the shotgun at hand, got closer to the fire. Her patient was breathing and sleeping peacefully. He looked like a monster. In the other room, Víctor and the travelers also slept while snoring peacefully.

At dawn, before the first light, the rooster crowed. Federico sunk in the hammock, continued breathing yet with some difficulty, occasionally gasping for air. Felisa left his side and went to the patio's stream to wash her face. The ice-cold mountain water produced little vapor clouds upon touching her warm, dark skin. She cleaned her eyes with the icy water and rubbed her hands over her apron to dry and warm them. As she approached the farmhouse she looked toward the city, observing the coming of dawn.

She loved the sunrise. From the hill, where the house was, she took part in the new day while enjoying the morning breeze and the pleasant coolness of the air, and followed the light coming down from the top of the willow trees as the sun climbed over the horizon. She listened to the chirping of the birds, the noise of the parrots that nested in the bamboo trees along the river, and the cackling of her chickens looking for worms and grasshoppers. In spite of having slept poorly, Felisa felt good and hugged herself as she adjusted her poncho to return to the kitchen. There, she checked on Federico and added some wood to the fire. As the coffee started brewing, she patted out a few corn tortillas and baked them on the sturdy iron grill over the fire.

Federico woke up when he heard noises in the kitchen. He hurt all over, but he was not in prison anymore. He breathed in the smells from the kitchen. Felisa helped him to sit up in the hammock by placing a couple of pillows behind his back and gave him a mug of coffee and a warm tortilla. Víctor, still rubbing his eyes, came out of his room attracted by the smell of coffee and hot food, and noticed that Federico was awake.

"How are you feeling?" he said, looking at Federico.

"Better, thank you. Tell me, where are Hernandes and Antonio?"

"They left around four to take advantage of the dark. They have a long trip ahead of them to deliver their cargo to General Bustamante."

The food and the morning breeze helped Federico to wake up completely. His head and his leg hurt, he had a fever, his face was swollen and his left eye was totally bloodshot, but he felt great because he was free. Meanwhile, Víctor got ready to go to town.

"Don Federico, I leave you in good hands. Rest, and eat when you can. You are so thin that you look like a poor's man donkey," said Víctor.

Federico tried to smile at the comment and made himself comfortable in the hammock. Shortly after, he again fell into a deep sleep. Felisa quietly took the empty cup from his hands and covered him with the wool blanket. He looked pitiful.

Víctor headed toward the market where he expected to receive a few fat calves a friend had promised; with luck, they would have meat for the business and for his home.

*   *   *

EARLY MONDAY MORNING, Constantino learned that soldiers sent by the governor and the prefect were looking all over the city for Hernandes, Antonio, and Federico. He was told that some pious old women had seen three monks with cassocks leaving the Church of San Francisco on Sunday morning before Mass. On a flier posted on the city walls, the prefect offered a reward of fifty pesos—to be paid in gold—for any information about the missing prisoners. The posted information accused them of being involved in the prison revolt and also of being responsible for the death of several soldiers and other prisoners.

*   *   *

AFTER DOMINGO'S FUNERAL ON MONDAY MORNING, Mariana opened the bookstore as a way to escape from her worries. How was Federico? And where was he? She had no idea. Agents from the prefect's office had come to the bookstore looking for the three missing prisoners. They also had been at Sofia's home and at the homes of other well-known families. They threatened imprisonment for anyone who could be hiding or helping the missing prisoners to escape from the authorities.

Arcila, having rested for a few hours, decided to pay Mariana a visit at the bookstore to let her know about Federico's situation. He found her sitting at her desk reading some papers, completely absorbed in her work. He noticed how beautiful she looked and knocked to attract her attention. She looked at him with worry etched on her forehead.

"Come in," she said. "I've been hoping to see you since yesterday. Clodomiro couldn't find you anywhere. I assumed you might be in hiding and I couldn't sleep for a minute thinking about Federico and all of you. The prefect's agents were here yesterday, snooping around and asking all kinds of questions."

"Do you mind closing the patio door?" asked Arcila.

"As you wish. If you like, I can close the front door also."

"No, leave it open. If somebody has been following me I don't want to appear as a suspicious character, I am just another customer."

Mariana understood his point, took two books from a shelf and opened them over the counter, just as she did with any other client.

"I have good news and bad news," Arcila said in a low voice. "Federico is free and is hiding in a safe place. He is wounded, although nothing we have to be concerned about at this time. He should recover soon from his wounds."

Mariana listened to him silently and intently. She didn't want to interrupt him. Arcila did not mention Pedro Lindo at all.

"Federico doesn't want anyone to know where he is. This is to protect his life. Besides, he doesn't want you to say a word about this to anyone. He just wants you to know he is alive and in good hands."

"Please, tell me where he is and who is taking care of him. I won't tell anyone," Mariana pleaded, and pleaded again.

"I'm sorry. I cannot and I must not tell you anything. It would put him in grave danger and would compromise you and those who are taking care of him."

"I will die if I cannot do something for him!"

"But you can do something for him. You and Sofia can go to see the prefect and ask for information about Federico. Scream and cry and supplicate to make sure he doesn't suspect that you know anything about your brother's fate. Tell him that you heard rumors about dead victims and wounded prisoners and also of three who are missing. Ask him what he is doing or can do to find Federico."

"If that is what Federico wants, I will do it. I am willing to see the prefect at any time. When do you want me to go?"

"Why don't you wait until I talk with Sofia? I am going to inform her about what I told you and I will ask her to help you as much as she can," said Arcila.

"This morning I saw her at Domingo's funeral. She came with doña Julia and with her uncle don Emilio. We went to try to comfort Zoila. She hasn't stopped crying since she got the news. We had to talk with the bishop to get his permission to bury Domingo in the cemetery. The parish priest was totally opposed to it. He said that Domingo was a liberal, an atheist, and a mason, and I don't know what else. But, of course, he had no problem pocketing the money that Zoila gave him to say some prayers for Domingo's soul."

"Did the priest celebrate a Mass at the funeral?" asked Arcila.

"No, Domingo would have come out of his casket if he had been taken to any church. They took him directly to the cemetery."

"Sorry, but I need to go. Please give my regards to your sisters," said Arcila, while looking at her tenderly. Mariana looked precious dressed in black, he thought.

Mariana was happy to know that Federico was free, alive, and in good hands. She trusted that Arcila was telling the truth, but the way he had looked at her made her wonder what he was thinking. He never had looked at her like that when Federico was present.

*   *   *

ARCILA FOUND SOFIA LOST IN DEEP SADNESS. Domingo's death, his funeral, and the uncertainty of Federico's condition were more than enough to account for her terrible anxiety. He felt compassion for Sofia when he saw her, but he had no words, didn't know what to tell her. She invited him into the parlor and offered him a cup of coffee.

"What a horrible thing! What are we going to do?" she said. "The damned Godos are finishing everyone off. We couldn't even see Domingo. They wouldn't allow the opening of the casket. If my mother had not talked with the bishop, they wouldn't have allowed us to bury him in the cemetery! Treating him almost as though he was a dog. Damnation!"

Arcila leaned back in complete surprise. He never had seen her so furious or heard her curse like that. She was so agitated.

"Calm yourself. I need you to promise not to share with anyone what I am going to tell you. Federico's life depends on it," said Arcila, playing nervously with his hat.

"I promise you anything you ask if his life depends on it. Where is he? Tell me, please. I can't wait!"

"I left him with people I can trust and he is in hiding. As you know, the Godos are looking for him and for Antonio and Hernandes."

"Yes, I know. The guards were here yesterday. My mother is furious with me. I cannot repeat what she said. I despise her when she talks to me like that. She is unbearable. Are Hernandes and Antonio with him also?"

"They were. Now they are far from where Federico is. As you know, we had everything ready for General Bustamante."

"And Federico didn't go with them?" Sofia asked.

"No, he couldn't. He is wounded and cannot walk."

"Wounded? What did they do to him? Tell me where is he. My uncle can cure him."

"No, I cannot tell you where he is. Federico doesn't want anyone to know where he is. His life, and mine as well, are dependent on your keeping this to yourself. Do not mention anything to don Emilio, to your mother, to your godmother, or to anybody that you know that Federico is alive and hurt. The only thing you know is that he is missing from the prison. Do you understand how important this is?"

"I swear I won't say a word," said Sofia. She understood the gravity of the situation and that she had to be compliant.

"Only you and Mariana know what I have told you. Now, I want you both to go and visit the prefect to ask for any information about Federico's whereabouts. It would be better if you go together. We need to know what he says."

She assented nervously.

"If you will pardon me, I need to leave right now. But I promise to keep you informed. Please don't look for me because there are spies everywhere. We all need to protect each other," said Arcila.

"You don't know the weight you have removed from my shoulders."

"He will decide when and where to meet with you. I will let you know, soon."

"Can I send him a note with you?"

"No. If they detain me it could be dangerous and they won't have mercy on anyone."

"That is what my godmother told me. Luis told her about the incredible atrocities. Tell Federico I send him my soul in a kiss."

"I will tell him that. I'll see you soon!" he said and departed. Sofia was left twisting her handkerchief between her fingers. She didn't know what to think. She trusted in Arcila like family. But how had Federico managed to escape? It was all a mystery. But thank God he was alive and free. "Damned war!"

*   *   *

THANKS TO THE GOOD ATTENTION he got from Felisa and Pedro Lindo, Federico recovered faster than expected. "The leg will take a while to heal," Pedro had said, but he told Federico to start walking as soon has he had strength to do so. He also returned don Nicomedes' ring to him:

the very one Pedro had removed from his finger when thinking he was dead. Federico couldn't believe it. That ring had saved his life.

After a week of rest, he managed to take his first steps with the help of a crutch that Víctor improvised from a guava tree branch. He feared his sisters and Sofia would see him as he was. He was pitiful, a living example of the Knight of the Sad Countenance.

Federico lived in constant fear. He was afraid of being imprisoned again and couldn't stop worrying what would happen to Pedro Lindo if they found out he had taken him out of the prison knowing he was alive. The only solution was to win the war and allow justice to take care of the criminals that had reduced him to a walking corpse, human waste. They had to win and they would do it!

XXIV: Sofia and Federico Meet Again

I swear by the most sacred thing in me and repeat what I have
said to you so many times: that in any circumstance I will prove
my passion to you.

—Sofia's second letter to Federico

OCTOBER–NOVEMBER 1900

That same afternoon, after Arcila's visit, Sofia and Mariana went
to look for the prefect at his home. The maid recognized the
visitors and said, "What do you ladies want?"

She had orders not to admit anyone without permission, but these
ladies were friends of doña Marisa and she felt obliged to ask.

"Tell Marisa that we need to talk with her!" said Mariana.

"Just a moment, ladies, I'll be back soon," she said, and ran to inform
her mistress that her friends Mariana and Sofia were waiting at the door.

"I already know what they are after. You may open the door and take
them to the parlor. Tell them to wait there for a minute; I don't want
anyone to see me like this."

As the maid accompanied the girls to the parlor, Sofia said, "Do you
know if the prefect is at home?"

"No, Señora, he left in a hurry, right after lunch. There has been a
revolution or something like that at the prison."

Marisa entered the room and, hearing the maid, said, "Stop being a gossip!"

The maid departed like a scared dog with its tail between its legs.

"It isn't gossiping, Marisa, because the whole city knows about it," said Mariana. "We came to see you because they didn't allow us to get even close to the prison doors. There are soldiers roaming around all over the city. Yesterday, they came to the bookstore and searched all through the house. Did your husband tell you anything? "

"He went to the Government House to a meeting with Luis. There are rumors over things I don't know anything about. Nobody knows what is happening."

"Didn't he tell you anything about Federico?" asked Mariana.

"I told you I have no idea. If you wish, why don't you come back tomorrow?" Anyone could see, looking at Marisa, the patience it took to be questioned over her husband's actions and to be petitioned for miracles she could not perform.

"I told you what we heard," said Mariana, who didn't believe that Marisa had no idea about anything.

"Could he be among the wounded?" asked Sofia.

"No, I truly do not have any information for you. I am sorry. This is all I can tell you. We are all in the same boat."

Mariana looked at one and the other, waiting for an opportunity to leave, before she was tempted to grab Marisa and strangle her.

"We need to leave now. I left Clodomiro alone at the bookstore. Thank you, Marisa."

"Good afternoon. I am sorry not to be able to give you better news."

Sofia was just as furious. She grabbed Mariana's arm and they departed.

Marisa felt great relief when they had left. She couldn't do anything for them, good or bad. The best thing was to keep her mouth shut. Her day had been impossible. She would order the maid not to open the door again, to anyone, known or unknown, friend or foe.

"They are all criminals," said Sofia as they hustled back to the store. "They invent a story, 'the official report,' and send some poor soul to post it on every corner. What drives me crazy is that they claim not to know anything. They lie! They must think I am stupid."

* * *

ABOUT THE MIDDLE OF OCTOBER, the governor and the prefect got news from their spies about numerous liberal troops crossing the cordillera, coming from the State of Tolima under the leadership of General Bustamante. They estimated the rebels had about 2500 well-armed men plus some peasants from the Tierradentro region who were joining them.

"We heard the same story before the Christmas attack," said the governor.

"Sir, we cannot allow them to get close to the city. Colonel Pinto put them in their place at Flautas. We must defeat them before they break into the city and rape every woman in sight," said the prefect.

"I will go in person with General Miguel Medina Delgado to the battle this time. What is coming this time is an army, not a bunch of fools," replied the governor.

The following day, he and General Medina Delgado started moving troops from neighboring towns—El Tambo, Timbío, El Bordo, Silvia, and others—in preparation for protecting the city at any cost.

* * *

THE TWO ARMIES RAN INTO EACH OTHER on October 20 of 1900, near Calibío, about 20 miles from Popayán. Both sides were determined to win. The war would be to the death. The government army, with close to one thousand men, defeated the liberals, butchered that day in what became known far and wide as the battle of Calibío. Some of the rebel survivors managed to escape over the cordillera by returning to Tolima, and others escaped to Ecuador. The local peasants and other fighters from the region, who supported the liberals, had to hunker down in their homes or hide in the mountains. The government troops hunted them, house by house and everywhere else. There was no clemency. Many were executed where they were found on the spot.

General Bustamante and some of his officers went south, looking for protection in Ecuador where President Alfaro offered them asylum and work. They were assigned to fixing the roads on the outskirts of Guayaquil to help pay for their expenses and to remain fit for the anticipated war in the Pacific.

The conservative government was vicious in the days following the battle. Captives were forced to identify their comrades; their relatives and friends were put in jail to create further fear. Their houses, land, and animals were sold in public auctions to government sympathizers at bargain prices. Many liberals went into exile to save their lives and whatever possessions they managed to take with them. At the end of October, the liberal resistance had been eliminated and in Popayán the government reestablished public order. But hatred remained alive, and the blood of the martyrs fertilized the growth of new fighters.

*   *   *

CONSTANTINO AND ARCILA remained in contact with Sofía and Mariana about Federico's progress. At each report, the news got better and one good day they were informed they could see him soon.

"If I don't see him very soon, I fear I am going to die," said Sofía to Arcila. She couldn't live without Federico and it bothered her to not even be able to write to him. But Arcila, inflexible in his position, kept his promise to Federico.

Federico had made enough progress to be able to walk using a cane. It was irritating to him to think he would have to use a cane for life. His head wound had healed cleanly but he couldn't move or touch his forehead without feeling a violent spasm between the wound and his eyebrows. Shaving resulted in similar contractions when he touched his cheeks. Thus, he stopped shaving, grew a beard, and allowed his hair to grow. After a few weeks the cane, the limp, the beard, and the long hair, plus a few more pounds on his wasted body, created a new Federico. This time he wasn't the Knight of the Sad Countenance but something resembling the Knight of the Lions.

"Where there is smoke, there is fire," said Arcila to Federico after the horrific events that followed the battle of Calibío. It was time for Federico to get away from Popayán. It was time to say goodbye to his family and Sofia. They needed to join General Bustamante and the surviving rebels that were in Guayaquil preparing for the coming war in the Pacific.

"We must be in Quito around Christmas," said Arcila to Federico. "The Liberal leadership has people in the United States who are looking for support against the conservative government. The Yankees are very interested in the Panama Canal and want the French out of there. We must take Panama as soon as possible, to guarantee their support."

*　　*　　*

ARCILA AND FEDERICO made a plan for visits with Sofia and his family. Felisa and Víctor would act as contacts to avoid any suspicion. On Friday, November 16, Víctor stopped by Sofia's home. He knocked at the door and waited, wondering if anyone was spying on him. Betsabé looked through the little window in the front door to see who was calling. Sofia had already informed her about what to expect.

"Good morning, is Señorita Sofia at home? Please tell her that it is Víctor."

"Yes, sir, she is waiting for you. Do come in, please," said Betsabé, and took him to the parlor before she bounded up the stairs to tell Sofia he was there.

"Good morning, señorita. I am Víctor."

"I was waiting for you. Thank you for coming," said Sofia.

"Here, I brought you this meat," he said, taking a package out of his shoulder bag.

"I am sorry you have gone to so much trouble and I thank you for it," said Sofia. In that time of rationing it was a wonderful gift, and she handed the large parcel to Betsabé, who took it to the kitchen.

Víctor waited until the maid had left, and from his shirt pocket he took out a handkerchief that Sofia immediately recognized. She had embroidered Federico's initials on it with her own hair. María, Pedro Lindo's wife, had found it in his soiled clothes.

"Señorita, my wife will be waiting for you at the church of San Agustín at five o'clock Mass next Sunday. She has a large mole next to her right ear. That will allow you to recognize her. I am sure you will."

"Yes, and I thank you. I'll be waiting for her. Tell her I'll be wearing a gray scarf, green skirt, and white blouse."

"I think she knows you. She told me that you buy herbs from her at the market."

"Oh, yes. I know her. Her name is Felisa."

"Yes, señorita, the very one. She will take you to see don Federico and will come back with you when you are ready."

Sofia said goodbye to Víctor and asked him to give her regards to Federico. When he left, she held the handkerchief with immense joy. She couldn't believe she would soon see him again. She had forgotten what joy felt like. Her ears felt warm. She couldn't stop the tears that flowed from her eyes and she dried them with the handkerchief.

Betsabé came back, wondering what to do with the meat, and found her mistress drying her tears.

"My little mistress, why are you crying?"

"Oh, it's nothing for you to be concerned about. Sometimes I think about things that make me cry." But truly, anyone could see that her eyes shone and her cheeks were flushed with pleasure. She was already dreaming about her visit with Federico.

"I tell you, the smell of that meat is delicious. It has been months since we have seen such a large piece of meat."

"Divide it in two, and keep one half for us," said Sofia, generous and in good humor, "And the other half will be for Mariana's family."

Soon Sofia left to take the meat to Mariana and her family and to inform her of the plan to visit Federico.

Mariana greeted her at the bookstore and was very surprised with both the gift of meat and the happiness that Sofia couldn't hide. They rejoiced in the news about being able to see Federico soon. Mariana confided in Sofia that she was afraid to think about how Federico would look after being wounded.

"Truly, I don't care how he looks, for he will always be my Federico," said Sofia stoutly. Mariana felt jealous of the love that Sofia felt for her brother. Nobody had loved her like that, without conditions.

"Make sure no one follows you," Mariana said. "It could be fatal. Think about what happened to those people from Calibío."

"After my visit, I will come to see you. I don't know where Felisa will take me. I plan to tell Betsabé not to wait for me for lunch because I will be visiting with you after Mass. If I don't tell her where I am going to be, she won't let me out of the house. You know her."

"I don't know Felisa or Víctor well, but Arcila and Federico trust them."

"They know what they are doing. If they didn't, those two wouldn't have selected them. I think people from humble origins are more loyal than our best friends and relatives. They don't have vested interests. They are good by nature."

Mariana looked at her and said no more. She wasn't that trustful. Anyone could be a spy. She had learned the hard way not to trust anyone completely.

*   *   *

THE FOLLOWING DAY was a day without end for Sofia. She felt like the sun would never set in the horizon. It seemed like a century since she had seen Federico, and that Saturday seemed longer than the many weeks she had been waiting to see him. She tried to picture him in her mind, and was only able to see his image in the portrait she had in her room. It was like his image, by some enchantment of the *camera obscura*, had taken away all her memories of him in person. She feared finding him looking like an invalid, and dreamed of seeing him younger and more virile than ever. She wanted to be with him alone, without interruptions, for a whole eternity.

"What will he look like? Will he have changed?" She tortured herself with questions she couldn't answer and finally decided to do something else to escape from her own mind. Thus, she started knitting and while doing so she got lost in the future she was waiting for. Knitting was the antidote for all her worries, her emotional eraser.

That night she didn't sleep. She tossed and turned in bed, she covered herself with her blanket and in minutes she had to remove it, unable to stand the heat. She slept in short intervals and each time she went to sleep she dreamed of being in Federico's arms, loving him unconditionally. She wanted to show him all her passion. Once, she woke up feeling very hot as though he was next to her. She cried tears of joy and of pain.

Finally dawn arrived and she heard noise in the kitchen. She got up, lit her oil lamp, and washed her face. The cold water removed all the worries from her mind. She put on a very tight corset that favored her figure and fresh cotton undergarments. Standing in front of the mirror she imagined her lover admiring her figure. She was feeling sensual and passionate. Her green eyes reflected the contents of her dreams. She put on a Scottish wool green pleated skirt, a white long-sleeved blouse with a high neck and lace cuffs, and an old gray cape to keep warm. She wore the American brown half boots her godmother had brought her from New York. They were ideal for a long walk: soft and sturdy. Finally, Sofia sprayed her forehead and temples with cologne and powdered her face. She wanted to be perfect for Federico. Happy with how she saw herself, she went to the kitchen to have a few sips of coffee to help finish waking up. She couldn't eat that early in the morning.

Betsabé observed her suspiciously. Sofia never woke up so early. Sofia looked at her maid, whose eyebrows were up as if trying to read her mind. She knew Betsabé was wondering what she was up to.

"I am going to five o'clock Mass, and after Mass I am going to visit with Mariana. I won't be back for lunch and I'll return in the afternoon. You take care of my mother."

Thus at a quarter before five, Sofia departed in the direction of San Agustín. The fresh morning air filled her with energy and emotion. She walked into the church and found a bench close to the image of the Virgin of Sorrows. Kneeling down, she observed the flickering lights of the votive candles that appeared to follow the rhythm of her heartbeat.

Suddenly, a thin woman all dressed in black knelt next to her. Sofia noticed the large brown mole next to her right ear: Felisa.

"I am Felisa. If you wish, we can leave at once."

Sofia stood up, took her by the arm, and they departed looking like a couple of old friends and left through the door facing the *Calle de San Agustín*.

Delfina the innkeeper was looking at them from behind her veil. She saw Sofia leaving the church, before Mass had even started, with a woman that looked familiar. She had seen her before but couldn't remember exactly where.

When they left the church, Sofia whispered, "Where are we going?"

"It isn't far. We live close to El Ejido. We have a little farmhouse across the river."

"And will Federico be there?"

"Yes, we will find him there."

Changing from one side of the street to the other, they went from the *Calle de San Agustín* to the *Calle del Empedrado* and eventually followed the *Calle de la Carnicería* and continued toward the river. Felisa, straight as a bamboo rod, walked without hurrying and answered the questions that Sofia asked by the dozens. Sofia felt an ineffable peace next to this humble woman and didn't know how to thank her for all she had done for Federico.

About half past six, they arrived at the farmhouse. The dogs, barking and jumping around them, came to greet Felisa. Sofia was terrified by the size of these two animals.

Federico had been waiting for them since first light. He was anxious to see Sofia and wondered about the impression his looks and the cane would make on her. The prison, the suffering, and the hunger had aged him. He had a few white hairs now. When he heard the dogs barking, he knew that Sofia and Felisa had arrived, and walked as straight and steady as he could to greet the women at the gate.

Sofia and Felisa looked like ghosts coming out from the mist. Overwhelmed, he walked to the gate and opened it. Sofia couldn't stop her tears when she saw him limping and using a cane. By instinct, she ran toward him. They were lost in a passionate embrace, filled with emotion. The cane fell on the ground. Felisa looked at them with happiness painted on her face, smiling. They were so happy!

Federico held her at arm's length and looked at her, spellbound and happy to have her next to him again. She looked at him without hiding her tears, filling herself with the new image of her man. He was no longer the handsome young bookstore owner, but a grown man: bearded, full of magnetism, with a deeper look and a strange light in his eyes. He contemplated her in amazement after having waited so long for this moment. He smelled like smoke, and very manly. By intuition, Felisa picked up the cane and gave it back to Federico, saying: "Excuse me. I have to go in to make some coffee." Sofia thanked her and turned back to Federico to embrace and kiss him again.

"You cannot imagine how much I have missed you. I almost fainted from emotion when I received your handkerchief. I couldn't sleep for a minute for two whole nights, thinking about seeing you again. If I had known you were so close I would have come to see you every day."

"I was more than eager to see you again also, but I couldn't allow you to see me before today. I looked like a monster when I came here. Felisa has taken care of me as if I were her son. It is thanks to her and others that I am alive," he said. "If the political situation was bad when I was in the prison, it is even worse since the battle of Calibío. The Godos have done horrible things. I need to get out of here as soon as possible. My life is not worth a cent if they find me."

Sofia looked at him, not even feeling the tears that ran down her cheeks. Her eyes were fixed on his but she listened to him without hearing what he said. Her heart didn't fit in her chest. She couldn't contain the desire to love him to madness. Federico looked at her as if she were a vision within a dream.

"Come into the house, please" said Felisa from the doorway happy to see them together again. "It is cold out there. The coffee is ready."

When they entered the kitchen, she served the coffee on the little table they used to eat their meals and told them she was going to look for Víctor at the stable where he was feeding the animals. They had to leave to go to work at the market soon.

"I will be back shortly after lunchtime. Víctor will come back later in the afternoon, before dinner. Make yourselves at home. There's soup by the fire and food in the pantry. Don Federico knows where everything is."

The dogs followed Felisa to the gate and then came back, looking for Federico. They didn't find him. On the table, the two cups of coffee, half-full, accompanied each other. The door to Federico's room was closed. The lovers had finally found an opportunity to be alone.

What happened then, any lover can guess. They loved each other outside of time. Eventually, Federico surrendered and without knowing how he went to sleep happily, feeling satiated and at peace because Sofia was with him.

Sofia, feeling victorious, looked at him tenderly until her mind was so full of him that she felt totally and madly in love. Incapable of staying awake after her long restless night, she also surrendered to sleep, allowing Morpheus to take possession of her naked body. She was in paradise.

*   *   *

AROUND ELEVEN THAT MORNING, the noise of rain awoke the lovers, who dressed and came out of the room to look for more coffee. Sofia washed the cups while Federico looked at her, completely amazed by her passion and her beauty.

"You don't know how much pleasure you have given me."

"I have been waiting for my whole life for this moment," she replied.

"Oh, really? I didn't know you loved to wash coffee cups that much."

"There are things I like even more," she said coquettishly. "Are you hungry? I'm starving. I haven't had anything to eat since this morning."

"I wouldn't say you haven't had a bite. You almost devoured me with your kisses."

"Don't say anymore," she said, blushing, and added more charcoal to the fire to make something warm to eat.

Federico continued looking at her, a bit in shock. *How could I have doubted her?*

"Felisa makes corn tortillas every day," he said, noticing she was looking for something. "They are in that yellow basket hanging from the beams. In the pantry there are eggs, cheese, sugar, fruit, and everything that has to be hidden from the mice. The iron pot is full of her famous soup. It has a little of everything in it: meat, vegetables, corn, and beans. A bowl of that soup is enough to resurrect a dead man. I know it from experience. Felisa is an excellent cook. In the month and a half I've been here I have gained at least ten pounds! I am now a robust man. When I arrived I was just skin and bones."

"I did notice that," she said, smiling maliciously, and laughed without knowing why. They ate and looked at each other as if they were seeing each other the first time.

Just before noon, a bolt of lightning fell close by and the rain suddenly became a deluge. The dogs, scared by the thunder, came in looking for Federico. The wind shook the willow trees, breaking branches and blowing them away over the fields. The bright light from the lightning illuminated the kitchen every few seconds. It rained and it poured. And it grew cold and humid in the little house.

Sofia looked for refuge in Federico's arms. She was very frightened by lightning. They were in the hammock where she sat close to him, and closer after each thunderbolt.

Federico enjoyed the show, rocking with her close to him in the hammock.

"Don't worry, if the lightning hits us, we'll never know what happened."

Sofia, nestled into his chest, felt secure. It was like a miracle to have Federico next to her. She looked at his hand that was caressing her hair, and enjoyed the smell of her man mixed with the aroma of coffee. She was the happiest woman in the world.

After lunch, they noticed that the river was over the banks and the rain didn't seem to want to stop. Better that way. They would have the whole afternoon and the night to love each other. After a nap in the hammock, they returned to paradise and lost all sense of time again. Fate had brought them together.

Víctor and Felisa couldn't return that night. The flood made crossing the river impossible. They had to spend the night at their neighbor's house across the river.

"They are not going to miss us," said Víctor to Felisa, winking at her. She smiled. They were still young enough to understand.

*   *   *

AT DAWN THE SUN FILLED the blue sky with its light. The storm was over. The river was approaching its normal flow. The race of the dogs out of the house told them that Felisa was back. She was looking for Sofia to accompany her to the city. Her relatives were looking for her. What would they be thinking?

XXV: After the Flood

> My happiness would be to call you my spouse and love you and
> adore you in our dream home where all my happiness would
> be to love you, serve you, and sacrifice myself if it would be
> necessary to make you happy, because that is what true love is.

—Sofia's Second Letter to Federico

When Felisa came into the kitchen it smelled like fresh coffee. The lovers, engaged in animated conversation while sipping their coffee, were waiting for her.

"Good morning," said Sofia and Federico in unison.

"They have been looking for you. It looks like Señora Delfina saw us coming out of the church of San Agustín and mentioned it to Betsabé. She went to see Víctor at the market and he told her that you were with me but because the river was over its banks it was impossible to reach us until the rain stopped."

"And where were you?" said Sofia.

"I was next to Víctor, hiding under a burlap sack. I could see her through the holes in the sack. She was the same one that comes to buy herbs and meat from us. Victor told your maid he would inform Señorita Sofia and I that she was looking for us, as soon as he could get across the river. If you so desire, I can accompany you to the city so that you to give your relatives peace of mind," said Felisa to Sofia.

Sofia realized the moment to leave Federico had arrived, but she had to say goodbye to him a few more times. She had no idea when they would see each other again. Both felt it could be the last time, but neither had the heart to share that premonition. If they had, it would have tainted the happiness they had shared in seeing each other again. A final long embrace, in complete silence, said more than all the words they could invoke.

In the mean time, Victor had left for the city to inform Arcila of all that had happened and to make him aware of the grave danger Federico was facing. Arcila told Victor they had to get Federico away form the farm immediately. There would not be time for a visit with Mariana. They would be leaving for Ecuador as soon as they could get ready for the trip. That same day Arcila would let Mariana and Sofia know about the new plan.

When she arrived at home, Sofia found a surprise: her godmother, her mother, and don Emilio were waiting for her and their long faces gave away their feelings. Only Betsabé received her with a big smile happy to see her again.

"My golly, we thought the earth had swallowed you. Thanks be to God, you came back safe and sound," said Betsabé, as Sofia embraced her godmother and her mother, and then greeted don Emilio.

"Tell us what happened, my dear," said doña Julia. Sofia had been thinking of how to answer this question for the last half hour.

"Early on Sunday, I went to Mass at San Agustín to ask the Virgin to help me with horrible constipation that was driving me insane," she began, choosing a malady they'd hesitate to check on. "I hadn't slept a minute the night before and had agreed to visit with Mariana after church. When I was on my knees praying to the Virgin, suddenly, Felisa knelt beside me and started praying her rosary. I greeted her and she asked me how I was. I mentioned my problem to her, wondering if she would know of some herb that would help me with the constipation. Then she grabbed me by the arm and said, 'Come with me. I believe the Virgin has sent me to help you.' I saw Delfina, but didn't have a chance to greet her when we left the church."

"Señorita Delfina told me that you had left the church with Señora Felisa. She is married to don Víctor, the butcher. He told me at the market me that you and Felisa were trapped on the other side of the river," said Betsabé.

"I couldn't believe what Felisa was telling me. It was a miracle. I followed her as if she were the Virgin taking me by her hand. We walked together to her farmhouse on the other side of the river. She made me an infusion of aloe vera and asked me to drink it as fast as I could. That, I did. Then, Felisa told me to rest there in the hammock. We prayed the rosary together, so that the Virgin would help us." Sofia paused a moment to calm her heart so that she would not sound as though she were lying.

"We prayed through all the sorrowful mysteries and then I went to sleep without realizing it. I had not slept well the night before and I needed the rest. When I woke up it started to rain cats and dogs. There was lightning and several bolts hit close to the house and at that moment the constipation was gone. The magic aloe vera infusion cured me. The lightning hit a tree that lost a branch that luckily fell the other way otherwise it would have killed us. That was a miracle of the Virgin."

Betsabé, looking at her with wide-open eyes, wondered. It was all she could do not to say, "She shit in her pants and it was the devil that got the tree branch down."

"It rained for hours," Sofia went on. "The river came over the banks and flooded the countryside. It was impossible to cross it. Felisa asked me to stay there overnight. Víctor came this morning to tell us that Betsabé had been at the market looking for me and that he had told her where we were, that there was nothing to worry about. Thank God you got his message, another miracle by the Virgin."

"Yes dear. I have to light a few votive candles to thank the Virgin for bringing you home safe and sound and for sending Felisa to cure you of your constipation. You have to give me the formula she used."

The godmother and don Emilio looked at each other with suspicion, clearly wondering what Sofia had been doing. They were not as innocent as doña Julia.

*   *   *

THAT MONTH SOFIA DID NOT HAVE HER PERIOD and it did not come again the next month. She had to urinate with annoying frequency and drinking coffee started to make her feel ill. She noticed that she had very tender breasts and didn't know what to do about it. Eventually, she decided to visit her godmother to ask for her advice. She was the only person she could trust with personal issues. Thus, Sofia told Betsabé where she was going and left.

"Niña Sofi, don't worry. I'll be praying for you," the maid said, watching the worry on Sofia's face. Sofia couldn't believe it. Betsabé really could read her mind.

Betsabé had noticed that since Sofia had visited with Felisa, her mistress' underwear had a new fragrance that Betsabé had smelled before. When she thought about it, she knew Sofia must be pregnant, and she couldn't believe it.

*   *   *

"HELLO DEAR! WHAT A PLEASURE TO SEE YOU," said the godmother, hugging Sofia and giving her two kisses. "You haven't visited for almost three weeks. Today you have to stay for the whole afternoon. We have so much to talk about."

"I had to come see you. I don't know what's wrong with me. I am always tired and have to use the bathroom constantly; everything I eat gives me nausea."

The godmother listened with great attention and couldn't hide the idea that came to her mind. All the indicators suggested Sofia was pregnant.

"Have you missed your periods?" she asked, frowning.

"Yes, I haven't had one for two months and this month I am already late."

The godmother calculated mentally, thinking about the girl's visit with Felisa, and said, "Did you make love with Alberto?"

Sofia didn't know what to say. She was in a trap. Her godmother always found out what had happened: it was useless to lie to her.

"Not with Alberto. Never! He is only a necessary evil for me. The only man I could make love to is Federico."

"Federico? Wasn't he missing? I thought he was dead but I didn't have the courage to say so to you. It would have been cruelty."

"Yes, he is alive. He escaped from prison and was wounded but now he is well, in fact, he is very well!" she said in a haughty and defiant manner.

"Yes, I understand," said Ana María, still frowning.

"You know that I love him with all my heart. I promised him I would prove my love under any circumstances and I made love to him with madness. We rejoiced for hours. I had to do it. I didn't know if I would ever see him again. I had promised to him in one of my letters, that I was ready to show him my passion under any circumstances."

The godmother looked at her in disbelief, words of surprise and many questions written clearly on her face: How daring to leave home to ask the Virgin for a miracle and give away her honor without thinking of the consequences. If Julia knew about it she would have Federico shot and then she would die of shame. The girl has ruined the family's honor, four hundred years thrown into the trash!

Then she looked at Sofia again and saw her as a woman for the first time. She envied her. She would have loved to love someone with the same intensity and determination. "To hell with honor!" she declared in her mind. "War forces us to live each moment with our whole soul in a continuous present, without yesterdays or tomorrows. One hour can have more value than a whole day. How long ago did you see him? Was it the day the river ran over the banks? It had to be."

"Yes, that same day," said Sofia.

"And where is Federico now?"

"I have no idea. Just as he showed up, he disappeared. I don't even know if he is alive. But it wasn't his ghost if I am pregnant and nobody is going to believe it was the Holy Spirit that got me in this condition."

"And does your mother know anything about this?"

"No, nobody knows about it, only you and I. If she finds out, she will kill me, or will die, or both. With the love she feels for Federico!" Sofia said sarcastically.

"The other day, I mentioned to her how much I missed him and she told me again not to ever mention that son-of-a-whore."

"Fortunately, she doesn't live in this world. She keeps talking to my father every day as if he were alive. I envy her. If Federico was a ghost I could see him every day at any time and I could love him without fears. Right now I feel he is alive and that's enough for me. He is at war. He is fighting for a new life for all of us."

Ana María nodded and said, "You are going to need the help of a doctor or a midwife. Do you feel something inside of you?"

"No, I don't feel anything unusual. But I don't know what to do. You have to help me. I am filled with fear and concerns about our future."

"We must talk to your uncle Emilio. He, as a doctor, is obliged to keep your secret and he understands that the dirty laundry is washed at home. He can prescribe something for your nausea and for the tiredness. The need to urinate so frequently will not go away until you deliver. If you want, I can talk to him in confidence."

"Yes, I think it is a good idea, but tell him to come to see me here. I don't want to raise any suspicions. Betsabé has a hunting dog's nose."

"You are right. That is a good idea. I will talk to Emilio as soon as I can. Go home and take a nap. You need to rest and sleep more to take care of that tiredness and you should eat anything you want."

*   *   *

ANA MARÍA TALKED TO DON EMILIO that same afternoon. She told him about Sofía's visit with Felisa on the day of the storm. The old man listened with great attention without interrupting her. He agreed to see Sofía when she came to visit Ana Maria, his cousin, the following Tuesday.

"These things are part of life, Emilio," she said. "Let us do our best to help her." He nodded at her and said goodbye calmly, and with his habitual courtesy he was on his way in a minute. In fact, he had a revolution going on between his temples. He had just found out that Federico Lemos was alive. Somebody had betrayed them!

When listening to Ana María talking about Federico as if he were alive—he couldn't believe it. He had seen the man dead and had asked Pedro Lindo to burn his corpse along with the others at the graveyard. Somebody was lying. But Ana María assured him that Sofía was telling the truth. It had to be don Higinio or Pedro Lindo or perhaps both of them. Who else? The question was, why? He would take care of them all. Soon they would learn how he, Emilio Carrasco, could handle tough situations.

XXVI: Don Emilio Attacks

> Taking unjust revenge (since no revenge can be just) goes
> directly against the Holy Law we profess which orders us to do
> good to our enemies and love those that hate us.

—*Don Quixote*, Second Part, Chapter XXVII

The next morning, don Emilio went to the graveyard and found don Higinio digging a grave for the Registrar's wife, who would be buried late in the afternoon that day.

"Good morning, don Higinio. I didn't know you were such an early riser."

"Don Emilio, what a surprise to see you here," said the gravedigger while drying his forehead on his shirtsleeve.

"I see you continue planting dead people in the ground, hoping they will sprout fully alive on resurrection day."

"Yes, sir. That day, I will receive my prize. Tell me, what can I do for you?"

"I wonder, do you remember those burlap sacks and some presents that Martín sent to you with Dr. Lindo?"

"Yes, sir. I helped the doctor to unload them from the wagon."

"And did you burn them as you always do?"

"Yes, sir, after the doctor left, I put a lit match at each dead man's feet to make sure they were dead and then let them burn out."

"And how many matches did you light?"

"One for each body, but I was a little drunk and I don't remember how many for sure, but not more than half a dozen. Years ago in the war of 1860 one of them stood up in flames and almost got me. I had to kill the devil with this shovel. That's why I use the matches to make sure they are really dead. It never fails."

"Did you recognize any of them?"

"No, I don't like to look at them. To avoid remembering their faces."

"And those shoes?" don Emilio said, gesturing at the yellow boots don Higinio wore.

"When I woke up from my nap I had them on and decided to keep them. They were in good shape. They must have been from one of those bodies, may he rest in peace."

"That's all, don Higinio. I think I have my accounts in order," said don Emilio, believing he was being lied to by the old man.

*　　*　　*

THAT WAS THE LAST TIME THEY TALKED. That afternoon, the sacristan found don Higinio dead next to the grave he had been digging for the Registrar's wife. He mentioned to the priest he had been surprised that the victim was wearing socks but his shoes were missing.

"Poor don Higinio, somebody killed him to steal his shoes."

*　　*　　*

DON EMILIO HAD A DIFFERENT TAKE on the story. They had betrayed him and had put Federico's shoes on some other corpse. He still had to talk to Pedro Lindo but first he had to consult with the governor, the prefect, Martín, and the magistrate Alberto Carrasco.

*   *   *

THE FOLLOWING DAY, DON EMILIO headed to Pedro Lindo's office. Noticing the door was half-open he entered without calling. Pedro was busy working at his desk.

"Pedrito, what's going on?" said don Emilio. "I haven't seen you for a while."

Pedro surprised by the intruder, stood up to greet don Emilio and said, "Don Emilio, what a pleasure to see you. I've been juggling so many balls I can't keep them all in the air. With all the duties of my accounting job and taking care of my patients, I hardly have time to breathe. Even though my clientele has doubled, the poor don't have a cent to pay for my services. One brings me a chicken, another a few potatoes, and most of them depend on my good heart. They are destitute. What brings you here?"

"Nothing in particular. I saw your office door open and decided to come in to say hello. Tell me, do you know anything about don Higinio? I just heard that the poor man was found dead in the cemetery."

"Poor man, indeed. He lived and died in poverty among the dead. They say that the sacristan went to see him about a grave he was supposed to have ready for the Registrar's wife's funeral and found him dead, with a sharp cut on his neck and without shoes. It looks like somebody killed him to steal his shoes."

"Today they kill you for any reason, even for some old shoes. I wonder if they belonged to one of the corpses you took to the cemetery?"

"It's possible, but I have no idea. I don't pay attention to those things. My duty is to care for the living. The gravedigger takes care of the dead."

"They must have been expensive if they were worth killing for."

"Could be, don Emilio. As I told you, I don't pay attention to those things. I am sorry, but, when you came in, I was getting ready to go to pay my respects to the family of don Higinio. He will be buried today. They are humble people who deserve our respect."

"Since the war started I have given up paying respects. I have better things to do. See you soon, Pedrito," said don Emilio while putting on his hat. He departed to talk to his accomplices and to the magistrate. They would figure out what to do with Pedro Lindo.

Pedro was perplexed by don Emilio's comments. The man never did anything by accident; he must have had something in mind.

As soon as Pedro got his ideas in order, he took his doctor's briefcase and his umbrella and went to visit the gravedigger's family. His head was full of questions, but he still felt pity for don Higinio.

* * *

PEDRO FOUND HIS FRIEND'S CORPSE stretched out on the dining room table, between two candles that illuminated the humble room. After he embraced the widow to pay his respects, he approached the corpse to say a prayer for his soul. When he bowed respectfully, he noticed that the corpse had a neat slit across the neck, under the right ear, almost as though done surgically. And then he was afraid. He made the sign of the cross and left. He opened his umbrella against the sudden rain and, walking as fast as he could, he left to find Constantino. They had to take precautions. Don Emilio knew something.

"Neither the death of don Higinio nor the visit from don Emilio were accidental," Pedro mumbled under his umbrella. "Don Emilio threw me the hook to see if I would bite; it's hard to believe how wrong I was when I thought that don Higinio was really drunk."

*   *   *

THAT AFTERNOON THE PREFECT'S SPIES were all over the city and in nearby places looking for Federico. Don Emilio, thinking furiously, remembered Sofia had spent the night of the flood at Victor's farmhouse. That same afternoon a team of soldiers arrived at the farmhouse. Felisa talked to them with an air of calm and answered the numerous questions they raised. As expected, they didn't find any evidence of Federico at the farmhouse. He and Arcila had been on their way to Ecuador beyond reach of don Emilio and his accomplices.

*   *   *

FOR REASONS UNKNOWN until the present day, Pedro Lindo left his position as accountant of the State of Cauca a week after don Higinio was found dead. Nobody could find out why he had to leave a position he had performed with brilliance for more than a decade. After leaving his accounting job, he dedicated himself to his true calling in life: the practice of homeopathic medicine in service of all social classes, making no distinctions about income or origin. He did this until his death in 1907, when he succumbed to a contagious disease contracted from a charity patient he had operated on.

*   *   *

ALBERTO COULDN'T BELIEVE what don Emilio came to tell him. He never imagined that Sofia would be capable of falling so low. To give herself to Federico, after rejecting Alberto for years, was a crime. Don Emilio proposed to him that he marry Sofia to save the family's honor, but Alberto couldn't agree to marry a woman who was not a virgin. He knew where to find that class of women but never considered marrying one of them. In the end he belonged to the noble Carrasco family that—he believed—had existed since before fountains and rocks came into being. He would find a way to make Federico and all his family pay for ruining his life's dream.

XXVII: Trip to Guayaquil

Don't you hear the neighing of the horses, the playing of the
clarions, and the rumble of the drums?
I don't hear anything, replied Sancho, but the bleating of the
sheep and the lambs.

—*Don Quixote*, First Part, Chapter XVIII

When Pedro Lindo left his position as accountant at the
Government House—after the Holy Week celebrations—Mariana received an order from the prefect to
report to his office the following Monday. She suspected the meeting
had something to do with Federico.

On Monday, when Mariana arrived to the prefect's office, he thanked
her for coming and said, "Mariana, I am sorry to have to inform you
that all of your property, including the bookstore and your home, will
be confiscated by the government to be sold at public auction. You and
your family are accused of conspiracy against the government by hiding
your brother Federico, who is accused of being responsible for partic-
ipating in the attacks on the city and in the revolt at the prison. As a
gesture of friendship for the services provided to the city by your family,
you will be allowed to leave the city with your personal belongings and

ten percent of the public auction income received by the government. You have until the end of May to depart from the city. The only way to change this order is to immediately inform the authorities of the location of Federico Lemos, or have him turn himself in to the government authorities inmmediatly."

Mariana was left breathless. She didn't expect anything like this. What would they do? She thought for a moment before talking.

"Señor Prefect," she finally said, "I don't have control over the location of my brother Federico and it is impossible for me to inform him of your order, or ask him to report to the authorities because I don't know where he is. Moreover, I wouldn't do it even if I knew where he was. Neither would my sisters. We only knew that the local authorities have reported him as missing since the revolt in the prison at the end of September."

"Mariana, I am sorry, but we are at war! I don't have any other alternative than to defend the lives of the citizens for whom I am responsible. For the same reason, I offer you and your relatives a dignified way of leaving the city. I am incapable of putting you and your sisters behind bars. Thus, I am trying to be as generous as I can."

Mariana was completely stunned when she left the prefect's office. Her only option was to find a way to get out of the city, as soon as she could put their affairs in order. They had to continue living, but not here. What did the future hold for them?

Walking across the Plaza Mayor, wondering what to do, she saw Pedro Lindo at the corner of the Plaza Mayor standing by La Torre del Reloj. When Pedro saw her, he knew there was something wrong and approaching her, he saw the tears in her eyes.

"Mariana, what is happening to you?"

She told him about her visit to the prefect and asked for his advice about what to do next. Pedro understood at that moment that his job loss, don Higinio's death and Mariana's challenges had a common origin.

"My advice to you is to stay away from anyone related to the Carrasco family. Be very careful with don Emilio, the prefect, the governor, and their relatives. Also, I want you to know that Delfino Alegría mentioned to me that recently, the magistrate Alberto Carrasco had visited with them several times since just days before don Higinio was found dead." However, Pedro did not venture to tell her that his job as accountant had already been eliminated. She had enough troubles of her own. She would learn about it anyway.

Mariana listened to him with fear in her heart. She never had imagined that the Carrascos would be her enemies. How could she not talk to Sofia? But she couldn't ignore the warnings of Pedro Lindo, whom she knew to be the holiest and most honest man to be found in the city of Popayán.

*　　*　　*

IN THE SECOND WEEK OF MAY a group of muleteers that worked for Aniceto Arcila arrived in Popayán. They were on their way to Guayaquil after delivering goods in Popayán and Cali and had been asked to help Federico's family to travel to Ecuador to join him.

Constantino sent a telegram to Federico describing the situation at the bookstore and the imminent departure of Mariana, Rosa and Lola, along with Mama Pola and Clodomiro. Besides, Arcila and Federico wanted them to come to Guayaquil for their own safety and to be close to their brother. Federico missed having Mariana and his sisters near him. Thus, Arcila sent his men at once to help the sisters travel to Guayaquil and to carry the family's personal belongings. Also, Arcila had other ideas in mind.

The third Monday of May, the Lemos family departed from Popayán on their way to Ecuador. The bookstore *El Libro* closed its doors in Popayán forever. Mariana was sad about not being able to say goodbye to Sofia, but she had no other option. It was all part of war: you sometimes had to stay away from your own friends when you needed them most. She couldn't ignore what Pedro Lindo had told her, but it hurt not to be able to trust one of her best and dearest friends. And it hurt to know that the magistrate Alberto Carrasco had bought their property at the public auction for next to nothing.

The muleteers had twenty mules and five horses to accommodate goods or merchandise. Four of the men had chairs tied to their backs to carry passengers who were unable to walk. Federico's sisters and Mama Pola traveled on horseback or walked, and only used the chair carriers for the most challenging climbs of the trip. Clodomiro traveled on mule-back and amused himself by using his spyglass to look at the landscape along the way. He thought it was marvelous to be able to see everything before arriving there. It was like living in the future and he constantly reported on what was yet to come. His parrots, in two cages hung from the sides of his saddle, were his companions.

The trip from Popayán to Pasto lasted for ten interminable days along impossible dirt roads. The best traveler turned out to be Mama Pola, despite being the oldest of the group. Fifty years before, she had moved from Tumaco to Popayán to serve old doña Domitila Lorenzo, don Nicomedes' wife. Close to Pasto, they encountered a shepherd guiding his sheep to better grazing fields.

Clodomiro, hearing the church bells ringing in the distance when he looked at them with his spyglass, said, "Don't you hear the ringing of the bells?"

"I don't hear anything but the bleating of the sheep and the muttons," said Mama Pola, who was hard of hearing. When Clodomiro heard her say that, he remembered reading the same words in Don Quixote. What did Mama Pola knows about Don Quixote? He wondered in disbelieve.

Arcila came from Guayaquil to Pasto to accompany them to Guaya- quil across the border. Federico hadn't come because he knew there was a price on his head. He feared being captured by the government spies who operated in the southern regions of Colombia. In Pasto they rested for three days before continuing to Guayaquil. There, they enjoyed the hospitality of the Delgado family, relatives of Arcila and President Alfaro. From Pasto, the view of the Galeras Volcano brought memories of the Puracé volcano in Popayán, and made them feel nostalgic for their ancestral home. Clodomiro seemed to have no remorse about the move as he spent hours studying the flight of the condors over the Andes with his spyglass. He dreamed of training the condors to carry him flying over the Andes and all over the world with his parrots some day in the future.

Traveling to Guayaquil with Arcila made the arduous trip far more enjoyable. He was well known in the region and had many friends along the way. He also often told them something new or interesting about the people they met, the topography, the climate, the crops, and the animals. They all enjoyed his company and Mariana, who got most of his attention, appeared to enjoy it more than anyone else. When they arrived at the Canyon of the Guáitara River, Arcila suggested they take a detour to visit the famous image of the *Virgen de las Lajas* shown inside a little adobe sanctuary on the side of the river. At the little church they learned from the local priest that in 1754 the *Virgen Mestiza* appeared to a little peasant, a deaf-mute girl named María, who told her mother in a sudden perfectly clear voice that the Virgin was calling her. Her mother couldn't believe that her mute daughter was talking and became even more overwhelmed when she saw the image of the *Virgen de las Lajas* imprinted on the stone. Mama Pola knelt down with the three sisters to pray there, asking the Virgin to protect them and to give their trip a happy ending.

From Quito, Arcila send a wire to Guayaquil announcing their arrival around the 21st of June. The sisters and their companions would live temporarily at his home, a two-story mansion with large balconies over the *Calle de Colón* across the street from the study of the famous photographer don Julio Bascones.

Federico had changed a lot since they had seen him. He now walked with a cane and was tanned by the tropical sun. His gray beard gave him a very distinguished look. He had been waiting for them since daybreak so anxious to see his family again and to hear the stories of the tragedy they had had to live through in Popayán. He embraced his sisters, Mama Pola, and Clodomiro with immense joy. Eventually, Mariana managed to take him aside and gave him an update about the painful closing of the bookstore and the humiliation of having to auction their home.

Federico described his escape from Popayán and told them about his new job as civil engineer in a government project supported by President Alfaro. He mentioned that Antonio Ramos was also working on the project and that currently, the liberals were waiting for their generals, Benjamín Herrera and Lucas Caballero, to return from El Salvador where they had traveled to acquire a war ship they would need to attack the city of Panama before the end of the year. A few days later, Antonio came to visit with Federico and his family and learned about the latest news from Popayán. He couldn't believe how they had been treated.

Shortly after their arrival, Professor Gustavo Adolfo Lemos Ramírez, a teacher at the *Colegio San Luis Gonzaga* next to the cathedral, visited them. His father, don Salvador Lemos, was don Nicomedes' nephew and had traveled with him from Galicia to Popayán before coming to Guayaquil. Rosita and Lola became instant friends with their cousin and joined his social circle as members of the extended Lemos family. The professor helped Mariana to get a job as a teacher at the *Colegio de la Inmaculada*, where the well-to-do girls from Guayaquil studied. Rosita and Lola became assistants to the photographer don Julio Bascones. Lola took over the accounting and Rosita became an expert in photographic equipment. Clodomiro joined Federico as an assistant in a road construction project. Mama Pola was convinced that all this good news was a miracle from the *Virgen La Mestiza.* They all had found things to occupy themselves and this contributed to the wellbeing of the Lemos family, a new life in peace. Well, in relative peace: Clodomiro's parrots never stopped talking. They were all happy.

XXVIII: *Sofia Gives Birth*

She, turned her face and addressed Don Quixote, saying: days ago, valiant knight, I gave you an account of what without reason a perverse farmer did to my beloved daughter, this unfortunate woman standing before you... and you promised to remedy this wrong... and I wanted that you would challenge this rustic and restless farmer to marry my daughter, complying with the promise he made to her to be her husband before he became the first to copulate with her.

—*Don Quixote,* Second Part, Chapter LII

POPAYÁN, MARCH–AUGUST 1901

A week after the funeral of don Higinio on Tuesday, Sofia went to visit her godmother after her siesta. She felt nervous and suffered from a terrible headache that not even a miracle from the Virgin would cure. Her stomach felt bloated and very tight.

Her uncle don Emilio had arrived early and had found his cousin Ana María traumatized by the assassination of don Higinio.

"Emilio, there is no respect for life anymore. Where is this country going to end up? My God! Such a good man is hard to find," she had said.

"You are right, Ana María. I live very close to these situations and know about them from experience. Until we get rid of these murderers, life will not be as it used to be."

She looked at him, confused, not sure of the meaning of his words.

"Sofía should be here this afternoon. I told Amelia, the maid, that you are going to examine me and asked her to bring Sofía into the room when she arrives," she said. The old man nodded and agreed to do what his sister was asking of him.

And so, when Sofía arrived, Amelia took her to Ana María's bedroom. Sofía waited until the maid left, then knocked on the door.

Her knees were shaking, just from thinking about her uncle's reaction. But she had no other choice: she had to face reality and she had to be brave. When her godmother opened the door, Sofía entered and greeted her with an embrace and a kiss. Then, she watched her uncle stand up and said in an insecure tone, "Hello, Uncle, you don't realize how much I appreciate that you have come."

It was the moment of truth, and she was very nervous.

"Your uncle is already informed about what you told me," said Ana María. "He will examine you now and I will be here to help you to relax. Whatever is said in my room is sacred. Just tell Emilio how you feel and ask him any questions you may have in mind."

"From what I understand you had sexual relations with Federico Lemos and Ana María thinks you are pregnant. What can you tell me?" the old doctor asked.

"Uncle, the whole thing started when I found out that Federico was alive. He had not vanished like the others had. As you know, the government was looking for him after the revolt at the prison. Much later, when I almost had lost hope of seeing him alive, I learned that he was in hiding and he invited me to meet him in a secret place. It was the greatest joy of my life to see him safe and sound."

"I assume that was the day of the flood, when you left with Felisa, the woman you met at church, correct?" said the doctor.

"Yes, Uncle, but she had nothing to do with it. Do you understand?"

"Yes, of course I do. But where is Federico?"

"I have no idea. We met that day and since then I haven't see him. I only know he was alive when we met. Today he may be in Peru or on the moon. I can't tell you where he is because I don't know. He is at war."

"And do you think that is how a gentleman behaves? He gets you pregnant and runs away, he gets lost."

"Uncle, I would say that it is not proper for gentlemen to insult those that aren't here to defend themselves. Federico has no idea that I am pregnant. I have been his girlfriend for ten years and he never had the slightest indiscretion with me. I am the only person responsible for my situation. I did it for love. I did it because I didn't know if I would see him again. God was in charge of what happened."

"Do you understand that you have put your mother, your godmother, and me, and the whole family in a very difficult position? We could be accused of treason and that could cost us our lives. Besides, you have become an ally of the governments' enemies and, to make it worse, you became pregnant by one of them, one that justice is pursuing! Do you know the meaning and the value of the family's honor? Four hundred years of tradition, no less! If your father were alive he would take you to the convent for life and he would kill Federico. Do you realize the mistake you have made and the mess we are in?"

"It is not a mistake, Uncle. I am the happiest woman on earth and if I have to go to the convent to save the family's honor I will go with pleasure."

Don Emilio was ready to call her impertinent but realized he wouldn't achieve anything by doing so. He took a deep breath and looked impassively at her. The best thing would be to keep an eye on her and try to trap Federico in some way. They had not been able to find him. Meanwhile, he proceeded to examine her and confirmed that she was pregnant, about three months. He washed his hands and put his instruments away.

"The birth, if all turns out well, should be in August. From what I see, you enjoy good health. Eat well and take a little walk every day, and make sure to rest. I will continue to see you every other week or more, as necessary. Ana María will let me know if you need me."

"Uncle, I don't want anyone to know about it. Promise me. If my mother learns about the pregnancy, she will kill me or will die of anger. I couldn't live with her sermonizing. I would have to kill her or just kill myself."

"Give thanks to God that your father is not alive; may he rest in peace. Ana María already mentioned to you that as a doctor I must respect your will. She can advise you, better than anyone, to make sure nobody knows about it."

Sofia accompanied her uncle to the door.

"If you don't want anybody to know about it, I advise you to stay at your home," he said with his hand on the doorknob. "You know how fast gossip can move around in this town."

She learned that her uncle was right a moment latter. When she was returning to her godmother's room, Amelia approached her with a question in her face.

"Niña, is my mistress seriously ill?"

"No, nothing to worry about. But she has to take better care of herself. My uncle will continue coming to see her to check on how she is doing. Women's issues, I think. Can you get us a little coffee with a few cookies or something?"

"Yes, Niña, I will be back soon. You go back to your godmother. God bless her."

Amelia was not convinced by this story. She had noticed that Sofia wasn't wearing the belt she had on when she came in. And Sofia noticed that the maid looked suspicious. *My uncle was right,* she thought.

*   *   *

SOFIA MISSED THE COMPANY of Federico's sisters and their conversation after they left for Guayaquil in the middle of May. Since their departure she'd had no news from them. Each day that went by she felt more alone and one day, for some reason, she couldn't stop thinking about them. During the night she dreamed that Federico had been killed in combat. She saw him slowly dying, bleeding and calling her as he choked on his own blood. The vision was so clear that she didn't question that he was already in the next life. The baby moved and kicked in her womb, just as if he had learned that his father had been killed. At dawn, she woke up soaked in sweat and found her water had broken. Scared, she called Betsabé to accompany her to her godmother's home. Luckily, the maid had just returned. She had gone to say goodbye to her own mother, who had been very ill with yellow fever. The woman died from it shortly after Betsabé's visit.

Ana María asked them into her room and sent Betsabé to look for don Emilio. In half an hour he arrived and took charge of the situation. The birth was imminent.

"Ana María, this young woman is going to give birth any time. Go to the kitchen and get me a large pitcher of hot water."

The godmother handed the pitcher to Betsabé and told her to go to the kitchen. "Amelia is there. Bring me the water as soon as it boils." Then she closed the door and got close to Sofia, who was in pain on her bed. The struggle was evident on her face.

"Her contractions are very frequent. She is dilated," said the doctor, and Ana María looked at Sofia in fear. Ana María was moving her head from side to side and her legs were shaking out of control. At that moment, she felt like fainting. She just couldn't take it.

"Emilio, as you well know I cannot tolerate the sight of blood. Let me call Betsabé. She grew up on a farm and she knows more about these things," she said, and left the room.

When she opened the door, she found Amelia lurking just outside the room.

"Did you help Betsabé with the water?" she said, furious to find Amelia spying.

"Yes, ma'am. She is in the kitchen waiting for it to boil," said Amelia.

"Tell her to bring it and right now!" said Ana María, flapping her arm to signal for Amelia to go at once.

The doctor saw that the baby was in the wrong position for birth. Sofia was pushing and breathing haltingly, gasping for more air.

"I'm choking! Uncle! Uncle, I am dying! I cannot do this anymore. Help me! Please!"

Betsabé came into the room carrying the water pitcher and was terrified when she saw Sofia. Poor dear! Sofia looked at her, eyes huge in desperation.

"Get me those big forceps from my briefcase," said the doctor, pointing at them.

Betsabé handed them to him and he applied them to correct the baby's position. In the middle of this procedure he accidentally cut Sofia with the forceps. She screamed in pain and passed out. The maid thought Sofia had died and made the sign of the cross.

"My God! My God! My mother has just died and now my Niña is going to die also!"

Don Emilio took advantage of Sofia's fainting and managed to accommodate the baby with the forceps. Betsabé, seeing the crowning of the baby's head, by instinct, took hold of it and received it from Sofia's womb. A boy. The doctor cut the umbilical cord as Betsabé held the boy. He had a yellowish complexion, as though made of beeswax. Sofia was paler and paler by the minute, bleeding profusely. The doctor put a spoon from the coffee tray in her mouth to keep her tongue down, to help her breathe. Her eyes had rolled back and she was struggling for air. It looked like she was dying.

Betsabé, with the yellowish baby in her hands, asked, "Is the baby alive, doctor?"

"Put him in warm water," ordered the doctor. She obeyed and submerged the baby partway in lukewarm water, cleaning the phlegm from his mouth with her finger. The baby jerked, emitted a sonorous cry announcing his arrival to the world.

When Ana María heard the baby's cry from the hall, she looked at Amelia and said fiercely, "You haven't heard or seen anything, understood? Nothing!"

"Yes, mistress," said the poor maid, scared by her attitude. She was terrified of Ana María when she was angry.

The godmother entered the room and found Betasbé cleaning the baby with a wet towel. He had Federico's black hair. This was the moment to get rid of the baby, before Sofía regained consciousness.

"Come with me," she said, taking the maid by the arm. Betsabé followed her, the baby in her arms.

"Go to the convent right now and give the baby to the Mother Superior. Do not mention it to anyone else. Do you understand? No one! You say a word and the *Patasola†* will get you! I promise you. I swear she will go after you!"

"Yes, I will do as you say," said Betsabé, frightened thinking about how the one-footed monster would suck her blood, and she departed with the baby wrapped in the towel. She hid him under her large scarf as they had hidden Sofía's pregnancy. She held him tightly against her bosom to keep him warm. When she arrived at the convent, the gatekeeper opened the door and went to look for the Mother Superior, who came immediately. She had been expecting this visit at any time.

---

†La Patasola: she is claimed to be a monster with one breast, a witch's nose, red eyes, and dogteeth that she uses to bite her victims and suck their blood like a vampire.

The Mother Superior received the baby from Betsabé and looked tenderly at him.

"Tell doña Ana María that the baby is now in God's hands and that we will be praying for Sofía's recovery," she said to the maid.

"Yes, Mother, I will tell her that," said Betsabé and went back to complete her mission. She felt terrible thinking about Sofía and wondered if she would live.

She had no idea that Ana María and Emilio had visited the convent, months before, to inform the Mother Superior of Sofía's situation, looking for her collaboration to protect the family's honor. When the Mother Superior agreed to help, don Emilio placed in her hand a small heavy leather bag, and the godmother gave her a pair of baby shoes as her present for the baby. The nun put the bag and the shoes away in her pocket, said goodbye to her guests and blessed them. When they left, she confirmed that the bag contained forty gold coins. She thought about Judas Iscariot and made the sign of the cross. It was the best donation of the year. The little black shoes for the baby had a bright red lining. The godmother, somehow, already knew it would be a boy.

Betsabé returned, as fast as she could run, to the godmother's house, arriving there within minutes. Amelia opened the door because she was waiting for her.

"My mistress is in the room with the doctor," she said, and ran to the kitchen. She didn't want her mistress to see her again.

The scene Betsabé encountered in the room was pathetic. Don Emilio, exhausted, was sitting in a director's chair next to the bed with his shirtsleeves rolled up above his elbows. His hands were all covered in blood. He had put the placenta in the basin, where it was floating in the bloody water. Ana María was trying to give Sofía a drink of water and Sofía was choking. She was clearly not fully aware of what had happened to her. The bedcover was on the floor, soaked in blood. Everything was in disarray, the room and everyone in it a total disaster. Without waiting for a question from the godmother, Betsabé whispered in her ear.

"The Mother Superior took the baby and she said he is in God's hands and she promised she would be praying for Niña Sofia's recovery."

"Not a word to anyone," the godmother ordered. "Do you understand? You know what the *Patasola* does to snitches. You do, don't you?"

Betsabé made the sign of the cross, for she really was frightened out of her mind. She almost burst into tears. Without saying another word, she started cleaning up Niña Sofia. The doctor and the godmother sat back, exhausted, and admired the dexterity and gentle hands of the maid. She took charge of disposing of the afterbirth when she got the room in order. She was marvelous. Sofia, sensing all was in order, settled into a deep sleep.

The doctor checked Sofia's pulse and said she appeared to have a slight fever but he wasn't worried about it. She was drained by her efforts and the loss of blood. He couldn't do any more for her at that moment and it was time to leave. He said goodbye to his sister and checked Sofia's forehead again before leaving. Ana María thanked don Emilio and accompanied him to the door.

"Emilio, Betsabé and Amelia were warned not to mention anything about the baby to anyone," she said. "Make sure to stop by the convent and ask the Mother Superior to send Sor Basilides to stay with Sofia. They get along very well."

"I was already going to do that. The Mother Superior promised she would send Sor Basilides after the baby was born. I'll make sure she comes as soon as possible. And I'll come back tomorrow to check on Sofia."

Ana María returned to the room and found Betsabé looking after Sofia, touching the girl's forehead with the back of her hand as the doctor had done, to check if she had a fever. She didn't feel anything. She was overheated with all the hustling and running and had no idea that she also had a fever, which she had caught from her own mother.

Sofia, half awake and half asleep, looked at her as though she were in another world and eventually closed her eyes, exhausted.

Then the godmother told Betsabé to go back home, and warned her not to mention a word of what had happened to doña Julia.

"If you tell her anything, she will worry to death. Tell her that Sofia is keeping me company. That I am not well."

Betsabé nodded and prepared to go home. She didn't know what was making her feel so bad. Probably all that excitement and running around. Or her nerves: she was also frightened thinking about what the *Patasola* could do to her.

Ana María summoned Amelia and told her once more to keep quiet about all that she had seen. Luckily, Luis was in Quibdó on a business trip and wouldn't return until the end of the month. The government needed money to keep the war going.

In about two hours, Sor Basilides came to accompany Sofia. The Mother Superior had asked her to do her best to take care of Sofia and to convince her to join the convent as soon as she recovered her strength. Ana María thanked God for her cousin Emilio, who knew how to move the world.

XXIX: After the Birth

Besides, she is indeed my sister, the daughter of my father
though not the daughter of my mother, and she became my wife.

—Abraham and Sara: *Genesis* 20:12

The Mother Superior told don Emilio and Ana María that Sofia's child had been adopted by a Christian family, but she did not tell them the identity or residence of the new parents. The only other person who knew that they were from Cali and knew their name was the Mother Superior's assistant, Sor Josefina.

Sor Basilides invested all her love and effort in keeping Sofia alive, treating her as though she were her own flesh and blood. They had a very special bond. Sofia had been her best student in the literature class at the *Colegio de María*. She loved Sofia's unique interest in Don Quixote, and how she shared her enthusiasm for the book with her classmates and her teacher. The good nun asked all the saints for help to keep Sofia alive and to allow her to find a way to convince Sofia to enter the convent as a novice. The Mother Superior needed candidates with a good dowry and missed no opportunity to remind her of that.

Sofia, somehow, endured weeks of hovering between life and death. She struggled with the memory of the pains of childbirth and the visions of the son she'd never held in her arms, the tortures of yellow fever, and persistent imaginings of Federico dying in the war. She didn't know if she was insane or so physically sick that she couldn't think or make sense of life anymore. Only a miracle could save her. And, eventually, Sor Basilides' efforts and prayers paid off and the miracle did happen. Sofia started to eat again and was able to sleep in peace. Don Emilio said the health of her pregnancy and the prayers and good care provided by Sor Basilides had saved her.

When Sofia recovered consciousness, her first question was "Where is my baby?" Sor Basilides lied and told her that the baby had been born dead and was buried in the convent. She asked God to forgive her for lying to Sofia. It was the thing to do.

"Perhaps your child's fate was an early death," Sor Basilides said, "and he now lives in peace in heaven with God and all the saints." Sofia didn't know what to say. Tears rolled down her pale cheeks and somehow the nun's words filled her with resignation. It was fate.

Feeling she was at peace, Sor Basilides decided to tell her about the untimely deaths of doña Julia and Betsabé, both victims of the same yellow fever. Sofia could neither believe nor accept so much tragedy; she cried until she had no more tears. For many days she wouldn't talk to anyone. In her brief moments of lucidity, she joined Sor Basilides in prayer, asking God to save her, to pardon her and to bring her to the convent if that was God's will. Together, Sofia and Sor Basilides prayed the rosary and imploring the Infant of Prague to help her to recover her sanity and her health. It was a miracle she knew He wouldn't deny her.

Federico was at war unaware that Sofia had given birth to a son and was struggling for her life with yellow fever and desperation.

Eventually, thanks to all the praying and the good care from Sor Basilides, Sofia decided she had to continue living. She wasn't alone, after all;

she had her godmother, who had promised to take care of her from the day of her baptismal ceremony and she had Sor Basilides at her side. She regained her appetite and prayed for Federico's health, hoping he would come home after the war was over.

Her godmother was happy to see Sofia in a better mood and beginning to think about her future. When she told Don Emilio about her progress, he felt the convent was the best place for her to go. In agreement, Ana María and don Emilio decided to visit with Sofia to discuss her future.

"Before dying your mother asked me to take you to the convent as a way of giving thanks to God, if he saved your life," Ana María said, leaning forward from her chair by Sofia's bed to deliver her message.

"Your mother told me that your dowry should be given to the Mother Superior, when you became a novice," don Emilio added. "Sor Basilides has promised us that when you become a novice she will take you to Spain, away from this war and this misery. She lives in constant fear of the brutality of this war, worrying daily about the fate of the novices if they should fall into the hands of the rebels."

"My dear, the only thing missing is your pledge to become a novice," said Ana María. "The Mother Superior has approved it and supports your move to Spain. Sor Basilides hopes to see her parents in Pamplona before you go to the city of Barcelona, where they have their Motherhouse."

"I would go happily to the convent, godmother," said Sofia, "because I promised this to God and to Sor Basilides. Nonetheless, my love for Federico is stopping me from doing it. When this war is over, I want to become his wife. I will tell him we had a son who died at birth, and then with God's help, we may have many more children. My dream has always been to be his wife."

"This thing about marrying Federico is something that Julia could never accept," said don Emilio, adopting a dramatic air. "Julia was terrified when she knew you were in love with him and she opposed your relationship by all means!"

Sofia interrupted her uncle, and said placidly, "Yes, Uncle, she was obstinately against our relationship. In fact, she hated him, because Federico was not Alberto, because he was poor and didn't belong to a famous family. But all of that means nothing to me because only Federico matters. I made love to him and for that same reason we had a son."

Don Emilio was not used to not getting his own way. He became so irritated that he lost his temper and hissed, "Stop, Sofia. You have no idea why Julia was so opposed to your relationship with Federico and why she could never accept him as your husband."

"And what was the reason why she couldn't accept Federico and I as husband and wife?" Sofia retorted.

Don Emilio adopted a thoughtful air—as though he didn't know if he should reveal what he knew or not—and after a few moments that seemed like an eternity, he told her:

"Federico's father wasn't don Gallardo Lemos. That was your mother's reason for calling him a son of a bitch so many times."

This was news not only for Sofia but also for Ana María.

"Then who was his father? Tell me, please!" Sofia screamed in a fit of anger.

Don Emilio again adopted a meditative posture. Finally he spoke.

"Federico's father was your own father, don Juan Francisco Usuriaga. Thus, Federico is your half-brother."

Ana María almost fainted when she heard him. How did she miss that?

Sofia broke into tears. She couldn't believe it and couldn't imagine her father having an affair with doña Micaela Beltrán. That was a horrible impossibility.

"Then are Mariana and Rosita and Lola my sisters?" she asked.

"No, only Federico is your half-brother. They are not your sisters," don Emilio said.

"Does Federico know this?" said Sofia.

"No, he has no idea. But he thinks that Clodomiro is his half-brother. He was old enough to realize that when Carlota became pregnant, there was no question that don Gallardo had done it, not the rooster *Don Clodomiro*, as the maids claimed."

"And Mariana knows it?" said Sofia.

"No, she only knows that Clodomiro is her half-brother."

"My God, godmother! I just realized I committed the worst of the capital sins. I conceived a child with my own brother. God punished us! This was incest! This town is a hell unto itself."

"Dear, for your actions to be called a sin you would have to have known what you were doing," Ana María soothed. "What you did, you did for love, with no malice. God is great and merciful. That's why the baby was born dead."

"Now do you understand why your mother wanted you to go to the convent?" don Emilio said, taking advantage of the silence of the moment.

Sofia looked at him and felt that a special light filled her. She bowed her head in a humble gesture, new to her, and said yes.

"Yes, Uncle. I will go to the convent. It is the best thing I can do. I am incapable of facing Federico again. I don't ever want to see him again. I couldn't explain to him what actually happened to us."

And in fact, the following day Sofia entered the convent to become a novice. Sofia Usuriaga died to the world and was born again as Sor Emma de la Concepción.

Don Emilio inherited the properties of his sister Julia Carrasco and her husband don Juan Francisco Usuriaga, excluding the dowry—one hundred gold coins—which he delivered to the Mother Superior with the godmother as witness.

Neither the godmother, nor Sor Basilides, nor don Emilio confessed to Sofia that her mother had not died of yellow fever, but from a fulminating heart attack when don Emilio told her that Sofia had given birth and the father of the baby was Federico Lemos.

The Mother Superior complied with her promise and—with help from the governor and the godmother—she allowed Sofia and Sor Basilides to depart for Spain, traveling from Popayán to the port of Buenaventura and from there to Bilbao in the ship named *Buena Esperanza* (Good Hope) early in November, 1902.

During the trip to Spain, Sofia couldn't stop thinking about Federico. She knew she would not see him again and also knew she would never forget him. Hidden in her luggage, she had the little book of Don Quixote with the letters in code that they had exchanged when he was in prison. Now she would be the prisoner, but he would not be able to send her more letters. She was condemned to live with her memories. What would be their fate?

XXX: The War in the Pacific and the End of the Thousand Days War

> It is difficult to sort out and identify the essential and profound causes of historical events.
>
> —Lucas Caballero, *Memorias de la Guerra de los Mil Días*

In Guayaquil, General Benjamín Herrera, Supreme Leader of the Liberals in the Pacific, departed for El Salvador to purchase a war cruiser—*Almirante Padilla*—and left General Bustamante in charge of his army with orders to take over the government garrisons at Barbacoas and Tumaco. The government of President Marroquín had declared war to the death, which meant that war prisoners could be shot on sight. They would have no other option but to be victorious or to die at the enemy's hands. With this incentive, General Bustamante and his soldiers started to win all their battles.

When General Herrera returned with the *Almirante Padilla* he found a most pleasant surprise: Bustamante and his soldiers had not only taken over the garrisons at Tumaco and Barbacoas, but had also procured large amounts of ammunition and the gunboat *Panama*. They also had captured one thousand prisoners.

Herrera left some of his men to protect the garrisons at Barbacoas and Tumaco. He departed for Panama with the rest of his army in the *Almirante Padilla* and the gunboats *Panama* and *Cauca* to take over the Panama Isthmus.

Federico was assigned to the general staff on the *Almirante Padilla* and joined the team in charge of the artillery battery. Hernandes and Antonio remained, defending the positions at Tumaco and Barbacoas.

The liberals' ships arrived at the isthmus in mid-December 1901 and anchored at Tonosí Cove, a strategic position south of Panama City. As soon as the liberals established a land base at *Antón,* General Herrera departed at once for Panama aboard the *Almirante Padilla.* He sent a message proposing an exchange of prisoners to his old friend General Carlos Albán, Governor of Panama and Commander in Chief of the government's armada in the Pacific and the Atlantic Oceans. General Albán, in what appeared to be a quixotic gesture, accepted the proposal and sent his officers fluent in English as his envoys to the battleship US *Philadelphia*—facilitated by the US Navy—with the specific mission of signing the peace agreement with Herrera.

After the agreement was signed—January 17, 1902—the liberal prisoners exchanged by Albán came back from Panama in the US *Philadelphia.* They informed Herrera that Albán had just taken *the Lautaro* by force. The *Lautaro* was a battleship owned by the government of Chile, and Albán obviously intended to use it to attack the *Almirante Padilla* by surprise. Herrera—feeling betrayed—decided on the spot to pay Albán in the same coin with a surprise attack before Albán had time to put his own plan in action.

During the night, the liberals departed at full steam, planning to attack Albán in Panama the next day at dawn. They had orders to attack the *Lautaro* but to avoid damaging the US *Philadelphia* and a merchant ship from Chile that were anchored next to it.

The same night, Albán had subdued the Chilean crew of the *Lauta-*

ro, who had rioted in protest from their temporary prison in the boiler room. Albán took them over easily and proceeded to repair the damages to the boiler. At about 2 a.m. he retired to his cabin to rest, unaware that the liberals were already on the way to attack the *Lautaro* at dawn. A night guard of the *Lautaro* woke Albán up when the enemy ship was only 1,300 feet from the *Lautaro*. There was no time for any response.

Early in the attack, Albán was shot in the abdomen and the left leg by bullets from the machine gun of the *Almirante Padilla*. The combat was brief. The liberals lost three men and had about thirty wounded. The government army lost many more soldiers, but its main loss was General Albán who, like a good captain, sank with his ship in the Panama Bay waters. His body was never recovered.

The US *Philadelphia* and the Chilean merchant ship took the wounded from both armies aboard and gave them first aid. The next day, the US *Philadelphia*, in a friendly gesture, took the wounded liberal soldiers to a site close to liberal's land base. That same day, General Lucas Caballero, second-in-command of the liberal army, was informed of the loss of the *Lautaro* and the death of General Carlos Albán. His death was one of the greatest losses for Colombia during the One Thousand Days War.

*   *   *

PANAMA, NOVEMBER 1902

THE LIBERAL VICTORY AT SEA IN PANAMA opened the doors for new victories against the government forces. In victory after victory, the liberals took over the Panamanian isthmus and in the end Herrera proposed that the governor negotiate a peace treaty as equals. The governor, who preferred death to defeat, declined.

Then something unexpected happened. The liberal's General Staff received a message from Rear Admiral Silas Casey, Commander of the United States Navy in the Pacific. It announced that the proposal from

General Casey had been accepted by the Bogotá Government and that he would act as a mediator for peace between the two parties at war. He proposed a meeting of the liberal and conservative leaders on the battleship US *Wisconsin* to work on an agreement to end the hostilities of the Thousand Days War. After arduous negotiations, the liberals created a final proposal that Herrera grudgingly accepted. Herrera put it succinctly: "The motherland is above the parties." He knew peace was more important than the differences between the political parties and more important than his ego.

The agreement was signed and approved on November 21, 1902, aboard the US *Wisconsin* by the two key men in charge of the conflicting armies, general Nicolás Perdomo and general Benjamín Herrera.

*   *   *

THE FIGHTING OVER, Federico took the first ship he could find back to Guayaquil to celebrate Christmas with his family. He had missed them terribly and was looking forward to being able to live in peace. Of course he also wanted to see Sofia again. He hadn't stopped dreaming about her since their last encounter.

On arriving in Guayaquil, he received a wonderful surprise: Mariana and his dear friend, Aniceto Arcila, were engaged. He was asked to be the best man in the wedding. Arcila had set up a new bookstore as a wedding present for Mariana on the *Calle de Pichincha* in Guayaquil. It replaced the old *Librería Española,* owned by don Pedro V. Janer, which had burned to the ground during the great fire of 1896, a fire that almost destroyed all of Guayaquil. Rosita, Lola, and Clodomiro had accepted the offer to resume the same roles they had held in the old bookstore in Popayán. Federico agreed to become the interim manager of the bookstore until the newlyweds returned from their honeymoon, a trip to several countries in Europe. Even though his desire was to depart at once to visit Sofia in Popayán, his friends convinced him to wait for a while, to allow the animosity remaining from the war atrocities caused by both armies to subdue. His sisters and Clodomiro didn't plan to return to Popayán.

After the celebration of the wedding of Mariana and Arcila, their friends Hernandes and Antonio returned to their old jobs in El Socorro and Popayán. They were longing to live in peace with their relatives and to start a new life. They expected that the hatred between the enemies would eventually die.

XXXI: *Federico Returns to Popayán*

Don't speak more, friend Sancho, replied Don Quixote
that the affairs of war, even more than others, are subject to
continual change. The more I think about it, I am certain that
the same sage Frestón who stole my home and my books, has
turned these giants into windmills, just to deprive me of the
glory of my victory.

—*Don Quixote*, First Part, Chapter VIII

POPAYÁN, APRIL 1903

When Mariana and Arcila returned from their honeymoon trip to Europe, Federico left his position as manager of their bookstore in Guayaquil and announced he would return to Popayán to ask for Sofia's hand. No one was surprised. They'd all expected that Federico and Sofia would be husband and wife once the war was over. Arcila had brought luxurious merchandise from Europe that he planned to sell for a good profit in southern Colombia and thought that Federico would be an ideal companion for that trip. But Mariana was concerned about what could happen to her husband and brother when traveling in a territory infested with lawless truants and runaway soldiers looking for ways to make a quick fortune. Eventually, Federico and Arcila convinced their relatives that they could travel to

Popayán safely. They would be accompanied by a seasoned group of well-armed muleteers that knew how to take care of themselves. In spite of all these arguments, the day they left, all the family members wondered if they would see them alive again. It was impossible to forget the war memories they all carried for the rest of their lives. Clodomiro wasn't invited to accompany the travelers. He felt immensely humiliated and rejected.

As Arcila suspected, he made a small fortune selling the imported merchandise. They arrived to Popayán on time, on Sunday, May 10, the day before Sofia's birthday. Antonio Ramos welcomed them to his home, happy to see his comrades again. Federico felt it was time to celebrate and asked his host to help him to find some musicians to give Sofia a surprise serenade that same night. Antonio and his relatives looked at each other and suggested that it would be better to rest from their long trip first. When Federico insisted, they proposed they had to have a drink first to celebrate their arrival. He couldn't refuse.

After the travelers refreshed themselves and shared a few drinks, Antonio thought it was time to bring his friends up to date about the reality of the moment. He told them that at the funeral ceremonies to honor the memory of General Carlos Albán, celebrated in Popayán the previous month, several dignitaries had mentioned that Albán had died from wounds caused by the projectiles coming from the artillery under Federico's command on the battle ship *Almirante Padilla*.

"You have been declared *persona non grata* in Popayán for the rest of your days," said Antonio. But Federico still insisted they had to find the musicians. Hence, Antonio was forced to tell him the whole truth.

"Federico, it is impossible. I must tell you that Sofia entered the convent as a novice and left for Spain in the month of November."

Instead of going out to give a serenade to Sofia, Federico ended up drinking with his two friends all night, looking for relief from his sorrow.

When he woke up the next day, he had a horrible hangover. His friends were not any better. Misery had brought them together once more.

The following day, May 12, Federico asked Antonio to help him to set up a meeting with Ana María Carrasco, Sofia's godmother. He knew she would do anything to please "her" Antonio and she would know all the details about the reasons that Sofia had to join the convent and leave without consulting with him first. In fact, she accepted and invited Federico to her home that afternoon after her siesta. She couldn't wait to see him.

As soon as Antonio had finished setting up the meeting and had left her home, she sent her maid Amelia to ask don Emilio to come have lunch with her and keep her company during the visit with Federico. Her husband Luis had left for Bogotá to a government meeting concerning the end of the war, and she felt incapable of facing Federico by herself. Don Emilio accepted at once. He wanted to see how Federico was after the war, and he felt he couldn't say no to the request since he and Ana María had been involved in Sofia's decision from the beginning.

The next day after lunch, Federico dressed in his best suit and prepared for the meeting with Sofia's godmother. He had so many questions he didn't know where to start. When it was time, he grabbed his cane and headed toward the governor's home. His appearance had changed so much that nobody recognized him as he walked nonchalantly along the streets of Popayán.

Federico's entrance to Ana María's parlor was dramatic. He didn't expect to see don Emilio there. The last time Federico had seen him was when the old doctor had come to the prison and had said that Domingo was sick and could leave, but that Martín had told him that nobody else was leaving. Neither Ana María nor don Emilio recognized Federico until he spoke and they heard his sonorous voice.

"Ana María, don Emilio, good afternoon."

They didn't know what to say. They all remained lost in a silence that seemed like an eternity. The godmother was stupefied. She had pictured Federico as the young man she'd known—she didn't expect to see an older man with a cane, a gray beard, and an imposing manly presence. Don Emilio looked at him and, in his mind, returned to the prison patio where he had seen Federico's body bathed in blood and had assumed him dead, next to Domingo's corpse. He felt that Federico had been resurrected and was coming back from hell to beat him with his cane. Finally Federico interrupted the silence.

"The day before yesterday, I learned that Sofia entered the convent and left for Spain in November. I came to find out what drove her to take such a radical determination. The last time I saw her I thought that as soon as the war was over we would be ready to become husband and wife. For that reason, I came to Popayán to see her with the intention to ask for her hand. I must admit I was dumbfounded by the unexpected news."

Don Emilio looked at Ana María, implying she should speak first.

"Federico, I am glad to see you alive and in good health but I am surprised to hear that you were coming to ask for her hand after ignoring her for more than a year."

"I think it is an insult that you dare to come into this house!" Don Emilio couldn't restrain himself any more. "You left her pregnant and ran away when you should have reported to the authorities and taken responsibility for your crimes."

"Sofia pregnant?" said Federico, and looked at the godmother and don Emilio, searching for a reply to his question.

"Yes, Federico. She herself told us about your encounter the day of the flood before you left to go to Ecuador and Panama where, as everybody says, you bloodied your hands by shooting Dr. Albán to death."

"I am sorry," Federico said. "I had no idea she was pregnant. And regarding what happened in the war, no one has the right to claim to be free of guilt. Fortunately, the Treaty of Wisconsin sealed the peace between the two parties at war and opened the door to forget our differences and return to live in peace. With such an idea in mind, I came to Popayán ready to start a new life with Sofia."

"Federico, I can appreciate your desire to return to live in peace again," Ana María said. "It is something we all need. I never was a friend of that senseless war. Regrettably, when Sofia found she was pregnant, she had to live in hiding to keep her secret from her friends and even her own mother, who never would have pardoned her if she had found out she had become pregnant out of wedlock. It would have been worse if Julia had learned that you were the father of the baby. To make Sofia's misery greater, the baby boy died at birth and she contracted yellow fever. It was a miracle she survived. Julia and Betsabé were not as fortunate as Sofia. They both died shortly after the baby was born, when Sofia was in the middle of her fight with yellow fever. The poor dear was left alone. Where were you?"

Federico, crushed and amazed to know he had had a son, was silent for a moment.

"But I don't understand why she went to the convent," he finally said. "I am sure she would have waited for me to return. We both dreamed of having many children together."

At that moment, don Emilio gestured to Ana María that it was his turn to talk.

"Dreaming costs nothing," he said. "But you were not born to be husband and wife."

"I am sorry, don Emilio," said Federico, wounded by these remarks, "but if we conceived a child together there was no impediment for us to be husband and wife. Besides, we loved and respected each other. That is the reason I came to see her and ask for her hand. If I didn't come before it was because I was at war, fighting for peace and law and order and a new world for our children."

"She didn't have any impediment until I explained to her why her mother, Julia, was always opposed to a romantic relationship between the two of you," don Emilio replied, beginning to lose patience again. "For that reason she decided to go to the convent."

"And what was that impediment?" Federico asked.

"If you didn't know it," don Emilio shouted, "Your father was not don Gallardo but Professor Usuriaga!"

In that instant it all became clear. Federico recalled the day when he was about fifteen and his neighbor Sofia Angulo had told him he didn't need to have his picture taken because he was a look-alike of Professor Usuriaga. Federico was not angry, but deflated. He didn't know what to say. In fact, he thought, this explained why doña Julia had told Sofia, each time she mentioned him, that he was a son-of-whore. He had foolishly even made a joke of it, signing his last letter to Sofia, after don Emilio's visit to the prison, in the exact point in *Don Quixote* where the Dueña called the poor Sancho Panza son-of-a-whore. He had been trying to be sarcastic and now he had to eat his own words. After a long silence, Federico, looking intently at the godmother, raised his eyebrows.

"So Sofia is my half-sister?"

"Yes, just as you have said," she replied. "Now you know her reason for going to the convent. She felt incapable of facing you again. She even thought she had committed incest. Fortunately, God took the baby to his glory. That is what I told her—truly, you didn't know what you were doing. So no, I don't blame you. I know you did it because you were in love."

"And my sisters, are they the professor's daughters?" asked Federico expectantly, looking at don Emilio.

"Not them. Only you. It was a great indiscretion that don Juan Francisco couldn't forget. He told me about it the day he came to ask for Julia's hand. That's why he only married her later in life. It was a miracle they managed to have Sofia."

Federico, noticing that Ana María couldn't hold back her tears, felt only pity for everyone involved in such a tragic story.

"Now I understand everything," he said gently. "I can't imagine how much Sofia must have suffered with this tragedy. I can't blame her for going to the convent. Her situation was impossible. She did the best she could under the circumstances."

The coffee service remained intact at the table. Nobody had touched it during the visit. Ana María stood up.

"I will never be able to live in peace knowing how much the poor dear suffered," she said. "The war, in one way or another, punished us all, the just and the sinners."

Federico approached the godmother and gave her a warm goodbye hug. As it turned out, they were never to see each other again.

Don Emilio extended his hand intending to say goodbye, but Federico ignored him, turning toward the door.

"Excuse me, I must leave." And he left unceremoniously without giving them the opportunity to say another word.

*   *   *

THE NEXT DAY, Federico went to visit with Pedro Lindo while Arcila took care of his business deals in Popayán. Pedro was more than happy to see his friend alive and in good health. He asked about Federico's sisters and in particular about Clodomiro, with whom he had a special friendship. He was delighted to learn about the marriage of Mariana and Arcila and also to know they had a new bookstore in Guayaquil. When Federico told Pedro about his visit with the godmother and don Emilio, Pedro insisted he should stay out of sight and leave the city as soon as possible.

"The reason that Luis and Alberto Carrasco left for Bogotá is that one expects to become the new governor and the other will occupy a ministerial position in the new administration. I understand Alberto hates you and blames you for the death of Dr. Albán."

The following day, Federico and Arcila departed for Cali. When they were crossing the *Puente del Humilladero*, Federico remembered that thirty years earlier, General Mosquera and don Juan Francisco Usuriaga—he could not yet think *father*—had had their picture taken there, posing for the photographer on the bridge where he was standing at that very moment. He felt a chill running down his spine. He decided that he did not need to feel that chill a second time. He never again returned to Popayán.

The atmosphere they found in Cali was different. There was general optimism about the importance the city would acquire when the railroad to Buenaventura was built and the Panama Canal was completed. Cali would then have a direct connection by sea to any place in the world.

*   *   *

GUAYAQUIL, 1903–1904

AFTER LEAVING CALI, Arcila and Federico traveled to Buenaventura where they boarded a ship to Guayaquil; it was a safer and faster route. On arrival at his sisters home, Federico encountered a mix of sweet and sour news. His sisters were dumbfounded when they learned that Sofia had entered the convent and had left for Spain. They could not believe she and Federico had had a son and that the baby was dead. They didn't know what to say to Federico. He didn't mention a word about don Juan Francisco. He was incapable of sharing his secret with them. They also had a surprise for him: Clodomiro had been missing since the month of July.

Apparently, since Federico had left to travel to Popayán, Clodomiro developed an attitude and started going to the pier to visit with the sailors from the merchant ships that arrived from all over the world.

"He couldn't talk about anything else. He befriended the captain of a merchant ship and one sad July day he left our home with his parrots in two cages before dawn, when nobody could see him, and he boarded a ship bound for Europe," said Mariana.

Federico didn't know what to say. He couldn't blame Clodomiro for leaving and looking for new adventures, to look for *what was yet come.* Like him, the dwarf had learned something from reading *Don Quixote.*

The following year, the captain of the *Targis*, a German merchant ship, confirmed to Arcila that Clodomiro had traveled on his ship to Bremen and had told the captain that he was going to Dresden to join the Sarrasani Circus. He dreamed of having a show with his talking parrots, speaking in many languages. And he added, "Clodomiro spoke during the trip in perfect German."

*   *   *

GUAYAQUIL, 1904–CALI, 1908

AT MARIANA'S BOOKSTORE, Federico met one of their best clients, Mr. Archer Harman, a contractor on the project of the *Ferrocarril del Sur* and director of the Guayaquil and Quito Railroad Company. His company had a contract—from 1899—to complete the railroad connection between Guayaquil and Quito, the most difficult railroad project in the world at that time. When he learned that Federico was an experienced engineer, Mr. Harman invited him to join the project. Federico accepted at once. He felt he needed something new in his life. Four years later, in June 1908, the railroad arrived to Quito. It was a memorable day.

At the ensuing celebrations he met don Pablo Borrero—the first governor of the new state of Valle del Cauca, created by President Rafael Reyes—who had been invited to the ceremonies inaugurating the new railroad from Quito to Guayaquil. Don Pablo proposed to Federico that he come to Cali to work on the railroad project to connect Cali with Buenaventura. The Americans were already working to open the

Panama Canal and he wanted to have the railroad ready when the Canal became a reality. Federico felt that once more, destiny was opening a new door to allow him to achieve his dreams.

His sisters applauded the idea and encouraged him to be part of the dream he had had in mind since he was fifteen years old. In August 1908, Federico boarded a ship in Guayaquil to return to Buenaventura. He was determined to finish the railroad to the Pacific port before the Americans finished the Canal. He had always dreamed of taking the train from Cali to Buenaventura, boarding a ship to Panama and crossing the Canal. He didn't need more.

Before departing for Buenaventura, he acted as best man for the marriages of his sisters, Lola and Rosa, in a ceremony that took place at the Cathedral of Guayaquil. They married two Italian brothers, nephews of Cardinal Lugarini. The papal nuncio officiated at the ceremony in the Cathedral of Guayaquil and consecrated their unions with a special blessing from the Holy Father.

*   *   *

CALI, 1908–PANAMA, 1914

WHEN HE ARRIVED IN CALI a friend told him about the unexpected death of Pedro Lindo. Pedro Lindo had left his position as accountant at the Government House, a job where he performed with distinction for more than a decade. For the good of all the members of the community, he dedicated all his efforts to his true vocation, the practice of homeopathic medicine until he became the victim of a contagious ailment, contracted from a charity patient, and died shortly after. The whole city attended his funeral ceremony and maestro Guillermo Valencia honored his memory with an unforgettable eulogy. As Antonio Ramos had put it: Pedro Lindo was a saint.

*   *   *

FEDERICO'S PLAN WORKED ALMOST EXACTLY as he had expected. The two great engineering projects were completed almost simultaneously. The Panama Canal was open to traffic between the two oceans on August 15, 1914, and on January 19, 1915, the railroad between Cali and Buenaventura was inaugurated.

Federico had to travel to Panama in July 1914, to receive the locomotives for the Cali-Buenaventura railroad. In the city of Panama, he ran into Monsieur Philippe Bunau-Varilla, who had been his boss and friend in the Panama Canal project around 1888, both working for the French Canal Company. The Frenchman told Federico that he had not been invited to the opening ceremonies of the Panama Canal which he considered an insult to France. He invited Federico to join him and they crossed the Isthmus from Cristóbal, in the Atlantic, to Balboa, in the Pacific, two weeks before the official ceremonies. Their memorable trip lasted only twelve hours. The two old engineers rejoiced, as they sipped vintage Champagne, brought from France to celebrate the special occasion, while contemplating their dream, now a reality. Moreover, the Canal had been built with locks above sea level, as they had proposed, and the locks had been made following Bunau-Varilla's designs. It was almost ironic that they had crossed from Cristóbal, where Columbus had landed 400 years before, to Balboa, where don Vasco Núñez de Balboa had set the Spanish flag in the Pacific Ocean a few years after Columbus' trip. For a moment, Federico thought he had seen the ghosts of Columbus and Balboa holding the Spanish flag on board while he enjoyed the Champagne with the Frenchman. He learned, later on, that neither President Roosevelt nor President Reyes had attended the inaugural ceremonies.

*   *   *

CALI/GUAYAQUIL, 1918–1920

IN 1918 THE WHOLE WORLD WAS AFFECTED by one of the most deadly pandemics in the history of mankind, the so-called Spanish Flu. It killed more than 100 million persons. Guayaquil a busy port with passengers arriving from all corners of the earth, suffered immensely from this plague. Sadly, Federico's three sisters all died from the flu within a few weeks, while talking care of each other. Federico buried them in Guayaquil accompanied by Arcila and the Lugarini brothers, who immediately after returned to Italy.

Federico came back to Cali, where he continued working for the *Ferrocarril del Pacífico* until 1920, when he had to retire due to numerous health problems—he was 66 years old and had lived a strenuous life.

Federico realized he needed a more sedentary occupation to keep himself busy. He decided to open a bookstore in the Plaza de Santa Rosa in Cali. From this bookstore, as he had done when he was 15 years old in Popayán, he spent the rest of his years contemplating the worlds past, present, and future, surrounded by his best friends: books. But destiny still had some surprises waiting for him.

*   *   *

YEARS AFTER OPENING THE BOOKSTORE IN CALI, Aniceto Arcila, his brother-in-law, came to Cali after a trip to Europe and told him the news he had about the fate of Clodomiro. His departure from Guayaquil had been motivated by a conversation he had had with Mama Pola, who had told him that his father was don Gallardo Lemos. In Dresden, Clodomiro had joined the *Sarrasani Circus* and the manager, Hans Stosch, encouraged him to develop the parrot show. This became one of the main attractions of the circus. It was there that a French dwarf woman, Mlle. Marlène, a baroness of Jewish origin and owner of a great fortune, who worked at the circus, fell in love with Clodomiro and soon they became husband and wife. In their elder years, they retired to her castle near Saint-Rémy-de-Provence. There, Clodomiro became fascinated with Nostradamus's work and dedicated the rest of his life to unravel his mysterious predictions and translated them into several languages. Then, he trained his parrots to repeat them by heart. Eventually, he set them free to fly all over the world. Clodomiro died happy of old age and was buried by his wife at the *Cimetière de Juifs* in the outskirts of Saint-Rémy. Visitors to the cemetery claimed to have heard the parrots that return there every year in the spring repeating the prophecies. They arrive accompanied by a crow that talks with them exclusively in English. An Indian intellectual claimed he heard the parrots reciting the prophecies of Nostradamus in perfect Sanskrit. He also heard them reciting the *Kadambari*, an Indian novel where a parrot tells a prince a love story.

*   *   *

XXXII: Sofía in the Convent

In a dark night, with love's desires inflamed,
O blissful fate! I left unnoticed,
Being my home already appeased.

—San Juan de la Cruz, *Dark Night*

Sor Basilides was the faithful tutor and companion to Sor Emma in the convent in Barcelona for almost thirty years after they left Colombia. In 1931, the old religious sister died there in holy peace, happy to have been useful to the sick, accompanied by Sor Emma de la Concepción, her disciple and faithful helper.

Days before dying, she called Sor Emma to her cell and invited her to pray. She needed help from God to be strong and be able to tell the younger nun something she had carried in her heart for years.

"Daughter," she said, "before long I will be with our Lord, and I cannot leave this world without telling you something you have to know."

Sor Emma looked at her, confused, wondering what she had in mind. "Mother, what would that be?"

"Please, bring me that tin that is over on my armoire."

Sor Emma gave it to her and waited for Sor Basilides to open it. She looked in the box and took out a little black shoe, lined with red felt, and gave it to Sor Emma.

"Take it, it's yours. It belonged to your son. Betsabé, your maid, took him to the convent when he was born. He didn't die as you were told. Sor Josefina told me that a couple from Cali, who couldn't have children, had adopted him." She paused to take a breath.

"After they took the baby with them, I found one of the little black shoes that your godmother had taken to the convent as a present for him before he was born. It probably fell off after they dressed the baby to give him to his new parents. I kept the little shoe as a souvenir. Pray for me and please ask God to forgive me for having lied to you. And pray for Betsabé, because she saved your baby's life."

Sor Emma almost fainted. In that instant she became Sofia Usuriaga again, thinking *my son should be about 31 years old, and if Federico survived the war, he won't know about our baby either. Could this be a signal from God the Father? Where could they be?*

Her mind became filled with memories, thoughts, and moments from her former life. A few days later, after Sor Basilides died, she asked her Mother Superior to help her to find a way to be transferred to Colombia. She wanted to return as a missionary. She had a debt to Betasbé, and she hoped for a miracle to be able to see her son and see Federico again.

Finally, she was blessed by the heavens. Her Mother Superior at the convent in Barcelona didn't have to think twice about it, for she had recently received a request from the Mother Superior of their convent in Cali, Sor Josefina, asking for volunteers to work as missionaries. Knowing that Sor Emma was a good nurse, and from Colombia, the Mother Superior saw that she would be an ideal candidate to go there. It was the right moment.

*   *   *

THE YEAR OF 1932 began in Barcelona with bad news for the Catholic Church in Spain. War was in the air. On January the republican government ordered the elimination of the Jesuits from Spain and confiscated all their real estate and property. Sor Emma had served their community for almost thirty years and it was in her best interest to go back to her motherland to serve as a missionary. Moreover, it would be unjust to have her live—or die—in another war. At her age, she deserved to go home.

Sor Emma received the order to travel from Barcelona to Cartagena in the spring of 1932. She packed her meager personal belongings, which included the tin with the little black shoe and the little book of *Don Quixote* with the secret letters to and from Federico. She didn't need anything else. Those were her treasures, the only things that she owned from her former life as Sofia Uzuriaga.

∗   ∗   ∗

CALI, 1932–1938

THE *COLEGIO DE LAS MONJAS* was a modern three-story building located close to the Cali River, a mountain stream that brings into the Cauca Valley clear waters from the mountains of the Farallones de Cali, part of the western branch of the Cordillera Occidental of the Colombian Andes. The building had a large central patio surrounded by broad hallways with well-polished tiles. The Mother Superior, Sor Josefina, received Sofia as if she were a miracle of Divine Providence. They instantly got along and found they were kindred spirits. They had a mysterious connection—felt like family to each other. She installed Sor Emma in the dormitory next to hers, around the corner from the chapel on the second floor. In the patio, a fountain attracted birds of all colors of the rainbow that accompanied an old turtle that Sor Josefina had inherited from Sor Delfina, the founder of the convent.

When Sofia became acclimated to the tropical environment, Sor Josefina told her, she would be assigned to serve as assistant to Father Martens—a Belgian missionary—in the jungles of the Colombian Pacific region that had been Betsabé's homeland. Sor Emma lived there for several years, traveling to those forgotten regions along the pristine rivers where the native population—including former black slaves and aboriginal natives—lived in humble wood huts with palm-leafed roofs, built high above the river's edge to survive the constant sudden floods. They traveled along those rivers in dugout canoes, propelled by slim black men who knew well the jungle channels and the rivers, and served as motors, guides, and fishermen to feed the missionaries and themselves. They moved from village to village, from hut to hut, to bring the Faith of Christ, to clean wounds, to give medals and rosaries away, and to bring news of the interior of Colombia to those men of ebony, descendants of slaves who had mined gold from those rivers for centuries. They shared their meals and taught them the Hail Mary, and told them how to pray to the Virgin and the Saints. They slept in their huts, in hammocks or on straw mats over the bare wood floors, lulled by the constant rains, while bats and insects flew around over their heads looking for food.

In the year 1938, Sor Emma returned to Cali to receive medical treatment. She had been infected with malaria and needed special help. Again, she was assigned to the room next to Sor Josefina's. But this time her Mother Superior didn't allow her to go back to the jungles: at her age she deserved a break. She was put in charge of the convent library to distract her from her sickness and allow her to recover. Later on, she was named as Counselor to the Novices in charge of the kindergarten children, girls and boys. Sor Valeriana, a young novice responsible for the boys, became her favorite companion. They shared a love for books and a love for teaching the children how to read and write.

Her new jobs were like a new dawn for Sor Emma. Her passion for the children and the young novices took her to the time when she was in love with Federico. In each one of the children she could see the son she had never met. In the fresh faces of the novices she could see the image she saw in the mirror the day she went to visit with Federico. But, behind the wrinkles and the thick lenses of her glasses she only had the memories of the beautiful woman she was when she was young.

On the weekends, Sor Valeriana took Sor Emma to visit the churches downtown and the second-hand bookstores in the Plaza de Santa Rosa, where they looked for bargain books for the children and for the convent library. Sor Emma soon became acquainted with the booksellers that operated in the plaza and its neighborhood. It was there that she noticed that one of the old book dealers, a good old fellow with beautiful white hair, known as *El Cojito*, was wearing a ring that reminded her of one Federico had inherited from his grandfather, don Nicomedes. He had been wearing it the last time she saw him.

When she went back to the convent she prayed in the chapel for hours, asking God for guidance to forget about her ideas regarding the old fellow. She couldn't stop thinking about Federico in the bookstore in Popayán and at the little farmhouse where she last saw him. She did her best, but couldn't avoid visiting his bookstore a few more times because Sor Valeriana insisted on visiting the old man, for whom she had her own special affection.

On one such visit, Sor Emma left with the sense that something in El Cojito's gaze was off. His eyes looked at her, yes, but more than that they looked inward — searching for a long ago buried memory. Did he recognize her somehow? If he did, why didn't he say something?

"No," she muttered as she shook off the feeling. "He's clearly senile, not quite all there."

Sor Valeriana wondered what had come over Sor Emma, standing there talking to herself. "The poor woman," she thought, "she's showing signs of senility, not quite all there."

XXXIII: Ramón and Sor Emma

I started my life, as I will undoubtedly finish it: in the middle of books.

—Jean-Paul Sartre, *The Words*

It was about the end of the summer of 1938 when Ramón's father, don Joaquín Bastos Romero, took him by the hand to the *Convento de las Monjas* for his first day of kindergarten. Sor Emma and Sor Valeriana were his first teachers; they taught him to read and write, guiding him through the discovery of the connection between words and the magic of reading and writing.

Sor Emma, who had acquired a Spaniard's accent, used to tell him, putting her teeth over her lips, "Ramón, my dear, we must say *vaca,* not *baca.* Look at my lips: Vvvvvaca! Vvvvvaca!" And he would laugh out of control thinking how funny she was.

"Ramón, dear, let us sing: Viva, Viva, Jesus my love." And he would mimic her, thinking how funny he was.

It was something the boy wouldn't forget. But he never learned to pronounce the v in *vaca* as the Spaniards do. He continued to say *baca.* Sor Emma understood. Love understands everything.

*   *   *

SOR EMMA AND SOR VALERIANA came back into Ramón's life many years later in the most unexpected way. It had to do with his father's health. Don Joaquín Bastos Romero was suffering from chest pains, and was resting in bed on orders from the family doctor, Dr. Pontón, who knew he was suffering from a serious aortic aneurysm. Ramón was sitting on his father's bed with his mother, doña Laura—the daughter of Antonio Ramos, Ramón's favorite grandfather—and his grandmother, Beca, when the telephone rang. He ran to answer it. Sor Valeriana was calling from the *Colegio de las Monjas* to inform don Joaquín of the death of Sor Emma. Ramón thanked her and mentioned his father's illness, asking Sor Valeriana for her prayers. She offered to pray for don Joaquín and said goodbye. When Ramón shared the news of the death of Sor Emma with his parents and his grandmother, he sensed they feared something: it was like an omen.

"Son, Sor Emma was your kindergarten teacher," his father said. "You should go to represent the family at her funeral. Don't forget that she and Sor Valeriana taught you how to read and write."

Ramón had no choice. He knew his mother wouldn't even consider leaving her husband alone for a moment and his grandmother didn't want to go either. She knew her son was dying. Dr. Pontón had confided to her that her son wouldn't last until Christmas. So Ramón had to go to Sor Emma's funeral alone.

Ramón put on his black tie and went to the convent, mildly looking forward to reconnecting with his kindergarten days when he had learned his first letters.

Sor Emma's funeral was unforgettable for many reasons, the main one being the awful surprise he got when he came back home. His father had died while he was attending Sor Emma's funeral. Ramón was devastated. His father was only fifty years old and Ramón had just started his career at the university. In just a few hours he transitioned from a teenager to a grown-up man.

The death of his father turned his mother into a different person. She became more distant each day, suffering from migraines and other ailments. The burden of her care fell mostly on his grandmother Beca. His time was consumed by his studies at the university and by odd jobs he took to contribute to the family income.

About three years after Ramón's father's death, Dr. Pontón discovered the source of his mother's health problems: she had a malignant brain tumor. His mother opted not to have surgery. She didn't want to become a vegetable. In a matter of weeks she died in her sleep.

Ramón's mother's funeral became another exquisite moment in the collection of his memories. As had happened with Sor Emma's funeral, he got a surprise when they came home from the cemetery, where they left her resting in peace next to her husband. His grandmother Beca asked him for a drink.

"Before my time comes to go the cemetery, I need to tell you something I never had the courage to share with your father and your mother. God bless them," she said.

Ramón brought her the drink and one for himself, wondering what she was going to say. She looked at him over the rim of her cup and took a deep breath.

"Your father wasn't our biological son," she said. "He was adopted. We couldn't have children. He was a son of the war, that's what the nuns at the convent said. We were in the middle of the One Thousand Days War and many orphans needed parents. We never found out who his parents were. The baby came from Popayán. The Mother Superior who helped with the adoption told us that the baby's mother was a special person."

Ramón didn't know what to say and decided he needed another drink. His grandmother Beca asked him for another one too, and after her drink she continued.

"When we got the baby home, I removed his blanket to change him and found he had come with only one shoe. Apparently, the other one was lost when the nuns got him ready for us. It was a little black shoe, lined in red felt. I want you to have it. Let me go get it, I'll be back in a minute." She made her way to her bedroom and came back holding several things.

"I also found a locket with your father's picture when he was a baby and a piece of his black curly hair." And she gave them to Ramón. From that day on, Ramón kept wondering who the biological parents of his father could have been. He couldn't stop thinking about it. He was full of questions about his lineage and about his real family of origin. What could he do?

*   *   *

HIS GRANDMOTHER BECA had known that she would die soon. A few months after his mother's funeral, Ramón returned to the cemetery to attend his grandmother's funeral.

On a memorable day in the summer of 1955, when he was about to finish his studies at the university, he went downtown on one of his wandering expeditions to look for old books. He had inherited this affection for old books from his father, don Joaquín Bastos Romero, who'd enjoyed taking him to the *Plaza de Santa Rosa* to buy biographies of important persons and textbooks at a good price. To look for old books was like being with his father again. It was then that he found, in the bookstore called *The Oasis* that was owned by his friend Hernando Tancredo, the little book of *Don Quixote* with the letters from Sofia and Federico written in code.

PART FIVE:

SEARCHING FOR IDENTITY

Who are you? Said the Caterpillar.

—Lewis Carroll, *Alice's Adventures in Wonderland*

XXXIV: A Late Surprise

And in less than a blink of an eye they carry him through the
air or over the sea where his help is wanted or needed: thus,
Sancho, this boat has been placed here for the same purpose;
and this is as true as it is nowadays.

—*Don Quixote*, Second Part, Chapter XXIX

UNITED STATES, 2002

A few years ago I was looking for the negatives of the photos
I took of the engravings in the little book of Don Quixote
when I was a student. Suddenly, I came across a box that held
various family treasures: my father's baby picture and the little black
shoe lined in red felt. My grandmother Beca had given me these things
after my mother died, when she told me my father had been adopted.
When I saw the shoe, I remembered her words: "These are the only
things I have of his from when he was a baby."

At that instant, I remembered the phone call from the convent invit-
ing my father to Sor Emma's funeral. I had been distracted by his illness
then, but now I wondered why the nuns had called my father to let him
know Sor Emma had died. I had never thought about that at the time
and I was very innocent.

These questions became an obsession. I told my wife Ann what I had in mind: I needed to travel to Cali to look for Sor Valeriana, the young nun I sat with at Sor Emma's funeral. If she was still alive she could help me to answer the questions about my parents and she could clear up the many doubts I had in my mind.

Paraphrasing Don Quixote, in less than a blink of an eye a plane carried me through the air and over the sea, and I was in Cali. The next step was to go the convent. I hadn't seen Sor Valeriana since 1950. Would she even still be alive?

Nervous, I rang the bell at the main door of the convent. In a few minutes the little window in the door opened and a nun asked me who I was.

"I am Ramón Bastos Ramos, an alumnus of the *Colegio*. I attended kindergarten here in 1938. I am looking for Sor Valeriana."

The nun opened the door and asked me to come into the waiting room, a small waiting area with three wooden chairs against the wall.

"I'll be back in a few minutes, Señor Bastos," she said.

After about ten minutes, the nun came back accompanied by an elderly nun I didn't recognize.

"The gatekeeper said that you are looking for me. I am Sor Valeriana," she said.

"Sister, I am Ramón Bastos Ramos and I wonder if you remember me."

"No, I'm sorry. I don't remember anyone with that name. But my memory is failing. I am getting old, they say I am 84 years old. Help me to remember you, please."

"I was at Sor Emma's funeral in 1950. You and Sor Emma were my teachers in kindergarten in 1938." The nun smiled.

"Now, I know who you are," she said. "Sor Emma loved you very much. It is sad you couldn't see her before she died. I will never forget her funeral. It was very special."

I mentioned that I had an almost perfect memory of the funeral, that it somehow was one of those things we cannot forget, that become points of reference to our past. Sor Valeriana listened attentively.

"If you allow me to take advantage of your good memory that is much better than mine," she replied, "I would like to propose that we review the funeral together to remember that day. Sor Emma was my mentor in the novitiate and I owe her my vocation and my life. She took care of me as though I was her daughter. She was a marvelous woman. But before we go over your memories, allow me to invite you for a coffee. The kitchen girls are making molasses cookies and it is almost time for our snack."

I was happy to be invited. The aroma of those cookies was imprinted in my mind as the aroma of kindergarten, stored next to the aroma of my mother's food and other childhood memories.

"I will join you with utmost pleasure," I said.

"Follow me, Señor Bastos, let us walk together toward the dining room, it is right next to the kitchen."

"Is the kindergarten where it was in 1938?" I asked.

"Yes, we will see it soon," said Sor Valeriana.

XXXV: Sor Emma's Funeral

The dead are not, no! Those that receive
on their stiff remains, the rays of light;
those that die with honor are the living,
those that live without it are the dead.

—Antonio Muñoz Feijoo, *One Thought in Three Verses*

CALI, 2002

While we enjoyed the delicious cookies and the coffee, Sor Valeriana said, "Can we go back to those days?"

"When my father was terminally ill back in 1950," I said, putting down my cup, "I was sitting on his bed with my mother, doña Laura, and my grandmother, Beca, when the telephone rang. I answered it. Sor Valeriana, you were calling to inform don Joaquín about Sor Emma's death. I thanked you, told you about my father's illness, and asked for your prayers. You offered to pray for him and said goodbye. You had an unforgettable voice."

"Yes. Now I remember, it has come back to me now. It takes a hook to get the fish out of the water," she said.

"On that day in 1950," I continued, "my father asked me to go to Sor Emma's funeral to represent our family. As you would understand, my mother chose to stay by my father's bedside, as did my grandmother Beca. She didn't want to go either, her son was dying."

"A very natural thing to do," said the nun, and I continued.

"Honestly, I went to the funeral in part out of curiosity to see the kindergarten again and in part to show my gratitude to Sor Emma, who occupied a special place in my childhood memories. She taught me how to read and write."

Sor Valeriana, displaying an angelic smile, said, "I was her favorite assistant. I stayed in kindergarten during all my teaching years."

"That day, after the phone call, I took a taxi to the convent and when I arrived, I rang the little bell, the same bell that my father rang when he took me—almost by force—to kindergarten for my first day of class. Sor Vicenta, a Swiss nun with red cheeks, opened the door and practically lit up the entryway with the light coming from her deep blue eyes. She directed me, as if I was again five years old, to the chapel where Sor Emma's body rested. She lay in a simple wooden casket with a glass window. She appeared to be sleeping and her face shone with profound peace. In her generous hands—that had always brought us candy during our obligatory naps—she held the same rosary with a cross that she always had hanging from her belt. Looking through the glass window at her, in her posture of eternal peace, my mind took me to kindergarten, and I saw again the image of the Infant of Prague lying on his back inside of a crystal box with his rosy cheeks and a permanent smile, like a German doll. Lost in my memories, I didn't notice that the chapel was filling with nuns, novices, students, priests. Even the kitchen help were there, and I also noticed the unforgettable smell of the molasses cookies we had in kindergarten and the bread coming out of the ovens. Father Martens, the robust priest from Belgium, offered a simple prayer for Sor Emma's soul. He invited us to accompany her to the Central Cemetery, where he would preside over her funeral Mass, and would give Sor Emma her final blessing before burial. Without further ceremony, he closed the coffin and invited those that were closest to carry it to the hearse that was waiting by the main entrance."

"Yes, I do remember it all now," said Sor Valeriana, and I continued the story.

"Without expecting it, I ended up being one of the pallbearers. I occupied the same position I used to have when we carried the Infant of Prague in processions around the convent. Following the same route we used in kindergarten, we went down the stairs, stopping at each one of the landings to turn the coffin carefully. The coffin was almost weightless. It seemed to me that a superior force was holding it by levitation. The nuns and the novices sang with their angelic voices, following us in procession. It was difficult to know where I was. The same force that levitated the coffin had erased time for me."

"Yes, we were singing *Christ have mercy on us, Lord have mercy...*" said the nun.

"After we put the coffin in the hearse, a 1945 dark-gray Cadillac, we followed it in three school buses and a few private cars. I sat by the window on the bench closer to the bus driver and in a few minutes a handsome nun sat next to me." I took a sip of coffee.

"I am Sor Valeriana, I said to you on the bus," the nun began, picking up the thread of the story for me. "Sor Josefina, our Mother Superior, asked me to call your family to inform your father about Sor Emma's death. Sor Josefina couldn't come because she is unable to walk, but she asked me to greet you and ask about your father."

I was fascinated by this new clue: Sor Josefina—for some reason—had been the one who wanted my father to know that Sor Emma had died.

"Yes, I remember it, clearly. You were a very handsome young man," she said.

"And you were a beautiful nun," I told her and carried on.

"Lulled by the nuns' Hail Marys, which sounded like buzzing bees, we drove toward the old part of the city, toward the cemetery. The funeral procession was so small that it didn't attract any attention. The city didn't have time to even take note of a hearse accompanied by three buses loaded with nuns. Two or three blocks after passing by the Ermita church, I noticed a black man, a very humble barefoot man wearing an old brown wool coat, standing on the sidewalk close to the corner. Showing immense respect, he removed his felt hat and he put it over his chest and slowly made the sign of the cross, keeping his gaze on the hearse. I imitated him without knowing what I was doing, and the man remained standing there until I lost sight of him. What a great prayer! What a great example of nobility! He was the ambassador at large of all the people that Sor Emma had served during her years as a missionary in the jungles of the Colombian Pacific coast." Sor Emma had told us stories of that part of her life: fascinating adventures that captivated a roomful of five-year-olds.

"May God hold him in his glory!" said Sor Valeriana, while carefully making the sign of the cross with religious devotion: from the forehead to the chest, and from the left shoulder to the right one, Amen.

"We entered the cemetery by a path flanked by above-ground crypts, where the dead were put to rest in boxes aligned like matches in a match-box. We continued to the chapel and placed the coffin on a table in front of the altar. The congregation occupied the wooden benches and Father Martens, wearing his usual white cotton cassock stained with wine, made a brief summary of Sor Emma's life of service. He talked about her life as a nurse in Barcelona and as a teacher of the kindergarten children in Cali and as a nurse to the people of the Colombian Pacific jungles. For Sor Emma they were all the same: children of God. Everywhere she had lived she had left a trail of gratitude because of her capacity for doing good without expecting anything in return, until she couldn't do it anymore."

"Yes, it is true. She couldn't do it anymore. Poor dear! May God hold her in His glory and may she rest in peace," said Sor Valeriana.

"Listening to Father Martens, I noticed, off to the side on a nearby bench, there was an old man with very white hair, a little stooped by the years he was carrying on his shoulders. He wore a white cotton suit with no tie and leaned on a carved wooden cane. I couldn't figure out if he was looking at me, wondering who I was, or if he knew who I was and couldn't remember my name and was trying to remember it. Each time I looked at him out of the corner of my eye, I encountered his restless look—full of questions—observing me from the other side of the central aisle. We had something in common, an affinity that appeared to be mutual. I decided not to look at him again but I couldn't stop feeling his presence. I felt as though he was still studying me in silence. I eventually regained my self-control and returned in my mind to Sor Emma and to my childhood memories, remembering her as my kindergarten teacher as if she were alive again. The ringing of the Consecration bells interrupted my thinking mind and I returned to the chapel. The old man in the white suit didn't go to communion. After the Mass, the priest invited those interested to accompany Sor Emma to her resting place. Then the old man with white hair, leaning on his cane and limping approached the coffin and took a flower he had on his lapel and put it on top of the lid of the coffin with his shaking hand."

Sor Valeriana, holding her coffee cup in the air, interrupted my story.

"It was a miracle," she said. "I remember well that flower. It was a yellow Catleya with a red cone in the center that looked like a heart," she said, and again she made the sign of the cross. I waited for a moment and continued.

"The old man looked at me again, with such intensity in his look that I will never forget it. He then left the chapel in no hurry, leaning on the cane with each step. Again, I noticed his limp. Those carrying the coffin followed the priest toward the burial site. I worried about the yellow flower falling off of the casket. Rain was in the air. Heavy black clouds announced a storm. When we arrived at the burial site, I noticed that the old man was looking at us from a distance. The sexton waited on his ladder, with a marble slab, mortar, and his tools ready to close the grave opening in the wall. Then the priest chanted the prayers for the dead while sprinkling holy water over the coffin and the yellow flower saying:

Réquiem aeternam dona ei Domine.
Et lux perpetua luceat ei.
Requiescat in pace.
Amen.

"After finishing the chant, we all said amen. We lifted the coffin to the height of the grave opening and the sexton pushed it halfway into the opening in the wall. At that moment, out of the dark clouds, a beam of sunlight came from the heavens and illuminated the yellow flower and the droplets of holy water that decorated it, filling the space of the grave with a biblical light. I remember I thought it must be Jacob's ladder coming from heaven to allow Sor Emma to climb and receive her well-deserved prize. I became totally fascinated by the miracle of light and heard a voice next to me that said 'Love, like perpetual light, is immortal.' It was your voice, Sor Valeriana! The same voice that called our home to tell us that Sor Emma had died."

"Yes, Ramón. I don't know where those words came from. Probably something I had heard or read somewhere."

I was anxious to finish my story, and said, "The sexton hesitated for a moment—like he was giving Sor Emma enough time to climb Jacob's ladder—and then he pushed the box slowly into the hole in the wall. You and I left, talking about the beauty of the moment and then I asked you who the old man was that had placed the yellow flower over the coffin."

"Yes, you did. He was a used-book dealer that we bought books from for the convent's library. He was a very good friend of mine and Sor Emma. I remember him very well. How could I forget him?"

"Why do you remember him so well? You didn't tell me anything about him the day of the funeral," I reminded her.

"That is another story," she said. "As I told you before, Sor Emma adopted me as her own daughter when she was put in charge of the novitiate. Just before she died, she handed me a little box—like those that used to come filled with imported cookies or chocolates—and asked me to give it to the book dealer, the one we visited together, after she died."

"And did you give it to him?"

"Yes, I did so myself. I went to his bookstore by the *Plaza de Santa Rosa* and gave him the little box. May God forgive me! He became so happy, so happy."

"Why did you ask God to forgive you for delivering the little box?"

"It wasn't because I delivered it. It was because I was so curious about its contents that I couldn't resist the temptation to open it before I took it to him."

"And what was inside, if you allow me to be curious also?" I asked.

"It had a little volume of *Don Quixote* and a tiny baby shoe. A little black shoe, lined with soft red felt."

At that moment, I felt that "somebody" was helping me.

"Do you remember the book dealer's name?" I asked her.

"They called him *El Cojito* but the day I gave him the tin from Sor Emma he told me his real name was don Federico Lemos. He was killed in the *Plaza de Santa Rosa* by a bus, a short time after Sor Emma's death. I only found out about his death much later. I was told he didn't have any relatives. Poor dear!"

"Tell me, Sor Valeriana, what was his reaction when he got the tin?"

"Nothing has moved me more in my life. As soon as he opened the tin and saw the little book he started browsing it, like looking for something, and I sensed he couldn't see very well, nothing as sad as seeing an old man in tears. I had to embrace him. The poor old man couldn't stop crying. 'God bless you, little sister,' he said and kept looking at me as if I was a ghost. He couldn't say more. Finally, I decided it was better to leave him alone and said goodbye. When I was about to leave the room, he said: 'I loved her so much, so much!' I didn't know what to say and I left." Sor Valeriana put her hand on her chest as though her heart was beating a little too fast.

Listening to her tale, I almost fainted myself at that moment. I didn't know what to say either. The only thing that came to my mind was to take out the little *Don Quixote* book from my coat pocket. When Sor Valeriana saw it, she blessed herself three times.

"Holy Trinity!" she cried. "It is a miracle! It is the same book!" And she embraced me.

Then, I asked her a last question before saying goodbye.

"Sor Valeriana, do you know what Sor Emma's name was before she entered into the religious life at the convent?"

"Yes, I do. Her name was Sofia Uzuriaga and she was from Popayán."

*   *   *

The End

Afterword

At the beginning of 2012, when the first draft of the novel was almost finished, I said to my wife, Linda: "I need to find out who Sofía and Federico were. I should go to Popayán to get a clear vision of the space where they lived and exchanged the letters. Will you accompany me?"

With these ideas in mind we made a plan to go to Colombia. We went in February to get away from the winter and enjoy the tropical climate. In contrast with previous trips we had made to visit family, this trip would be a trip to do research.

We began in Bogotá, visiting my friend and colleague Miguel Wenceslao Quintero[13], an authority in Colombian genealogy. He helped me to find out who Dr. Cajiao was. He was Domingo Cajiao Caldas[14], who was a member of the Liberal leadership of the Old Cauca around 1900 married to Zoila Candia Velasco. He had been in prison during the One Thousand Days War in Popayán and in Bogotá. It was an important piece of information, because when Federico was a prisoner with doctor Cajiao, Sofía asked in one of her letters if he wanted her to talk to Zoila in reference to making slippers for Domingo. Doctor Domingo Cajiao Caldas turned out to be at the same time one person, Doctor Cajiao and Domingo, Zoila's husband. These were characters mentioned in the letters that for me in the novel were two different people. Federico referred to him as Doctor Cajiao and Sofía called him Domingo. This suggests that they had different relationships with him.

With these new clues we had found we travelled to Cali where we visited with friends and relatives for a few days. It was time to go to Popayán to look for key pieces of information related to the letters and the novel in the Historical Archives of the Universidad del Cauca.

The beauty of the landscape along the valley of the Cauca River—sugar cane fields, cattle-grazing lands, lagoons filled with flowers, majestic white herons, little adobe farmhouses with plantain and coffee trees, and the Cauca River meandering like a brown snake on the green landscape of the Cauca Valley—took us into the rolling hills in the proximity of Popayán, the land of Sofia and Federico.

My wife didn't like the room at the hotel we had reservations at and we decided to look for a better place to stay. It was a last minute change that turned out to be marvelous. We took a room at the traditional Hotel Monasterio. This hotel preserves its original colonial-style architecture. It is a true historical jewel and a key part of the historical sector of Popayán. There, we experienced *in vivo* the contemporary ambiance where the letters were written. According to Professor Arboleda Llorente[15], the hotel building dates from about 1570, when the Franciscan friars started its construction. The building has served as a monastery, a convent, the mint, a military barracks, a jail, a school, the Government House, and finally the current Hotel Monasterio. It is adjacent to the Church of San Francisco.

The bewitching air of the old city took us without effort into the space where Sofia and Federico had lived between the middle of the XIX and the onset of the XX centuries. From the window in our hotel room, I could see the house across the street where I was told my maternal grandparents had lived in the early part of the XX century.

The next day, after a traditional breakfast with that magical coffee from the Cauca farmlands and hot bread fresh from the oven and tropical fruits, my wife and I walked toward the Historical Archives building, not far from the Plaza Mayor, the main plaza of Popayán. We had an eight o'clock appointment with the director.

The director, Hepi Hartman Garcés, turned out to be the most charming person and a true professional and expert in her field. She welcomed us with open arms as if she had known us forever. Two of her assistants took care of supplying us with any archival documents we requested, making our task easier and faster.

The strategy I had in mind to find the identities of Sofia and Federico is based on the English aphorism—'follow the money'—a well-known investigative approach used by journalists. The plan was to look for real estate transactions, official documents that had the names of any person named Sofia or Federico with any family name. Given that the Pedro Lindo named in the letters was 31 years old in 1900 and was contemporary with Federico and Sofia, I decided to look for documents in a bracket of sixty years, from 1870 to 1930, to identify data that might reveal persons fitting the identities of Sofia and Federico and that was in agreement with the story within the six letters in the little book of Don Quixote.

The Historical Archive was created under the direction of Doctor José María Arboleda Llorente, the director's mentor. When I mentioned our strategy, her eyes brightened up.

"Juan, I have exactly what you need!" she said enthusiastically.

She turned around and from a bookstand near my table she reached for a collection of notarial indexes, with brief references that included the location of the documents in the archives, the date of issue and the names of the persons involved. With help from my wife we looked for the business transactions in alphabetical order and stopping where we found reference to any Federico or Sofía. With the references we found in the indexes, we had the assistants find the original documents, written by hand on official paper, sealed by the Republic of Colombia.

The tension we felt when browsing through pages and pages of data, reading as fast as we could, had something in common with mystery movies. More than tension was a feeling that something surprising was going to happen 'on the way to El Toboso.'

Soon we encountered in the real estate indexes the names of persons known to my family, and also people whose names I had heard in family conversations. But we decided to ignore them to keep the search focused on a single objective. Pedro Lindo's name appeared in various transactions, selling and buying real estate properties. That was encouraging and we knew we were on the right track. The morning came to an end without any significant lead. In a few documents we found persons named Federico X or Sofia Y, but the contents did not connect in any way with the letters or the story. These were put on hold, to determine if later on we could tie them with other hints.

At noon, we took an obligatory break to have lunch: the archives close from noon until two in the afternoon. Well-fed and rested, we returned at two to the archives, observing the people on the sidewalks and the plaza and the buildings of interest. The view of the beautiful clock tower, on the south side of the Plaza Mayor, made the walk worthwhile.

We both agreed that the search wasn't easy. It demanded lots of effort and we had nothing to show for the intense morning's work. To search for information we had to wear gloves and masks as key precautions when handling priceless old documents. This forces the investigator to adopt a surgical reverence for the documents about the lives and miracles of people from bygone times; this reverence—almost liturgical—for the task at hand, was demanded also by the statue of Archbishop Mosquera—brother of don Tomás Cipriano—who, from the stone patio of the archives, observed us impassively.

I knew quite well the low probability of success in our adventure. But we continued our task driven by my optimism as a researcher trained in many impossible projects, and by the intuition that in one of those volumes containing documents written by hand more than a hundred years before, Sofia and Federico could be waiting for us. I didn't know how many stories could be hidden in the Historical Archives in Popayán, which houses documents dating from the early 1500s—before don Miguel de Cervantes was born—to our days. But I was certain that, of all of them, I was interested in only one: the story of Sofia and Federico. With that idea in mind, we continued our research fighting against the drowsiness that comes after a good lunch in the tropics.

Around three o'clock I found a document of interest[16]: Federico Lemos and Sofia Uzuriaga—as she wrote it in the document—were selling a parcel, including an oven to make clay bricks, to be paid in gold coins, in a negotiation with Bolívar Mosquera, the last son of General Tomás Cipriano de Mosquera. The document was from 1901, in good agreement with the period when the letters were written. My heartbeat accelerated: I finally had an interesting lead. I showed the document to my wife.

"I think these people could be them," I said. "But we still have to prove it."

"Juan, what else do you need?" said Linda in an impatient tone.

Inside of my mind my intuition said: we have them. But, next to the intuition the fairy of the sciences said: "Intuition proves nothing. Continue searching. Proof, to be acceptable, must be unquestionable, absolute."

We sped up the search. In addition to the two first names Sofia and Federico we now had two family names: Lemos and Uzuriaga. Not less important, Lemos was the family name of doña Antonia Lemos Largacha, the wife of don Miguel Wenceslao de Angulo, whose signature written in invisible ink is on the title page of the little book of *Don Quixote* that contains Sofia's and Federico's hidden letters. This was an important connection with the letters, the book, and the names of the lovers. All of these connections were of significant interest.

Like fox hounds attracted by the smell of their prey we continued looking for the elusive animal. One hour later—feeling wasted by the effort of speed-reading documents—I found another real estate transaction. It had the names of Federico Lemos, Sofia Uzuriaga de Lemos and Constantino Usuriaga—note the difference in spelling. I knew we had arrived at El Toboso! The emotion of that moment was immense, unforgettable!

My pupils dilated looking at the *Escritura*[17] document to confirm I wasn't wrong. It was true: there were Sofia, Federico and Constantino, together again. Federico had mentioned Constantino in his last letter to Sofia. This was not guessing anymore. I had three key persons named in the letters in one document and two of them in the other one. They were the same persons found in the transaction with Bolívar Mosquera.

Without doubt these were the same Sofia and Federico of the letters. And it was a great surprise to find—later on—that Constantino was Sofia's brother, something I had not guessed from the contents of the letters. Apparently, Sofia decided to write her family name with a *Z* instead of an *S* like the other members of her family. She was different. Special. I already knew that.

I confirmed that the two documents in the archive reinforced each other and were in good agreement with the contents of the letters. The long search had come to a point when we observed the signatures of Sofia and Federico in the documents found in the archives, and compared the calligraphy in the documents with the few letters they wrote in pencil in the book. They were identical. This was additional and critical evidence to confirm the connection between the letters in the little book and the signatures in the documents found at the archives.

The documents found in the archive and the copy of *Don Quixote* in our hands had been in the hands of Sofia and Federico more than a century before that day. We also found that in one of the documents, dated 1901, Sofia had signed as Sofia U. de Lemos, indicating they already were husband and wife. Of course this differs from the novel, where the author chose a different path. So they did marry during the war. The connection of Sofia and Federico with don Wenceslao de Angulo and doña Antonia Lemos, that had been merely intriguing at that moment, was confirmed later in the genealogy book by Gustavo Arboleda quoted before. Doña Antonia and Federico were part of the same Lemos family.

It was time to celebrate. So we stopped the search and went to see the director to share with her the happy findings. She was fascinated by the good news found in such a short time.

Back in our hotel room after a few gin and tonics, I thought about how Federico had slept for months no more than three hundred feet away from where we were now, in a similar room to our room on the same second floor of the hotel. The ghosts of the lovers from a century ago were floating around and I could not go to sleep. My imagination took me along the silent corridors of the hotel feeling I was accompanied by Federico, who wanted to show me the cell he had occupied. On the way to the prison, he and I saw Sofia walking by, across the street from the hotel, on the same sidewalk we had used that morning to go to the archives. I was not quite sure if I was dreaming, imagining, or seeing what was real in my mind. It didn't matter. I felt it and that's what counts. It was a marvelous encounter. The magic of the city at night had taken possession of my mind. I was even welcomed by other ghosts floating around the room. They wore garments from the early XVII century. They could have been the ghosts of Don Quixote and Sancho accompanied by the city founders. It was hard to tell.

The following day, after a good breakfast with plenty of coffee, we returned to the archives at eight o'clock to continue the search for new surprises about Sofia and Federico. This time the expectations were different. The road was known. We just had to arrive.

Around ten in the morning my wife Linda found a new document[18] with the names of Federico, Mariana, and Dolores Lemos. Given that in Sofia's first letter she mentions Federico's sisters, and Mariana was mentioned in another letter, Dolores was probably one of the other sisters. A new person had been found and two were related to Federico. Linda was overjoyed by her discovery and the addition of another person to the story.

Later we verified in Gustavo Arboleda's book that Federico had several sisters: Rosa—unmarried like Mariana and Dolores—and Avelina, married to her first cousin Francisco Antonio Arboleda. We also confirmed that Federico had several brothers. In total his family included twelve siblings, eight men and four women. Federico was the youngest of the men. This additional information cemented the authenticity of the connection between the documents and the letters.

Just before lunch, I came across a thick document of succession[19] from Dr. Juan Francisco Usuriaga, Sofia's father, but I didn't have time to examine that document before the archive closed for lunch. My wife and I talked over lunch about the incredible progress made in our research at the archive in less than two days. We ate without knowing what was on our plates, lost in the historical space a hundred years before that moment, in the time of Sofia and Federico. After lunch I returned to the archives to read the succession documents of Dr. Juan Francisco Usuriaga. Linda went to the hotel to take a nap for both of us. I could not wait to see the succession papers. I was suffering from mental itchiness or discovery anxiety sickness.

Shortly after two in the afternoon, when I was sitting by my work table—with my surgeon's attire, mask and gloves included—reflecting on the best way to look at the large book that was open in front of me, the director arrived accompanied by a man I didn't know.

"Juan, I want you to meet an old friend who stopped by unexpectedly," she said. "I have not seen him for a long time." The gentleman extended his hand to greet me.

"I am Víctor Usuriaga," he said.

Víctor was a man with a sincere look, authentic and easy-going. I felt an electric charge, just as if Sofia and Federico were shaking my hand

and not Víctor. I felt that this was a real live connection with the key persons of the letters.

Víctor turned out to be the great-great grandson of the Dr. Juan Francisco Usuriaga –who was Sofia and Constantino's father. Neither the director nor Víctor knew that I had, right there on the table, a collection of documents related to the estate of his ancestor. As we shook hands, I thought, *this goes beyond probabilities. This is almost a miracle. Someone must be helping us.* It was an eerie feeling, mysterious to say the least.

I got goose bumps. I told Víctor and Hepi what I had on the table, and they could not believe it either. Then I couldn't talk for a moment, looking at Víctor and wondering if it could be true. It was an eternal moment as I sat paralyzed, once again outside of time. I was in the presence of a direct descendant from don Juan Francisco Usuriaga!

After I recovered my composure, I offered my chair to Víctor to allow him to look at the documents of his ancestor. I showed him the details of the page that had the name of Dr. Juan Francisco Usuriaga in large letters in black ink. Linda arrived soon afterward, rested after her nap, and we shared with her the marvelous moment. She sat with us on the benches along the corridors around the patio, across from Archbishop Mosquera's statue, while I told Víctor about the letters in which his great-grandfather Constantino had been mentioned. Like me, he was stupefied.

The next day Víctor returned to the archives with a paper where he and his aunt had written all the details of their family tree, showing the names of his ancestors in sequence from Dr. Usuriaga to the present day. Víctor was indeed a direct descendant of Constantino, and the great-great-grand nephew of Sofia.

At that moment I realized that I had not just the family names of Sofia and Federico but I also had documents with their signatures, before and after marriage, their handwriting, and the names of their relatives and descendants. To complete the package, Víctor and his aunt were the only members of the Usuriaga family still living in Popayán, a city of about 350,000 people.

After Víctor left the archives, I continued reading the documents on the table. There it was mentioned that Julia Velasco Cajiao was Sofia's mother. She was the daughter of Manuel Velasco López and María Ángela Cajiao Pombo, as was later confirmed in the Gustavo Arboleda's book quoted before. In that same book I found that one of Julia Velasco's brothers was Emilio Velasco Cajiao, married to Ana Vargas. He very likely was the uncle Emilio mentioned by Sofia and Federico in the letters, the doctor who reported that Domingo was very ill but that Federico was well. It was he who betrayed Sofia and Federico.

I realized that because Emilio and Domingo were related, both of the family name Cajiao, Uncle Emilio had reported his nephew as very ill. But he did not do the same for Federico as Sofia had hoped he would. Presumably he was not fond of Federico as a potential family member, as is suggested by the contents of the letters.

I also found that Gustavo Arboleda's book lists a Delfina as one of the unmarried sisters of Julia Velasco, Sofia's mother. It is possible that this Delfina was the lady mentioned in the first letter of Sofia to Federico, the lady that—in the letters—refused to help with Hernandes' escape from the prison. This may explain also why they went to see her: if she was related to Julia Velasco, there was a family connection and an obligation to help. However, this idea did not fit with the language used by Sofia in her letter, where she refers to *Delfina* as *that lady*, suggesting she did not care much for Delfina or that Delfina was not her aunt but somebody else. Another key person named in the letters, more than once, is Alberto, who was going to help Federico. I found an Alberto[20] Velasco Cajiao, another relative of Sofia, who got his degree in jurisprudence in 1880.

This collection of historical details accumulated during the visit confirmed beyond any doubt the identities of Sofia and Federico. The evidence was solid, incontrovertible, just what was requested by the muses that were helping us. But there is more.

On the last day of our visit to Popayán, the director decided to look on the Internet for information about Federico Lemos. After doing so, she came to see us with a smile that hardly could fit on her face. She had made a surprising discovery. There was a person selling a collection of historical documents related to Colombians from the XIX century, and among the long list of dozens of people was the name Federico Lemos. At once, I sent a message to the seller to determine if he wanted to get together, if he was living in Popayán. He was actually in Spain and replied to the message about a week later. He wanted a large amount of money for the entire collection of documents and in his reply he included copies of fragments of the three documents about Federico Lemos.

One of them attracted my attention. It related to a request made by Federico: in a letter dated February 3, 1900. He petitioned for a delay of his imprisonment (Fig. 8). The date of Federico's letter was in perfect agreement with the historical moment and the content of the six letters. I could not believe it. Now, a totally unknown person from across the ocean—and from Spain where Don Quixote had come from—was helping me with an important date and a document in Federico's handwriting to define the exact days when Federico became a prisoner. This was another outstanding coincidence.

In this letter[21], dated February 3, 1900, Federico thanks the governor for his help in reference to the prefect's demand to put him in jail. Federico said in the letter: 'This can only relate to intrigues by someone who doesn't care for me at all.' He also asked the governor to request a delay of imprisonment until he recovered from his illness.

Interestingly, that governor was General Luis Enrique Bonilla, married to Ana María Velasco-Velasco, Sofía's relative. Hence, this family connection on Sofía's side was being exploited to try to force the governor to use the power of his office to influence the prefect. Judging from the history of that time and place, we can guess that Federico was probably involved, or presumed involved, in the assault on the city of Popayán by the Liberal soldiers on Christmas 1899, just a few weeks before the letter was written.

We can deduct from the letter to the governor and the coded letters that the prefect prevailed and Federico was taken to prison sick or well.

After one year of conversations with the owner of the documents in Spain, I managed to convince him to sell me the original letter by Federico, dated February 3, 1900. The signature in the letter is the same as the one found in the historical documents (Fig. 8) both written by the same hand. This evidence and the documents found at the archives provide a good collection of facts to prove that we had indeed found who Federico and Sofia were, and a lot more.

We had arrived to Popayán at the precisely correct time for an appointment set up more than a century before we met at the Archives. I estimated that the probability of our encounter was lower than the probability of winning the first prize of the lottery. I also knew that things like that only happen to Knights-Errant lost on some enchanted adventure.

Where else? In Popayán!

*   *   *

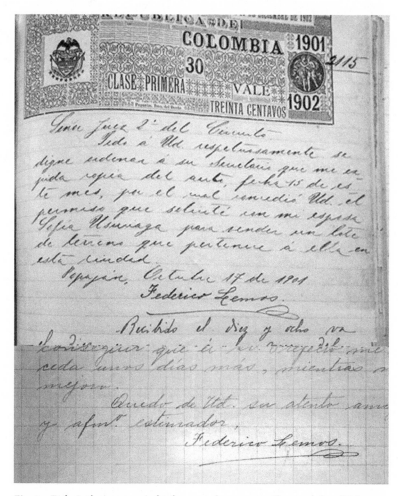

Fig. 8—Federico's signature in his letter to the governor (bottom) dated February 3, 1900 and signatures of Federico and Sofia and other witnesses in a notary document from 1901.

Acknowledgements

I most sincerely thank all those persons that in one way or another contributed to this book. Starting with Hernando Acevedo, owner of the bookstore *El Banco del Libro* where I purchased the little book of *Don Quixote* with the secret letters of Sofia and Federico. He put me in touch with don Emiliano Rivas, the previous owner of the book that and he had purchased from "El Cojito" another dealer in second hand books whose business was near the Santa Rosa Plaza, in Cali.

Ana Luisa, my paternal aunt, Sor Emma in the convent, whose life of service to mankind and whose funeral ceremonies inspired various events of the book.

Antonio Muñoz Obando, my maternal grandfather—a veteran of the One Thousand Days War—who invited me when I was a child to enter into his magic world of the enchanted mirrors, the kingdom of imagination, where I continue to spend a good part of my time.

My parents, brothers, sisters, and their spouses and relatives provided support and suggestions. My father, Joaquín Garcés Caicedo, told me that in 1905 he had as a classmate in Popayán a son of Pedro Lindo. This defined the site and time of the story and a connection with my own family. My mother, Laura Muñoz Obando, introduced me to the traditional families of the Old Cauca State. My brother, Christian, a fan of *Don Quixote,* edited the manuscript in Spanish. They shared anecdotes about the people and the life in Popayán in the XIX and early XX centuries. From our family maids I learned as a child about their traditions and expressions. They inspired some of the characters in the novel.

I am indebted to many friends for reading the manuscript. Pedro Valencia, classmate since first grade and always a close friend, edited the novel and provided useful insights and data. Miguel W. Quintero, colleague and expert genealogist, provided professional advice. Ramiro Velásquez, my student and friend, shared inspiring comments about the story. Pilar Caicedo, my friend since college days, raised good questions about the plot and put me in contact with literary agents and publishers. Manuel Quintana, great friend and colleague, shared key insights on the structure of the novel. María de Laburu, a friend and Spaniard by excellence, loved the story and inspired me to publish it. Likewise, Lilian Escudero, a dear friend, shared her gut feelings and observations about some aspects of the novel.

In Popayán I benefited from the collaboration of Hedwig "Hepi" Hartmann Garcés, my relative and Director of the Historical Cauca Archive, who oriented our search for the identities of Sofia and Federico; Giovanni Castrillón shared city photos from the early XX century; Víctor Usuriaga, artist and great-grandson of Constantino, Sofia's brother, shared his family records; Tomás Castrillón Valencia, a relative and professor at the Universidad del Cauca, shared architectural photos of the historical sector of Popayán.

In my immediate family, my wife Linda is an integral part of every aspect of the novel in both languages. Her interest in the project and her support through the writing and editing process has been invaluable to me. Our daughter, Marcela, a Spanish professor, edited the manuscripts and offered valuable ideas. Martha, our youngest daughter, was in charge of the book cover and its overall artistic design and all the publication details. Her husband, Tom Nehil, a journalist, reviewed the first draft of the novel. In addition to the overall design, Martha collaborated with my son Andrés and his wife, Sabrina Marques, to adapt a painting by

Sabrina, titled "Amor Eterno" to create the image that appears in the cover. Other family members and their spouses and even some of our grandchildren have cheered me on along the way, providing the moral support I needed to keep writing.

Professor María Sablo Yates edited in great detail the first draft of the novel. I do not have the words to describe my gratitude to her for unmatched patience and constructive criticism. Professor Elvira Sánchez Blake, read and provided wise commentary on the novel. My two editors, Claire Allen, in the USA, and Víctor J. Sanz, in Spain, transformed the novel in its English and Spanish versions into material ready for publication.

I cannot close this note without thanking other friends who kindly volunteered to read the manuscript and provided valuable comments: Tim Davis, Karen Clark, Jody Bunce, Stacey Trapani, Howard Means, Marie Zuckerman, Elizabeth Mayette, Larry Levy, Liz Grose, and more recently Andrés Suárez. All of them, and others that I may have missed or were not mentioned here, walked with me along the way on this pilgrimage and marvelous adventure.

*   *   *

CHARACTERS

Ramón, his family & friends

Ramón Bastos Ramos, the narrator of the novel, a university student, the son of don Joaquín Bastos and doña Laura Ramos, he discovered the letters in code written by Sofía and Federico in an old edition of Don Quixote from 1844.

Don Joaquín Bastos Romero, professor and Ramón's father. He was the adoptive son—unknown to him—of don Ramón Bastos and doña Beca Romero, a family without children who lived in Cali.

Doña Laura Ramos Téllez, Ramon's mother, the wife of don Joaquín and daughter of don Antonio Ramos and doña Rosa Téllez, a couple from Popayán.

Don Antonio Ramos, a native of Popayán, lover of Sofia's godmother, doña Ana María Carrasco, the governor's wife. Don Antonio married doña Rosa Téllez in Popayán and later moved to Cali where he told Ramón stories about his adventures as a liberal soldier during the One Thousand Days War.

Doña Rosa Téllez, wife of don Antonio Ramos and mother of doña Laura Ramos, Ramón's grandmother.

Doña Beca Romero, the adoptive mother of don Joaquín Bastos Ramos.

Don Ramón Bastos, the adoptive father of don Joaquín Bastos Romero.

Don Emiliano Rimas, adopted Ramon as a friend and told him that he had purchased the little book of Don Quixote from El Cojito, a used books seller, owner of a business at the Plaza de Santa Rosa, in Cali.

Hernando Tancredo, retired anthropologist and owner of *El Oasis*, books and antiques seller.

Sofía, her family & friends

Sofia Uzuriaga Carrasco, daughter of professor Juan Francisco Usuriaga and doña Julia Carrasco. Sofia was the lover of Federico and co-author of the letters in code in Tome III of *Don Quixote*. She studied at the Colegio de María and was the accomplice of Federico during the One Thousand Days War.

Don Juan Francisco Usuriaga, a medical doctor and professor at the university, he was interested in ancient languages and married late in life to doña Julia Carrasco Argüello. He was the Lemos' family doctor.

Doña Julia Carrasco Argüello, the wife of don Juan Francisco Usuriaga. She had the unique ability to talk to don Juan Francisco after his death when he was busy in his office studying ancient languages. She wanted Sofia to be married to her relative, Alberto Carrasco Maisterrena, a lawyer and important political figure in Popayán. Her brother, don Emilio Carrasco, the prison's doctor, betrayed Sofia.

Betsabé Balanta, a woman of African descent, who served Sofia's family and was her maid, friend and confidant.

Doña Ana María Carrasco, Sofia's godmother, the cousin of doña Julia Carrasco and of don Emilio Carrasco. She suggested to Sofia and Federico to communicate using coded letters written in an old edition of *Don Quixote*. She was the wife of the governor and the lover of Antonio Ramos and used her position to ask Sergeant Llaves to pass the little book between Sofia and Federico.

Alberto Carrasco Maisterrena, prominent layer, first boyfriend of Sofia and relative of doña Julia Carrasco, who wanted to see him married to Sofia. He was Federico's rival in his relationship with Sofia and an ally of don Emilio.

Don Emilio Carrasco Argüello, a doctor. He was opposed to Federico's relationship with Sofia and betrayed Sofia when he refused to help Federico when he was a prisoner. He probably killed don Higinio, the gravedigger.

Delfina Bocanegra Beltrán, owner of an inn next to the prison. She didn't want to cooperate with Federico and Sofia to help Hernandes, a prominent liberal prisoner, to escape through her inn. She was the lover of Martin Cienfuegos, the prison's Sheriff.

Federico, his family & fiends

Federico Lemos Beltrán, a political prisoner during the One Thousand Days War, one of the authors of the coded letters found by Ramón Bastos in an old edition of *Don Quixote*. He ran the bookstore *El Libro* with his family members, and fell in love with Sofia when she came to the bookstore, accompanied by her mother, doña Julia Carrasco to purchase a book for her birthday. He was known as the son of professor don Gallardo Lemos and doña Micaela Beltrán.

Don Gallardo Lemos Lorenzo, the son of don Nicomedes Lemos, founder of the bookstore *El Libro* and doña Domitila Lorenzo. He married doña Micaela Beltrán, the love of this life, and, after returning from the bloody war of 1860, became an alcoholic and eventually a madman. He sired a son, Clodomiro, with an idiot servant, Carlota, who worked for his family.

Doña Micaela Beltrán, the mother of Federico, Mariana, Lola and Rosita. Died when delivering her last child. She was don Gallardo's wife and only love.

Don Nicomedes Lemos, migrated to Popayán from Galicia, Spain, with his pregnant bride, doña Domitila Lorenzo, and opened the bookstore *El Libro*.

Mariana Lemos Beltrán, was the sister and accomplice of Federico during the One Thousand Days War. She became a good friend of Sofia and married late in life to Aniceto Arcila.

Pedro Lindo, a boy of humble origin who was hired by don Nicomedes as a helping hand at the bookstore when Federico left Popayán to work as a civil engineer in the Panama Canal Project. He was an avid reader and had a brilliant intellect. He graduated in medicine when still in his teens. Clodomiro was his favorite person at the bookstore.

Clodomiro, a dwarf, the son of don Gallardo Lemos and Carlota, the maid in charge of the chickens and the parrots of the Lemos family. He inherited his name from a rooster, known as don Clodomiro, who presumably, according to Mama Pola, the oldest maid, had impregnated Carlota.

Mama Pola, the oldest maid of the Lemos family. Was hired as a servant by don Nicomedes' wife doña Domitila Lorenzo when they arrived from Spain.

Prison Personnel and members of the Liberal Resistance

Hernandes, a political prisoner, a liberal officer from Santander, in charge of delivering a shipment of weapons from Ecuador to general Bustamante. Sofia and Federico collaborated with the liberals to help Hernandes to escape from the prison.

Constantino Zambrano, telegraph operator, ally and accomplice of Federico in the liberal resistance.

Víctor and Felisa, farmers living in the outskirts of Popayán, collaborators with the liberal cause. He was a butcher and she a sold herbs at the market.

Domingo Cervantes, Federico's cell mate. Married to Zoila, a good friend of Sofia. Domingo was killed at the prison during a revolt in 1900.

Doctor Cajiao, leader of the liberal party in Popayán during the One Thousand Days War. He had been President of the Universidad del Cauca.

Aniceto Arcila, businessman from Guayaquil, an ally and relative of the President of Ecuador don Eloy Alfaro, and a good friend of Federico. He married late in life with Mariana, Federico's older sister.

Martín Cienfuegos, the prison's Sheriff, lover of Delfina.

Sergeant Llaves, prison officer who collaborated with Sofia and Federico to exchange the little book of *Don Quixote* with their secret letters in code.

The governor, don Enrique Zorilla, married to doña Ana María Carrasco.

The prefect, Saturnino Belalcázar, the City Mayor, married to Marisa.

Sergeant Orlando Barbosa, took Federico to prison by order from the prefect.

Lieutenant Froilán Bordón, took Federico to prison.

Salustio Guzmán and Evaristo Rengifo, friends of Federico. They liked to read books for free.

Delfino Alegría, army payroll manager and friend of governor Enrique Zorrilla and Federico Lemos.

Don Higinio, the gravedigger, an innocent victim of the war.

Members of the convent

Sor Emma, name adopted by Sofia when she entered the convent.

Sor Basilides, teacher of Sofia in Popayán and the mentor of Sor Emma at the convent in Barcelona. Her family was from the Basque region in Spain.

Sor Josefina, assistant to the Mother Superior in Popayán who negotiated with don Emilio and the godmother the adoption of the baby born to Sofia.

Sor Valeriana, assistant to Sor Josefina and teacher of Ramón in kindergarten. She was a friend of El Cojito and introduced him to Sor Emma at the bookstore.

Father Martens, a Belgian priest who officiated at Sor Emma's funeral.

References

1   Arboleda, Gustavo, *Diccionario biográfico y genealógico del antiguo departamento del Cauca*, 1926.

2   Arboleda, Gustavo, op. cit.

3   Reyes, Rafael, *Memorias 1850–1885*, Compiladas por Ernesto Reyes Nieto. Fondo Cultural Cafetero. Bogotá, 1986.

4   Morris, Edmund, *Theodore Rex*, Random House, New York, 2001.

5   Rivas, Raimundo, *Historia Diplomática de Colombia 1810–1934*, Imprenta Nacional, Bogotá, 1961.

6   Aragón, Arcesio, *Popayán, Ciudad Procera*, Bogotá, Imprenta Nacional, 1941 (p. 185).

7   Maya, Rafael. *Poesía* (Don Quijote muere en Popayán), Banco de la República, Bogotá, 1979 (p. 491).

8   Uribe Uribe, Rafael, *Documentos Militares y Políticos Relativos a las Campañas del general Rafael Uribe Uribe*, Imprenta del Vapor, Bogotá 1904.

9   Caballero, Lucas, *Memorias de la Guerra de los Mil Días*, El Ancora Editores, Bogotá, 1982.

10   Uribe Uribe, Rafael op. cit.

11   Museo Negret, Popayán.

12   Uribe Uribe, Julián, *Memorias*, Toro Sánchez, Edgar (Editor), Bogotá, Banco de la República, 1994.

13   Quintero Guzmán, Miguel Wenceslao, *Linajes del Cauca grande: Fuentes para la Historia* Primera edición, Bogotá, Ediciones Uniandes, tres tomos, 2006.

14   Arboleda, Gustavo, *Diccionario biográfico y genealógico del antiguo departamento del Cauca*, 1962.

15   Arboleda-Llorente, José María, *Guía Turística de la Ciudad de Popayán*, U. del Cauca, 1963.

16   Índice *de Escrituras Popayán 1897–1923*, Folio 2110, Escritura 456, p. 149, 1901.

17   *Archivo Histórico del Cauca. Escritura: Federico Lemos, Sofía Uzuriaga de Lemos y Constantino Usuriaga*, Folio 5352, p. 152, Escritura 1370, 1904.

18 *Archivo Histórico del Cauca, documento: Federico, Mariana y Dolores Lemos,* Escritura 2, Folio 4, Vol I, 1901.

19 *Archivo Histórico del Cauca. Usuriaga, Juan Francisco. Sucesión*: Escritura 314, Folio 1102, Vol. 2, 1899.

20 *Monografía Histórica de la Universidad del Cauca, Octubre a Diciembre 1977,* Tomo II, no 71, 1977.

21 *Letter from Federico Lemos to Gobernador Luis Enrique Bonilla,* February 3, 1900. Personal documents of the author.

Made in the USA
Coppell, TX
19 February 2023

13116079R00198